DREAMS OF FURY
DESCENDANTS OF THE FALL
BOOK IV

AARON HODGES

Edited by Genevieve Lerner
Proofread by Sara Houston
Illustration by Eva Urbanikova
Map by Michael Hodges

ABOUT THE AUTHOR

Aaron Hodges was born in 1989 in the small town of Whakatane, New Zealand. He studied for five years at the University of Auckland, completing a Bachelors of Science in Biology and Geography, and a Masters of Environmental Engineering. After working as an environmental consultant for two years, he grew tired of office work and decided to quit his job in 2014 and see the world. One year later, he published his first novel - Stormwielder.

FOLLOW AARON HODGES...

And receive TWO FREE novels and a short story!
https://aaronhodgesauthor.com/newsletter

ALSO BY AARON HODGES

THE KINGDOMS OF HUMANITY

PROLOGUE
THE SOVEREIGN

Standing atop the marble balcony, Lukys looked down into the amphitheatre of the Sovereigns, down at the thousands that had gathered below. The citizens of the capital were dressed in every colour of the rainbow, though Perfugian blue was most prominent. In one corner, a group of yellow cloaks marked where King Nguyen and his Gemaho waited.

A lump lodged in Lukys's throat as he felt the weight of all those eyes upon him, the hush of expectation. He had not expected so many to accept the invitation, not with the events that had led to this day, and the woman who stood beside him. And yet...come they had, from all across Perfugia, come to witness the inauguration of their new Sovereigns.

Lukys struggled to swallow the lump in his throat, and his stomach tied itself into a knot instead. A buzzing filled his inner mind, the whisper of a thousand voices, generations of lives lived, the knowledge of every Sovereign that had come before him, all screaming to make themselves heard. He clenched a fist and fought to press them down, to ignore his own inadequacy compared to those that had come before him...

All Sovereigns before this day had been chosen at birth for their strength as Melders—humans who had inherited the mental abilities of their inhuman ancestors. The chosen were trained to rule, prepared for their elevation to Sovereign, when the minds of all who had come before would be passed to them.

But for Lukys and the woman beside him, the process had been almost accidental, a desperate act committed by their dying predecessors. Now he felt exposed, a fraud before the gaze of his people. Surely they would see the truth beneath the purple robes, that he was nothing and nobody, a failed recruit who had been destined to die on the frontlines fighting the Tangata.

At that thought, he reached out an unconscious hand for the woman at his side. Sophia. Warmth touched him as she entwined her fingers through his and he felt the reassurance of her consciousness against his own. Smiling, he exchanged a glance with his lover, the woman with whom he had chosen to share his life.

The grey eyes of the inhuman Tangata looked back at him, though...he no longer saw the Tangata as inhuman. More...distant relatives, long lost to human history.

A glint appeared in Sophia's eyes as she smiled, and in that look Lukys saw a flicker of the knowledge she possessed —that they both now possessed. Memories, stretching back to before the founding of Perfugia, before even the creation of the kingdoms of the mainland. So many lives, they could each spend a lifetime sifting through the memories, and still not know them all.

So far, those memories had revealed much, and nothing. They were so convoluted, flickering of images without rhythm or reason. Some things they had managed to piece together—confirmation that Lukys's theory had been correct, that the first founders of Perfugia had been Tangata, not human.

In a way, those memories meant Sophia deserved to stand as she did, more so than Lukys himself. After all, the abilities of the Melders came from her people. But there was no convincing her of that. Even now, he could sense her fear, a doubt that matched his own reservations. The title of Sovereign was sacred amongst his people, a line of secretive, powerful rulers that had protected Perfugia since its founding.

But of course, that secrecy had only been a means to an end, a way to conceal Perfugia's true ancestry from its people. It had also protected those few amongst Perfugian society fortunate enough to possess the abilities of the Tangata—Melders like Lukys, though his ability had not been discovered until his first encounter with the Tangata on the frontline.

But that was all in the past, and forcing the memories aside, he leaned in close to Sophia. "Are you okay?" he said out loud.

A grimace crossed Sophia's face but she nodded. *Yes,* she whispered into his mind. Then turning to face the crowd, she opened her lips. "I will...be okay."

The words came out with the hesitation of someone unused to speaking. Indeed, even now the hairs on the back of Lukys's neck tingled to hear his partner's voice. No Tangata in living memory had possessed the ability to speak aloud, something that had no doubt contributed to their conflict with humanity. Now though, with the knowledge passed onto her by their predecessors, Sophia had rediscovered the ability to speak.

Lukys smiled back at her, savouring the musical accent to her voice, strangely similar to his friend Cara's. Something stirred in his mind at the thought of the Goddess, some long-forgotten memory of the Sovereigns, but now was not the time to delve into that labyrinth. Giving Sophia's hand another squeeze, he turned towards the stairs leading down into the amphitheatre.

Their guard responded immediately, men and women dressed in blue-stained armour falling into step around them, surrounding the two Sovereigns in a ring of steel. The guard in the lead glanced back before they started down, and Lukys glimpsed a cheeky grin on Travis's face. Lukys's fellow recruits and their Tangatan partners had seemed the logical choice for their guard. They were family now, the only ones either of them could trust.

When they didn't immediately start down the steps, another face looked back. "If you two are quite done dawdling, I believe you have a pair of crowns to accept," Dale grunted.

Lukys drew in a breath and nodded. "Let's get it over with then."

"About time," Dale muttered.

Their guards went first. Silver spears and kite shields in hand, they advanced down the stairs to the floor of the amphitheatre, clearing a path for the new Sovereigns. Silence gave way to whispers as the crowd parted before the blue-garbed warriors, their heads lifting in search of a glimpse of their new rulers.

Lukys shivered as they descended the great steps. The unpredictable Perfugian spring had chosen to gift them with a rare day of sun. Despite the warmth, Lukys couldn't help but feel exposed as they approached the floor of the amphitheatre. After months of war and battle, he was used to a spear and shield in hand. To stand before so many in nothing but a simple robe, defenceless...he felt naked, though with Sophia at his side, he knew no human assailant would dare attack.

And the gift of the Sovereigns had added something to Lukys as well. Not the raw strength or speed of the Tangata, but another sense almost, an awareness of their surroundings that neither he nor Sophia quite yet understood, but which he hoped might aid them in times of need.

Certainly Lukys's own talents as a Melder seemed amplified by the Sovereign gift. And so as they approached the crowd, he reached out with his mind to examine the aura of his people. They flickered before his inner vision, multicoloured hues augmented by their colourful clothing. Purples for fear and courage shone, pinks for love and greys for doubt, even some blues of sadness shimmered in the minds of his new subjects. Thankfully, the reds of anger and greens of hatred were blessedly rare.

It was surprising, the power of truth.

There had been resistance, of course. For centuries, the Sovereigns had spread tales of the barbaric Tangata, of a monstrous species that sought only to destroy humanity. But the reality Lukys had discovered in the south could not have been further from that lie. Sophia and her companions who stood with them now wanted nothing more than a life of their own, a chance to raise their children in peace, to create rather than destroy.

And those they'd left behind in New Nihelm…well, that was a worry for another day.

Lukys did not doubt there were still those who disbelieved the revelations, who refused to accept their Tangatan ancestry. But from what he glimpsed of those below, the people who had come here did so out of curiosity, rather than anger. After all, the public had never been invited to an inauguration for their Sovereigns. Perhaps that alone had been enough to quench their trepidation at Sophia's presence.

Or maybe they just wanted to see the monster.

Lukys's head whipped around at Sophia's whisper.

No, he said immediately, catching her gaze. *To see the Lady and her partner.*

A smile touched her lips at his words and they continued down the stairs, doing their best to move in what they thought was a regal fashion. The long robes were more than just uncomfortable—Lukys feared they would actively hinder them should it come to a fight. Only with his friends and their Tangatan partners around them had he agreed to the ceremony—and even then, only because Nguyen had pressured them. The King of Gemaho had insisted that an official coronation would help the people to accept their strange new rulers. Much to Lukys's irritation, the reaction of the crowd suggested that the old king had been right.

He caught a glimpse of the man himself now, standing amidst his Gemaho guard. Nguyen had shaved the unkept beard he'd grown over the past weeks, though he still looked more the part of a scholar than a king. The man kept his face carefully blank as they approached, though Lukys could see the sheen in his eyes, the amusement behind the mask. Even as he watched, the king gave a subtle wink. The man was enjoying their discomfort.

At Lukys's side, a snort of laughter came from Sophia. He shook his head, a smile of his own tugging at his lips. The pair had formed an inexplicable bond, even before Sophia had learned to talk. Since their ascension to the Perfugian throne, the king couldn't hear enough about her people and their past, their wants and dreams. It seemed Nguyen was as fascinated with the past as the Archivist Erika had been, though no one had heard news of the woman in weeks. Neither had they heard of Cara, and

Lukys was left wondering what had become of their quest to find the City of the Gods.

Again a memory tugged at him, but they were approaching the floor of the amphitheatre now, and quickly he pushed it aside. Hand in hand, Lukys and Sophia stepped onto the stage and started towards the stone slab that had been placed in its centre.

A shiver touched him as they walked amongst the crowd, the line of their blue-garbed guards keeping them back. He couldn't help but remember another day just a few weeks ago, when their fate had seemed far grimmer. Standing alone in a ring of swords and Melders, Lukys, Sophia and his friends had faced off against the old Sovereigns—and convinced them to cast aside their hatred.

The bloodshed might have ended there but for one of the royal guards. Consumed by her hatred of the Tangata, Tasha had refused to accept the decision of her Sovereigns. In her desperation to save Perfugia from what she saw as monsters, she had struck down the last Sovereigns, then used her powers as a Melder to turn the rest of the guards against Lukys and the Tangata.

But he had defeated her, struck her down with mind and spear, and in doing so had claimed the memories of the dying Sovereigns.

Now he and Sophia stood where those ancient rulers had, preparing to receive their crowns as thousands watched on. He could feel their minds now, pressing in from all around, adding to the strain of those secret memories locked within his head. What must these people think, watching the Tangata walk amongst them, seeing a monster from their childhood about to be crowned Sovereign over all of them?

Even now, he half expected the calm to break, for their rage to be unleashed, to see them surging forward against the thin line of blue steel. Yet there was only silence, only that hidden curiosity, only the waiting. He supposed this was the first time most had ever set eyes upon the Sovereigns. When the rulers were so remote, so mysterious, they might have been Tangata all along for all these people knew.

Besides, through the academy every child entered at eight years of age, Perfugians were accustomed to obedience, to accepting the decree of their superiors. If the last Sovereigns had chosen a Tangata and a failed recruit as their next rulers, would they even question it?

Lukys couldn't help but feel there was a wrongness to that. After all, was that not how the Old One had conquered New Nihelm? The Tangata there had been ruled by a Matriarch, an ancient creature of strength and wisdom. But the Old One had turned the Matriarch's guards against her, slaughtering her in order to take her place. That should have mattered to the Tangata, that betrayal. Instead, they had bowed to the Old One's power without question.

Coming to a stop before the granite slab in the middle of the amphitheatre, Lukys looked upon the silver crowns that rested atop the stone, awaiting their new bearers. Adorned with a fortune in sapphires, they were only ceremonial, a show for those gathered to watch, an object to give legitimacy to their rule, as Nguyen put it. The true Sovereign gift had been passed to them as their predecessors lay dying, just as it had for every pair of Sovereigns before them.

Lukys shivered as he sensed cold eyes looking down from the pillars that lined the amphitheatre. Atop each pillar stood two statues, Sovereigns of ages past, stretching back centuries. He knew each of their faces now, had *been* every one of them. A strange sensation, that.

Turning from the statues, he and Sophia paused before

the crowns. Their minds were closer than ever now, almost as one since the transformation, their thoughts aligned by the hundreds of lifetimes they had shared. It scared a part of him, to sense her presence so close, always on the edges of his consciousness. Yet it was a comfort too, the knowledge she would always be with him, that he would not be left alone.

As one, they reached down for the silver circlets. Despite the sun, the metal was cold to the touch as Lukys lifted the first above Sophia's head, and she did the same for him. There they paused, and their eyes met, grey of the Tangata to his own plain brown. Time seemed to stand still, and Lukys felt he stood on the edge of an abyss, that this moment would forever change their lives, tie them to a path they might grow to regret.

Yet what choice did they have? The Old One was coming with her Tangatan army. No kingdom could stand against her, not alone. If they did not act, did not lead Perfugia to unite humanity, the Old One would prevail. The kingdoms would fall, one by one, and his people would be exterminated, enslaved. One day, there would be nowhere left for them to run, nowhere left to hide.

He saw the same thoughts reflected in Sophia's eyes and momentarily, he wondered if they were truly his own, or hers, or one of the hundreds they had collected in their fragile minds. A shudder shook him, but they could not look back now, could not pass on this burden.

As one, they lowered the silver crowns onto each other's heads.

And turned to greet their subjects as the new Sovereigns of Perfugia.

THE TANGATA

A light snow was falling as the Tangata moved from the mountains into the Calafe foothills. The cold did not touch Adonis as he paused to watch the passage of his people, but he couldn't help but be reminded of their last journey through these hills, the desperate march of the Tangata as they followed Maya into the unknown heavens, driven on by her Voice, by the power of the Old One.

A tremor raised his hackles as he recalled the swirling snow, the faces of those who had succumbed, of men and women, of the children who had fallen in the snowdrifts, never to rise again. The journey had taken a terrible toll on the Tangata, on his people, and more than once he had found himself doubting his partner—though he had helped raise her to Matriarch.

Now though, after their glorious victory in the mountains, Adonis joyed in her power, in the fall of the Anahera, of the creatures that humanity had named Gods. The cost had been terrible, but in the end, to watch the Anahera kneel at their feet, cowed by mere Tangata…it had been a glorious sight.

Smiling, Adonis looked up at the creatures, soaring on their cursed wings. They served the Tangata now, keeping watch for the enemy. Faced with Maya's power, the creatures had made their choice, had bowed to the Old One, surrendered their liberty to preserve their future.

Adonis turned as the sound of rattling chains carried above the soft patter of falling snow. The elation of their victory left him as he saw the group of prisoners approaching, watched closely by their Tangatan guard.

The children of the Anahera—fledgelings, as the creatures called them—marched with heads down, each chained to the next in line by collars of steel fastened about their necks. They walked in blessed silence, heads bowed and stumbling in the deep snow, cowed by the power of their captors, by the thrum of Maya's Voice, always present now, as she walked at the head of their column.

Adonis clenched his fists as he watched the fledgelings trudge past. They might have left them imprisoned and under guard in the Anaheran city, but Maya wanted to keep them close, needed them to ensure the obedience of her new slaves. Not even her Voice could keep so many of the adult Anahera in check without the threat against their youth.

His heart twitched as one of the fledgelings tripped and fell into a snowdrift. The icy stuff had ceased to fall, but the ground was thick with the last of winter's storms, making passage difficult for the young. And their wings, still too young for flight, only seemed to hinder them further on the ground.

Adonis couldn't help but wonder at a species whose youth were so defenceless. The moment he had caught one within his superhuman grip, the fledgeling's life had hung in his hands. No wonder the rest had surrendered so easily.

Most of the fledgelings barely stood taller than Adonis's

waist, and with the chains binding them together, the journey through the mountains had been difficult. It would only get worse. Now that they had reached the lowlands, the pace would increase. And if their parents resisted Maya's orders...

At least the Tangata were strong. From a young age, they were able to fend for themselves. And the Old Ones...legend whispered of their offspring, of new-borns able to walk within days, fight by their first year. Adonis felt a thrill of excitement at that thought and looked around for Maya. Her pregnant belly had grown large in the weeks they'd spent in the mountains, and he wondered whether it was right that they continue with this mad rush, that they hurl their strength upon the defences of humanity now, rather than wait. But Maya had been insistent.

A shout from the fledgelings drew his attention back to the captives. Another at the rear had fallen, his chain pulling short so that the others stumbled. Shouts came from their Tangatan guards, then one of his brethren strode forward. He held a rope in one hand and with a flick of his wrist, he sent it hissing at the fledgeling's back. A scream punctuated its impact as the youth's wings thrashed against the snow, becoming entangled in the chains. The Tangata raised the rope again, but a shout from the back of the line gave him pause.

"Hey!"

Adonis flinched at the coarseness of the human language—not so much the words themselves, but the manner in which they communicated. The creatures spoke aloud, so that all the world could hear their thoughts. Indeed, he had come to suspect they enjoyed the fact that their speech made it all but impossible to be ignored. Certainly this individual did not want for silence.

"Bastard, why don't you pick on someone your own size?"

Stifling a growl, Adonis marched to the rear of the line where the human was sitting up in her stretcher, waving a fist at the Tangata with the rope-whip. The human had been injured in the battle for the Anaheran city, twisting her leg in a terrible fall. For now, Maya had permitted her to live, though if she did not cooperate when they reached the human lands, her protection would not last.

Swathed in furs, only the human's golden complexion and long black hair was visible, but that was more than enough to show her displeasure. The two Anahera that had been assigned to carry her stretcher struggled to keep from tipping their burden into the snow at her erratic movements.

Adonis shook his head as he approached. They were such vulgar things, these humans. This one called herself Maisie, but Adonis rarely bothered to recall their names. He couldn't understand how so many of his brethren had taken them as assignments. Despite the old Matriarch's urgings, he could have never stomached the thought of bonding with one, let alone procreating—though until recently that had been the only way of preserving the Tangatan lineage.

For Adonis, even the Anahera would be preferable, cowardly as they had proven. At least they were powerful, elegant, maybe worthy of the Tangata. That had been his hope once, a union between their species, one that might save the Tangata from extinction.

Then he had discovered Maya, and the future of his people had changed forever.

Approaching the stretcher, Adonis looked to the Anaheran woman who was helping to carry the human.

Translate for me, slave, he said, then turned to glare at the human.

"You," the human spoke before Adonis could relay his

admonishments through the Anaheran woman. "I know you…you're the first one, the one the Old One used to take the fledgeling."

Adonis scowled. *"I am Adonis, partner to the Matriarch of the Tangata,"* he hissed, and the Anaheran woman relayed his words. *"And you will speak only when commanded, human."*

To his surprise, the human only rolled her eyes, a gesture he'd come to learn was one of disrespect. A growl rumbled from his chest and he took a step towards the creature.

"I hope you're happy," the human said, ignoring his warning and lying back in her stretcher. She gestured to her bearers. "I can't say I was the biggest fan of the Anahera, but to enslave an entire species…" She shook her head. "That's almost *human.*"

"Quiet, prisoner," Adonis snapped, irritated despite himself. How dare this creature compare his people to their kind? *"Or you will soon outlive your usefulness."*

"Ha!" Maisie snorted. "You and I both know I'd already be as dead as poor Farhan and his son if that was the case. Your master clearly needs me for something."

Maya is not my master, Adonis snapped back.

The human only stared at him, as though she had not caught the meaning of his words. It was a moment before Adonis realized the Anaheran woman had not relayed his words. Snarling, he swung on the creature.

Slave, why have you not translated?

The Anahera blinked, shaking her head as though coming out of some trance. "I…I…" she stuttered, seemingly unable to put together the words. Her face had paled, and he noticed now that her eyes were red, as though she had not slept in a long while. "I am sorry, Tangata, the human…she mentioned my partner…and my son."

Her face twitched at the words—then to Adonis's

horror, tears spilt down the woman's face. Images flickered in his mind, of Farhan's death by Maya's hand, crushed by her power. Then the youth in his grief, bowed over the fallen Anahera's body. The son. Maya had sent him to kill his sister, the young Anahera that had escaped, but he had never returned. Adonis had no doubt that meant the son was as dead as the father. Such was the power of Maya's Voice that the boy would not have stopped until the sister was slain, or he himself was dead.

"I am sorry," the Anaheran woman said softly, struggling to straighten, to contain herself. "I…it is just…I do not know what became of Hugo. He so wanted to please his father…"

Your son is dead, Adonis said harshly. False hope would not help the woman now, as he knew was the human way. The woman's son was dead—no amount of lying would change that truth. *Likely his sister killed him. I suppose you can be pleased by that at least: your daughter lives.*

The tears had returned to the Anaheran woman's face, but she froze at his last words. Then she was shaking her head, fists clenched, her whole body trembling. "Cara…was not my daughter," she mumbled. "She was…the daughter of Farhan's first partner. She would not have…could not have…no, she was headstrong, but she would not have killed one of us, not Hugo, not her own brother—"

The Anahera broke off as Adonis struck her hard across the face, sending her crashing to the snow. Anger raged within him as he looked down at the creature's shock. She would be far stronger than him, faster, more powerful, but the steel collar about her throat revealed the truth of her nature. She had bowed with the rest of her kind and now her strength meant nothing. They were his, all their kind. Their lives belonged to the Tangata. How dare she waste his time with her tears.

Yet, as he looked into her eyes and saw the grief there, Adonis felt the harsh words wither within him. Instead, he only shook his head and glanced at the human.

Pick up your burden, slave, he said, adding venom to his words despite his sudden regret. *Perhaps hard labour will help you to forget the loss of your foolish child.*

The human watched him as the Anaheran woman rose from the snow, her simple tunic now damp from melting ice. She had not heard his words, could not have understood half the conversation, but knowledge still shone from Maisie's eyes as she watched him. A shiver passed through Adonis at that look, and he couldn't help but wonder at Maya's wisdom in keeping one of Maisie's kind alive. They were intelligent, scheming creatures. So long as this human lived, she was a danger to them all.

But he could not go against the wishes of his Matriarch. So instead he turned back to the Anaheran woman as she picked up her end of the stretcher. The second Anahera had remained silent throughout the exchange, and he couldn't help but think he'd picked the wrong translator. Even so…

You had best get used to the pain, Anahera, he said as she lifted the stretcher. This time his voice lacked anger, and his tone was soft, without antagonism. He spoke only truth. *I fear the suffering of your people has only just begun.*

❧ 2 ❧

THE PRISONER

Erika's world was pain. Agony, drilling into her skull, searing her flesh, twisting her very bones. Darkness engulfed her, the pitch-black offering no escape, no fleeting distraction from her suffering. Even when the convulsions subsided, and her mind began to return, she would hear the footsteps on the stairs, the soft creaking of boards beneath booted feet, the rasping of the queen's laughter.

And the sound would begin again. That terrible, soul-rending shriek that set her whole being aflame. No matter that Erika pressed her hands to her ears, that she screamed to drown it out—the sound found her anyway. Through cloth and flesh and bone, even in the depths of unconsciousness, it sought her out. There was no escaping the fiery lashes of the queen's power, no relief. Time fled in that dark place and reality with it, until there was nothing for Erika but the ebb and flow of her pain.

The pain—and the whispers of the queen.

"Give up, Erika, surrender, and be free."

Lost amidst the agony, Erika began to wonder why she still resisted. The insidious words crept their way into her soul, murmuring their promises of freedom. She wept at the thought of relief, of a world without the shrieking, without the agony.

But something within Erika would not allow it, a tiny fraction of her consciousness, one that remembered the queen's lies, that recalled the woman's treachery. And she knew the promises were ash, that the only relief the queen offered was the cold embrace of death.

So instead, all Erika offered her enemy were her screams.

Queen Amina didn't seem to mind. Between flashes of red and white, in moments of brief clarity, Erika glimpsed the woman's face, the cruel grin twisting her lips. The queen didn't care that Erika resisted, only that she had her revenge. Then the madness would rise once more, an ocean of agony sweeping Erika away on dreams of suffering.

She could not have picked the moment when the end finally came, when the tide of her pain receded—and did not return. Consciousness came to Erika slowly, her soul creeping back to the broken husk of her body, as though fearing some trap, a trick by the queen to catch her unawares.

But when Erika finally cracked open her eyes, she found herself alone in the hull of the ship. Pain still rippled through her body when she tried to sit up, aftershocks of the queen's magic, but for the first time since being taken captive, the raw agony had vanished.

Drawing in a breath of stale air, she sought to pull the scattered fragments of her thoughts together. Memories collided in her mind as she recalled her struggle to convince the Anahera to fight, to resist the Tangatan attack. Never could she have imagined that the noble creatures, proclaimed as Gods over humanity, could have submitted so readily.

In the end, only Farhan had resisted. Cold, uncaring Farhan. But he had proven his love for his daughter, twisted and controlling as it was. He may have saved Cara from the Old One, but only after coming so close to condemning her, to robbing the Goddess of the wings that gave her life, freedom.

Yet, what did it matter now? Farhan was dead…as was his son Hugo, who had perished at the hands of his own sister, Cara. A shudder shook Erika as she recalled that desperate struggle. Through the agony of Erika's broken arm and Cara's shattered wing, they had fought poor Hugo, Cara's half-brother, to the death. Driven mad by the Old One, he had fought as though possessed, screaming that he was helping Cara—even as he slammed her skull against the stones.

Now he was dead, drowned in the mountain stream, his body carried away by the currents. And Erika and Cara had found themselves a fresh prison, a new tormentor in the form of the Flumeeren Queen. How Amina had come to take the lands of the Gemaho, Erika could not comprehend, but it hardly seemed to matter now. They had fallen into her clutches, been conquered by her magic. There would be no escape now.

Erika still wasn't sure why she was even alive. The queen wanted the magic gauntlet Erika wore, but why not prise it from her corpse? Why go through the hassle of torture, of the demands for Erika to remove it? Unless…the magic could not be taken against her will. Erika hadn't considered that possibility, but now she wondered…

The squeal of hinges drew Erika's attention to the boards above her head and she flinched as a ray of light swept the gloom beneath the deck, illuminating stairs leading up to a trap door. Feet descended, followed by the queen herself.

Erika's heart raced as she watched the woman's approach, but there was nowhere to hide in the hold. She shrank into a corner, as though if only she could make herself small enough, she might avoid the queen's wrath. But there was little hope of that, and balling her fist, she tried desperately to reach for the power of her gauntlet.

Pain seared through her wrist as the broken bones grated together, still mending from the injury she had taken in the mountains. Despite the pain, a brief flickering of light appeared in the links of her gauntlet, but it quickly died, as Erika's energies flagged. She couldn't remember the last meal she'd eaten—even before their capture, she and Cara had barely scavenged enough from the land to stave off starvation. She had discovered in the mountains how the gauntlet fed off her own strength. Without sustenance, its power was useless to her.

A smile crossed the queen's thin lips as she watched Erika's pathetic attempt at resistance. Then she raised her own gauntleted hand and squeezed it into a fist. Light burst from the metallic links, so bright it was nearly blinding. Erika flinched from the display of power, her own mind withering at the pain it promised, the agony that would follow. A moan drew from the depths of her throat as half-mad, she turned and clawed at the boards of the ship.

Erika herself had once used that same power to dominate friends and enemies alike—to strike down Cara and the Tangata, even Farhan, the leader of the Anahera. Now that she found herself on the receiving end...she could barely hold onto her own sanity.

"So my Archivist awakes," the queen murmured, raising her burning fist.

The woman was dressed for war, with heavy chainmail draped across her lithe frame, a helm with a golden circlet set in the brow carried in her free hand. A sword hung from her side, though with the power of the ancient gauntlet, this woman had no need for such a primitive weapon.

Erika shrank further into her corner at the woman's voice, tears springing to her eyes. She could already feel the onset of the pain, the return of the madness. Those Erika had tortured with her own gauntlet had perished quickly, their insides torn apart by her magic. But Queen Amina had obviously spent time refining her power, had learned such control that she could torture Erika for hours without her victim succumbing to the silent embrace of death.

A sob tore from Erika's throat as she shook her head, scrunching her eyes closed. Now that she had regained her sanity, had escaped the pain for even a few hours, the thought of its return...

Laughter rasped in her ears and a brilliant light seared at Erika's eyelids, as though the queen were gathering even more power. But then the light faded and footsteps approached. Another tremor shook Erika as she clenched her fists, struggling to keep from screaming.

"Such bravery," the queen's voice whispered from close by.

Cracking open her eyes, Erika found the queen crouched alongside her. The woman's emerald eyes seemed to pierce Erika to the soul. There was a sharpness about the queen's face that spoke of power, of her unyielding will. This was a woman who had defied the Tangata, who had traded and manipulated and battled her way across the kingdoms of humanity, until all lay conquered at her feet.

Where had she come from, this warrior queen of Flumeer? Her father had been king before her, but he had not shown any inclination towards war—had overseen years of peace for Flumeer, in fact. Little was known of her mother, only that she had succumbed to a wasting fever when Amina was yet a child at the breast.

Somehow, the pair had created a conqueror.

Light bathed Erika's face as the queen reached out with the gauntlet and pressed a finger to Erika's chest.

"Why do you still fight, little Archivist?" Amina whispered. "You know you cannot resist. Eventually you will give me what I want, you must know this. So why suffer? Why put yourself through this agony? In the end, the result will be the same."

Fire lit in Erika's belly at the queen's words, at her arrogance, to think that Erika could not stand against her, that she would surrender so meekly. Staring into the queen's eyes, she found a spark of courage and bared her teeth.

"Because I am a princess of Calafe," she snarled, "because I will never surrender to the murderer of my people."

"Calafe?" The queen seemed surprised by that as she rose. "Since when? Did your people not chase you from your lands, steal the rightful crown from your head? Did you not come to me yourself and kneel as a citizen of Flumeer, swear yourself to my cause as Archivist?"

"That was before I knew the truth," Erika snarled. "Before your assassin revealed himself, before he told me about my father."

"Ah…" the queen sighed. "So Yasin found you in the end. I take it he is dead? A shame; men of his quality are difficult to find. Though he always did have a loose tongue."

"He killed my father on your orders!" Erika screamed, her rage coming alight at the queen's casual tone.

"A means to an end, my dear," the queen said, dismissing Erika's anger with a flick of her hand. Turning away, she clasped her arms behind her back. "While other leaders have fought and squabbled amongst themselves, I alone knew of the danger that was to come." She spun suddenly, golden eyes seemingly aglow in the dim light beneath the ship. "Tell me, Archivist, what did you discover in those mountains? What did you learn of *their* kind, of the Anahera?"

Erika's retort caught in her throat at the queen's words. "How...how do you know that name?" she whispered.

That was a name known only to the Anahera themselves. Surely Cara had not told her? No...looking into the queen's eyes, at the anger simmering those golden irises, Erika sensed there was more to this woman than she had realised.

"*They* were the ones who betrayed us, Archivist," the queen murmured, crouching before Erika. "The Gods we have worshiped, whom my father so loved—it was they who cast down humanity, who schemed to destroy our ancient ancestors." She paused, eying Erika a long moment, before nodding. "Yes, I can see it in your eyes; you found them, discovered the truth."

"How can you know?" Erika whispered, barely able to manage the words. The queen's words...they spoke a truth Erika had only learned from the Old One when she had invaded the city of the Anahera. How could Amina possibly...

"I have always known," the queen murmured, looking away. "My father discovered the truth. He knew they would come one day, that humanity's growing power would threaten them, and they would seek to destroy us again. He raised me to prepare for that threat, for the coming of the false Gods." She smiled bitterly. "When I heard your Goddess had revealed herself above the waters of the Illmoor, I knew that day was upon us. Alas, if you live, it means Yasin and his assassins failed. Time is short, Archivist. I will need every power at my disposal to defeat them. Come."

The last word was an order and Erika flinched, her

beleaguered mind unable to process the command. How did the queen know all this? Cara would not have told her such secrets, no matter the pain Amina gifted with the gauntlet. Only the Anahera and the Old One had known the truth.

"*Come*," the queen said again, and this time Erika managed to stagger to her feet.

The queen went first up the stairs. When she disappeared into the light above, Erika might have slunk back to her shelter, might have tried to hide again in her corner, but then the queen would only send her soldiers to drag Erika out. And besides, she had a yearning to see the world again, to discover what had become of Gemaho and its people now that Amina had conquered them.

Emerging onto the deck, Erika squinted against the brilliance of the day. The sun shone high overhead, announcing the noon meal—not that Erika would be offered anything. Her head swam as she looked around, finding massive cliffs stretching above the river on which they sailed.

Erika recognised their surroundings immediately—there was only one place like it in all the kingdoms of humanity. They were sailing down the Illmoor through the pass that connected Gemaho and Flumeer.

"Come and look upon the fate of those who defy me, Archivist," the queen called to her from the bow.

Erika swallowed at the power in the woman's voice. Her back was turned and the crew on the ship did not seem to be paying Erika much attention. She might have fled to the railings and hurled herself into the racing waters. But Erika was weak in mind and body, and instead she found herself staggering across the ship to where the queen waited, her spirit crushed, defeated.

Amina gestured to the shore as Erika joined her. A dozen ships sailed around them, each flying the scarlet sails of Flumeer, while a hundred yards away, an army shadowed the fleet on the banks of the Illmoor. They too bore flags of Flumeeren red, the conquering army returning to its homeland. Their numbers hardly seemed diminished from the force that had stood outside the Illmoor Fortress and demanded King Nguyen to surrender. She wondered what had become of the man, how he had been defeated so quickly.

Then the ship sailed around a curve in the gorge, and Erika looked upon the truth.

Ahead lay the Illmoor Fortress itself, whose walls had defended the lands of the Gemaho. For generations, those walls had defended the kingdom against Tangatan and human foes alike. No foe had ever breached their granite expanse.

Now the fortress lay in pieces, great holes torn through the stone of its walls, as though a giant had swung his club to break them. Blocks the size of small houses lay scattered around each breach, and part of the citadel had been broken too, crumbling before some vast power. Black ash scorched the stone blocks, suggesting some fiery explosion had been behind the fortress's fall.

"Your Archivists Guild finally proved itself useful," the queen announced. "After your departure, I had my guard tear their school apart in search of any secrets you might have hidden from me. Turns out they had secrets of their own. Black powder. Seems you used it for minor excavations, but my engineers saw other possibilities. The Gemaho never knew what struck them."

A shiver ran down Erika's spine at the destruction the queen had wrought. If the Illmoor Fortress could have fallen so easily…

"You see now, Archivist?" The queen's words echoed Erika's thoughts. "You see the truth? There is no one left to save you, no one left to stand against me. Nguyen, your father, they stood in my way. Now they are dead. Whatever it takes, I will unite the kingdoms beneath me against the Anahera. There is no reason left now for you to resist, nothing left for you at all, but surrender."

Looking upon the ruin, Erika knew it to be true. She closed her eyes, her body trembling. She imagined returning to the stale air of the hull, to the torture and pain, to the unending agony without even a hint of hope. No one would come for her. Nguyen was gone, his kingdom fallen, the Gods made slaves to the enemies of humanity. Her future held only agony, and death.

But the queen was wrong. There was still one person left that Erika cared about, one good deed she might yet fulfil.

"Okay," she croaked, eyes still closed, unable to meet the queen's gaze. "I'll give it to you. But first, I must see Cara."

❧ 3 ❧

THE SOVEREIGN

"Well, I can't say the past few weeks went quite as I imagined when I set out from Gemaho," Nguyen said to those gathered in the room.

Holding a glass of whiskey in one hand, the other tucked behind his back, there was regal manner to the way the king paced the room while Lukys and Sophia sat together on a velvet sofa. Lukys tried to hold himself a little straighter to mimic the king's posture, but it was only a moment before he slumped back into the soft cushions. It was no use—Nguyen had trained all his life in the ways of royalty. Lukys couldn't hope to achieve the same poise in the span of a few days.

"You mean when you *fled* from Gemaho, right?" Travis interjected. Standing at attention by the door, he seemed to take his Sovereigns' silence as an opportunity to speak himself.

A scowl crossed Nguyen's face as he glanced at the newly made royal guard. "It's customary for guards to keep their silence in a gathering of monarchs," he said with a scowl.

"It's also customary for a king to have a kingdom," Travis shot back, face blank.

For a second, Lukys thought the king might explode at his friend's impudence. The moment stretched out as Nguyen stared at the guard, teeth bared. Then suddenly the man let out an explosive laugh. Waving a hand, he turned his back on the gathering and continued his pacing.

"Might be your man is right, Lukys," he said, glancing at their sofa. "Regardless of how we came to our current circumstances, we have what we wanted: Gemaho and Perfugia united."

"It won't be enough," Sophia spoke up.

Lukys looked at her sharply, his consciousness already extended, sensing the familiar fear she had carried since that day in New Nihelm when Maya had slain her Matriarch. There was more to Sophia's fear now though, augmented by the knowledge they had acquired, though they had still only glimpsed a fraction. The rest lay buried, like the iceberg concealed beneath the waters. But what they had uncovered so far of the Old Ones filled Lukys with terror.

Sophia did not reply to his silent enquiry. Instead, she reached for the table beside their sofa. Taking up her glass of rum, she raised it in silent salute, then downed it in one go. Lukys raised an eyebrow as he sensed ripples of the alcohol's burning from his partner. She seemed to have developed an appreciation for Nguyen's various liquors over the last week, though Lukys understood from the Sovereign memories that a Tangata's sense of taste and smell were far more sensitive than humans.

Letting out a sigh, he took a measured sip from his own glass. Unlike Sophia, he did not have the metabolism of a Tangata, though...it might have been his imagination, but his senses *did* seem augmented now, as though the imbuement of all those lifetimes had passed something else onto him. He held the rum in his mouth, savouring the caramel tones overlaid by wood smoke. Memories stirred at the taste, an image appearing in his mind, of shacks built of wood clinging to cliffs, a hundred at most, a broad harbour stretching out beyond.

Ashura, as it had been long ago.

Lukys shivered. Nguyen claimed to have uncovered the cask in the Sovereigns' private cellar, a vintage over a century old. The image in his mind suggested it was even older than that, stretching back to a time not long after their ancestors had first arrived on the island.

The king did not return Sophia's salute, only stared at the Tangatan Sovereign, as though he were still trying to communicate in the telepathic manner of a Melder. Finally he shook his head and crossed to his own chair. A servant stepped forward to fill his glass from the decanter as he sank into the soft leather.

"What would you propose, My Lady?" he murmured.

"I do...not know," Sophia replied, her eyes drifting to the open window that overlooked the harbour. Outside, in place of the shacks Lukys had seen, buildings of stone stretched across the cliffs. "Only that we must stop Maya before..." She trailed off, and Lukys shuddered as fresh images flickered through their minds, of a land overrun, of fields, forests, an ocean aflame.

The king sighed. "How many Tangata will this Old One bring against us?"

"Maya will have thousands from New Nihelm," Sophia replied, "but...others have been moving north to occupy Calafe. My people once had a bond with that place, with its people, in centuries long forgotten..." She shook her head at the distraction, at the memories rising from the depths of their minds, struggling to restore her train of thought. "If she gathers more on her way north, they could number ten thousand by the time she reaches the Illmoor."

Her words sent a chill down Lukys's spine. "Even amongst the younger generations, it would take thirty thousand human soldiers to match that force." The younger the generation of Tangata, the more their lines were mixed with humanity. Sophia was of the fifth generation, the others they had brought with them mostly sixth. "Perfugia has only three thousand regular soldiers," he finished finally.

"And my fleet six thousand," Nguyen added grimly. "What of your citizens, though? If we could recruit—"

"*No*," Lukys cut him off, turning hard eyes on the king. "I will send no more untrained innocents to be slaughtered in a foreign kingdom."

The king scowled. "You would prefer them to be slaughtered in their houses when the Tangata come?" he snapped.

"I would prefer them not to be slaughtered at all," Lukys replied.

He thought the king might dig in his heels, but instead Nguyen waved a hand. "Fine," he said curtly. "Then what do you propose? A guerrilla campaign? We know the Tangata cannot easily replenish their number. If we retreat into the mountains and forests, avoid a pitched battle, we could whittle them down over a few years. It will cost Flumeer everything, of course. Turn the entire kingdom into a battleground, but I am prepared to play that game."

Lukys's skin crawled at the king's words, at the thought of condemning an entire kingdom to years of open warfare, to armies rampaging across their lands, resisted only by small freedom forces, striking the enemy where they could. He could never countenance such an option, even for the warlike Flumeerens. But there was another reason the king's strategy would not work; it was the reason the war needed to end, and end quickly.

"No," he replied softly, his tone so low that all eyes in the room turned to him. "We cannot afford to delay."

The king raised an eyebrow, but when he said nothing, Lukys swallowed and went on.

"It's different with this creature, with the Old Ones," he said, digging into those ancient memories.

The Sovereigns had only been created on their arrival in Perfugia, but even before then, the ancestors of the Tangata had passed knowledge between their generations.

"Maya, the Old Ones, they're fertile, virulent. In ancient days, they would gestate for a matter of months before giving birth to litters of half a dozen or more. Those children would grow to adolescence within two years, but even before that they could be dangerous. If you think *one* Old One is terrifying, wait a few years, and there will be dozens."

Lukys trailed off. A silence had fallen, heavy with the weight of his words, with the spectre of the danger that haunted them.

"Not even the strongest of the Tangata could stand against Maya's power. Give her time, and she will give birth to an army of her own kind, superior in every way to our soldiers, *and* the Tangata." He paused, those other memories stirring in the back of his mind. "Maybe superior even to the Gods."

There was more there, a flickering in the back of his mind, a memory of Cara soaring above, and others, winged figures in the sky, soaring through mountain peaks…

…then it was gone, slipping beneath the surface of a hundred others. He looked around, meeting the eyes of his friends, of the king, and let himself fall silent. Slumping into the sofa beside Sophia, he waited for someone to speak, to offer a plan, some semblance of hope. That had been his task for so long now, first as they marched south of the

Illmoor on the Archivist's mad quest, then again on their desperate flight from New Nihelm, on the ship amidst the storm, even here in Ashura, when they had faced the condemnation of the old Sovereigns.

But now...this time Lukys couldn't see where to begin. If she chose it, Maya could remain at the seat of her power, safe in New Nihelm, far from any danger humanity might pose to her. Their only chance was the rage of the Old Ones, that her hatred for humanity would drive her to attack, to place herself at risk.

"You're right," Nguyen said finally, his voice reassuringly calm, though Lukys didn't know how anyone could keep their cool when faced with such an existential threat. "We cannot let this Maya go to ground. She must be destroyed... even if it means going through ten thousand Tangata to get to her."

Lukys nodded, but before he could ask what the king planned, a fresh wave of emotion struck him, a surging, bubbling, rippling red, of anger, of rage. He looked sharply to Sophia at the abrupt change in her state, though...it came not just from her, but others in the room, from the blue-garbed guards, from her brethren Tangata.

Sophia had grown so pale Lukys feared she might lose herself, might surrender to the uncontrollable rage of the Tangata. Silently he reached for her, but she jerked away and swung on him, eyes wide, shining.

"You're talking about my *people*," she said, and hearing her voice break, Lukys knew suddenly the grief that lurked beneath her rage. "About slaughtering thousands of innocents. How can you be so casual, so calm, as though they were no more than numbers on a piece of your paper?"

"They are the enemy now, My Lady," Nguyen replied softly, leaning forward in his chair. "They have chosen their side."

"They have chosen *nothing*," Sophia grated. "Maya controls them, just as she would have controlled me, or any of my sisters and brothers in this room, had she turned her mind against us." She shook her head, and Lukys's heart twisted as a tear streaked her cheek. "You don't understand, *can't* understand…"

She trailed off and Lukys reached for Sophia with his mind, seeking to comfort her, to reassure her that he was there, that he understood. But for the first time since they had been granted the gift of the Sovereigns, he was met by a wall of grey, so thick he sensed not a hint of what hid beneath.

The sudden absence of her mind made his heart begin to race and he sat frozen for a second, unable to focus, to pull his thoughts together. Sophia's grey eyes swept the room, and in them he saw the emotion she hid, anger and fear, and confusion too. She knew the threat Maya presented, the danger the Old One posed to all their kinds. Her people were not the only ones that would suffer should the Old Ones return.

But they would be the first, if humanity moved against Maya.

Abruptly, Sophia rose. Without another word, she strode from the room. Movement came from around them as the other Tangatan guards followed her out, until only the humans remained.

Letting out a long sigh, Nguyen sat back in his chair and entwined his fingers. "There is a time in every ruler's reign when he comes to realise a terrible truth."

"Oh, and what's that?" Lukys snapped. In Sophia's absence, he found himself suddenly agitated, anxious about their separation. He could feel the memories pressing on him, an enormous ocean on which his consciousness floated, waiting to swallow him up. He feared there were more perils to the Sovereign gift than either of them knew.

The king raised his eyebrows at Lukys's tone, but when the Sovereign did not offer an apology, he went on with his explanation.

"There are many who call me a coward, who hate me for my actions following the southern campaign."

Lukys frowned at that. The king was not wrong. Just over a decade ago, the four kingdoms had led an invasion into the Tangatan homeland—only to have it go disastrously wrong. Barely half of those who had marched south had returned. Afterwards, Nguyen had withdrawn from the alliance, leaving the other kingdoms to face the wrath of the Tangata without Gemaho's aid.

"Most would have had me remain faithful to the alliance," Nguyen continued, his voice soft. "To send more Gemaho soldiers south to the frontlines, to be used as fodder in the battle against the Tangata."

Lukys frowned, surprised by the admission. "It *was* a cowardly act, abandoning the alliance."

"Perhaps," the king replied evenly, "but also a kingly one. Others do not understand, but before all else, a king's duty is to his people. Our own wants and desires, our pride and vanity, our past loves and friendships, all of it must be put aside before the weight of duty." He looked away, gaze sweeping out to the ships at anchor in the harbour. "I faced the Tangatan charge once, on the plains south of Calafe. After the events of that day, I knew they could not be defeated, not in open battle. Resistance would mean deaths by the thousands. That was a price I was unwilling to let my people pay."

He looked back at Lukys, and in that moment he saw the pain in the man's eyes, the guilt at what he had done.

"And so I ordered the Gemaho to withdraw. I abandoned the lands of Calafe, the kingdom of a man that had been my friend. Had it only been me, I would have fought to the end to protect those lands. But as king…" He trailed off, spreading his hands as though he had said everything that needed saying.

Lukys swallowed as Nguyen's emerald eyes watched him, until finally his gaze fell to the floor. A lump lodged in his throat and he shivered, thinking of all that stood before them. The challenge they faced was daunting, the thought of protecting all of Perfugia, of defending the shores of this peaceful archipelago all but impossible. And yet…

Swallowing, Lukys rose to his feet and nodded to the king. "I'll talk to her."

❧ 4 ❧

THE TANGATA

S tanding in the centre of the village, Adonis felt the very
air thrumming with the Voices of the Tangata, with the
growing excitement that always came before Maya's arrival.
This was the third Tangatan village they had visited since
reaching the lowlands. And it would be the third they left
empty, abandoned as its occupants marched north, just as its
former owners—the Calafe—once had.

Only the Calafe had fled before the Tangatan invasion,
while Adonis's brethren would march north for conquest.

The murmur of Tangatan voices swelled to a roar in
Adonis's mind, though beneath he could still sense the
beating of Maya's own Voice as she worked her power on
the crowd, feeding their anger, their lust for revenge against
the humans that had tormented them. Old memories of the
human invasion swelled in his mind, of brethren who had
died to human blades, of youth put to the sword.

Despite knowing the source of those images and his
strength as a third generation Tangata, Adonis's blood
began to pound in his ears. He clenched his fists, letting the

rage sweep through him, his own bloodlust surging along with that of his brethren. And yet…he was growing accustomed to his partner's presence, the pressure upon his mind, and finally he exhaled, relaxing as the anger flowed from him.

A shiver touched him instead as he scanned the faces of those gathered, and he glimpsed the prisoners in the rear, the human and her Anaheran bearers. How much longer must the human be carried, he wondered. A Tangata would have healed long ago. How such flawed creatures could have resisted his people for so long, he could not understand.

But it was not the human Adonis sought. His eyes settled on the Anaheran woman and he frowned. He had been harsh with her, forced her to confront the loss of her son. Adonis did not regret that, but…there was another guilt in his soul, a remorse for what Maya had done to the Anahera's son. Young and untrained in the powers of the mind, the young Anahera had never stood a chance against the powers of the Old One.

Silence fell in Adonis's mind, the Voices of the Tangata abruptly cut off. Only the dim pounding of Maya's Voice remained. Now it swelled to a crescendo as she walked amongst the low built stone buildings. The Tangata parted like water before a human ship as she strode to where Adonis stood.

Adonis's heart raced at her approach, at the sight of her swollen stomach. Smiling, she reached out a hand to cup his cheek, then pressed her lips against his. In a rush of heat, Adonis's concerns were swept away, consumed by the touch of her mind against his own, by the *roar* of her Voice.

Then the warmth faded, and he found himself standing fixed in place, watching as she turned to face the crowd. She raised her arms to them, her grey eyes, so like those of his own people, aglow with the power of the Old Ones.

"*My children!*" she spoke aloud, but beneath the human tone, her Voice carried to every mind in the village, caressing them, calling them, inviting them to join her. "*Come, hear me. The age of the Tangata is upon us!*"

At those words, the crack of wings came from overhead and half a dozen Anahera fell from the sky. Those of the Tangata who had not noticed Maya's prisoners gasped and leapt back as the creatures landed amongst them. They might not have worshiped the Anahera as humanity did, but even the simplest of his brethren knew of the creatures, that their power was not to be trifled with.

Now the Tangata of the village watched in awe as the Anahera fell to their knees before Maya, sinking into the soft mud at the centre of the Tangatan village. Standing over the kneeling creatures, the Old One raised her hands again to Adonis's brethren.

"*See how even the mighty Anahera bow before us?*" she cried. "*They have accepted the power of the Tangata, the power of your new Matriarch!*" Her eyes seemed to glow as she looked out over the crowd, and Adonis shivered at the thrumming in the air, the hiss of her voice upon his mind. He didn't feel the same elation he once had, watching her display, but he was still touched by her aura, by the glory of her promise. "*Soon, all the world will bow to our will,*" she went on. "*The humans that have plagued our people for so long will be vanquished, enslaved by their betters, as they were always meant to be. My children, join me in their conquest, in the heralding of our new world.*"

A roar sounded in Adonis's mind as the Tangata that had followed Maya from New Nihelm responded. It was only a moment before those of the village joined in, merging their minds with the crowd, with the collective of the Tangata that marched beneath the banner of the Old One.

Hearing the glory in their Voices, the ecstasy, a tremor shook Adonis. Witnessing their rapture, he found himself wondering if these newcomers would meet the same end as their predecessors. Would they too be left behind when she judged them weak, cast aside as though they held no more worth than the human they dragged with them?

Shivering, he looked again at Maya. Her Voice rung above the din of the crowd, silencing any doubters, those who might deny her. His blood stirred as he stared at her swollen belly, the life that grew within her, and he felt his own doubt subsiding. The weeks were passing rapidly now, and it would not be long before his children took their first steps into the world. What possibilities then, with a new generation of Tangata, invigorated by the power of the Old Ones?

Adonis found himself dreaming of the days that would follow, when his children would stand alongside him in battle. Together, they would lead their people against the enemy. Whatever remained of humanity would crumble before their power.

Are you well, my mate?

Shaking himself, Adonis looked around, surprised to find that Maya had returned to his side. Concern was etched into her brow and he saw now that the crowd had dissipated, gone to prepare themselves for the journey, to gather their children and elderly and leave behind this place they had made their home…

…to be led to their deaths.

Shuddering, he shook his head, frowning at his mate. He felt her mind pressing against his own, the vastness of her strength, but for once he resisted, did not capitulate to the power of her Voice.

I…confess I am concerned, he said softly, taking a step towards her and placing his hand on her engorged stomach. *Our path forward, this campaign against the humans…are you sure it would not be best if you returned to New Nihelm? You could wait in safety, while I lead our forces against our foes.*

A smile touched his mate's lips and reaching down, she entwined her fingers with his. As she held his palm to her stomach, he felt the soft movement of the life within. Tears stung his eyes as images of a future yet to be flickered before his mind.

They are but a few weeks away, my mate, she said softly. *These children will be everything you have ever wanted.* She hesitated, her eyes growing uncharacteristically distant. *But I cannot do as you suggest.*

Why? he asked, reaching up to cup her cheek. *The fate of our entire world rests upon your survival. Should the humans strike a lucky blow, should you fall…*

I will not fall, Maya replied, a soft smile upon her lips. She turned away then, eyes drifting to the mountains above. *Still you do not understand what is at stake, Tangata,* she said. *Once, my parents delayed their assault upon the humans, sought safety that my siblings and I could be welcomed into this world. It cost them everything.* She turned abruptly, her deep grey eyes catching Adonis's. *They are a plague upon this earth, the humans, a flame that grows brighter with every day we delay. Did you not see the magic the one in the mountains wielded? Grant them time, and soon a hundred such will come against us.* She shook her head. *Or worse, rediscover the magics of their ancestors. No, we must crush them now, grind them back into the mud from whence they came.*

Adonis shivered at Maya's words, for they were accompanied not only by her Voice, but images of her past, of a man and woman standing in a cave, of skies stained red, of horizons turned black with ash, an abyss that would never be filled. He swallowed, wondering at such a time, at a world twisted by the old magics of humanity.

A warm hand touched his cheek, drawing him back, and he found himself staring into the dark eyes of the Old One. For a second he glimpsed something there, a flicker in her mind, a hint of yellow fear, of doubt. But what did Maya, a being capable of defeating even the Anahera themselves, have to fear? Surely she did not truly consider humans such a threat?

Maya stroked his cheek again, then smiling, she moved away, calling for the Tangata to join her, to make ready for the journey, for the next desperate race across the wilderness. They couldn't be far from the great river that marked the border of human territory, just a few more days. Would they meet the humans there, or would their human captive's words prove true, and they would find the creatures busy warring amongst one another?

Adonis shook his head at the thought. Maya might fear them, but it seemed to him that if anything, humans had become like the Anahera—a shade of their former greatness. How could a species that spent half its time murdering one another possibly pose a threat to the Tangata?

But there was no arguing with the Old One, no dissuading her with his own Voice. So they would march north and fall upon the enemy, slaughter them where they stood.

And then he would welcome his children into a new world…

"She's using you, you know."

Adonis started as a voice carried from the shadows. The soft tapping of wood against rock came from a nearby building as the human, Maisie, appeared. While she still required bearers to carry her across the endless wilderness, her twisted leg had healed enough that she could hobble around the village with the aid of a wooden crutch. Only one guard was with the human, but Adonis was irritated to see it was the woman, Nyriah. At least she kept her face stoic today, her grief concealed.

Scowling, Adonis swung on the human woman. *What would you know, human?* he snarled, before realizing belatedly that she could not hear him. Cursing, he gestured for the Anahera to translate.

Maisie laughed before Nyriah could finish. "Your words might be hidden from me, Adonis." He started at the use of his name, but the human went on before he could interrupt. "But the body language between you and your master does not lie. You get to know these things, when your survival depends on reading those around you." She leaned casually against a building, appearing relaxed, though she faced a creature capable of tearing her in two at a whim. "Yep, no doubt about it, she's using you."

A pounding started in Adonis's ears at her words and he felt the Tangatan rage coming upon him, felt its burning, the longing to grasp the pitiful creature before him and throttle the life from her.

In an instant, he snapped, launching himself forward. The human's eyes widened—then he was upon her, catching the woman by the throat, hauling her into the air. A squawk escaped Maisie as she struggled, but it was little use. Her face contorted in pain as Adonis shook her, her injured leg bumping against his shoulder. Gasping, she slumped in Adonis's grasp, helpless before his rage.

Still trembling, Adonis dumped the woman to the ground, not caring about the scream as she struck. Lips drawn back in a snarl, he faced the Anaheran guard.

Translate, he snapped, then turned to the human without waiting for a response. "*You know nothing, human. Maya is the only reason you still live. You had best show more respect to the Matri-arch of the Tangata if you wish to see another day."*

The human lay panting on the ground for a long moment after the Anahera translated his words, gasping, moaning as she struggled against the pain of her leg. Adonis felt no remorse—she was only a human, a plague upon this world, as Maya had said. What need had he to pity such a creature?

"It was obvious…even back in…the Anaheran city."

For a moment, Adonis did not recognise the words amongst her gasps. When understanding finally dawned, he blinked, shocked at her continued defiance. Did this crea-ture have a death wish? He frowned. Was that what this was about, a way out for her, to make a quick end of her imprisonment?

"She makes you do her dirty work," the human rasped, "had you capture the fledgeling, has you stand with her at each village. One of their own, mated with a creature of legend. All so they will not question, so you will not realise the truth—she cares nothing for any of your people."

"She is our Matriarch," Adonis snarled. *"She will lead us to glory."*

"She isn't even one of you," Maisie replied.

A growl tore from Adonis's throat and he fought the desire to haul her from the ground and shake her again. But lying on the snowy ground, unable to stand or even lift herself to a sitting position, Maisie was too pathetic to be worth his effort. Adonis could only shake his head at her wretched figure.

"She will be the mother of my children, of a new generation of Tangata."

To his surprise, Maisie began to laugh, though lying there in the muddy snow, it sounded like sobs, might have even been both, given the undoubted agony from her leg.

A growl rumbling from his throat, Adonis advanced on her. "*Why do you laugh, human?*"

Her eyes snapped up, brown against the pale white of her face. "It's only, I didn't realise the Tangata were so gullible," she replied softly, shaking her head. "After all, what makes you believe the children are your own, Adonis?"

✣ 5 ✣

THE PRISONER

The queen's cabin was everything Erika's confinement in the hull of the ship was not. The interior was small, but had been filled with an opulence the queen rarely displayed in public. A golden chandelier dangled from the low ceiling, candles swinging slowly in rhythm to the ships rocking, and several silver-framed paintings had been hung from the walls. Papers decorated a mahogany desk in the corner, the etchings almost unreadable to Erika, and she wondered again at the queen, the secret knowledge she had hidden from the rest of the world.

Erika shivered as her eyes passed over a standing mirror and she saw herself for the first time in weeks. The long blonde hair she had once so prided herself in now hung in a tangled mess, ends split where she had hacked it shorter with a knife. Shadows hung beneath her sapphire eyes, and looking into their depths, she searched for the woman who had set off into the mountains all those weeks ago, determined to save the world.

But the truth was, that woman had perished in those mountains, crushed by the weight of her discoveries, the knowledge of the Gods' betrayal. Her spirit had faltered, and now she could not bring herself to stand again, to face the evils that threatened.

Shivering, Erika swallowed that despair, and forced her attention to what had brought her to this place.

In the other corner of the queen's chambers, Cara crouched in a steel cage so small the Goddess could not even lie down properly. At least it was tall enough for the Anahera to stand, but her auburn wings hung limp, unable to stretch within the bars of her confinement. Erika was relieved to see the wing Cara had injured in the mountains had at least straightened. Did that mean the Goddess could fly again?

Cara didn't look up at the entrance of Erika and the queen, and Erika swallowed, wondering what torments her friend had suffered at the hands of the queen. Though... after what Cara had faced in the mountains—the condemnation of her father, the subjugation of her people, the brainwashing of her brother...who then died at her own hand...

"Cara." The whisper slipped from Erika before she could contain it.

The Goddess flinched at Erika's voice, but it was a moment before she finally lifted her head. Her movements were slow, lethargic, as though she hardly retained the will to move. Amber eyes, once so full of life, met Erika's gaze, now vacant, empty.

A tremor shook Erika, and ignoring the queen, she slipped across the room and fell to her knees beside the cage. "Cara," she said again, trying to reach the Goddess through the bars. "Cara, what has she done to you?"

But Cara only looked away. Defeat hung about her like a cloak, and Erika couldn't help but recall her own despair on the deck above, the realisation that she was doomed, that she could not hope to stand against all the power of the queen.

And yet…seeing her friend's pain, Erika recalled their desperate battles in the mountains, how they had stood against the wills of Farhan and Maya both. Erika had defied the Gods themselves—and lived to tell the tale. She had saved her friend from a fate worse than death. That had to count for something.

"Cara," she whispered, gathering her courage. Managing to reach through the bars, she wrapped a hand around the Goddess's fingers and squeezed. "Be strong. I'm going to get you out of this."

Cara didn't so much as lift her head this time. Erika's stomach twisted, but giving her friend's hand one last squeeze, she straightened.

Queen Amina shook her head as she approached the cage, emerald eyes on the Anahera. "I thought the Gods would be regal, when they finally came for us. Still, I cannot ignore the danger they pose. It is fortunate you uncovered our people's lost magic, Archivist."

Erika swallowed as she faced the queen. How did Amina know such things, secrets that had been kept from humanity for centuries? It had been Cara who had first revealed to Erika the origins of the gauntlet she wielded, that it was born of human magic, centuries past.

Created in a time before the Anahera and Tangata had worked together to manufacture the fall of the world—and the destruction of human civilisation.

Tightening her fist, Erika faced the woman down, though the flicker of light that came from her gauntlet only set her swaying on her feet. Her vision swirled, as though she'd just run several miles on an empty stomach. Watching the queen, she wondered how the woman had come to master her own device so quickly, what poor souls she had tortured to perfect its use.

"How do you know about our ancestors, about the Anahera?" Erika demanded.

The queen waved a hand. "The source of my knowledge matters not—you cannot deny its truth. The Anahera will come for us with their Tangatan allies, just as they did in ages past. Humanity lies divided, unprepared and ill-equipped to face them. Our people will perish unless they unite beneath my rule."

"You're a traitor," Erika spat.

Amina snorted. "In more ways than you could possibly know," she replied, "but it matters not. The people believe the Anahera to be our saviours, that they will come at the hour of our greatest need, but you and I know the truth. They will turn on us when the moment comes. I must prepare the kingdoms for what they truly are."

At that the queen spun, a flash of light bursting from her gauntlet. Erika flinched away, a scream on her lips, but for once the magic was not directed at her.

Instead, it caught Cara in its terrible light.

Shrieking, the Goddess thrashed on the floor of her cage, back arched, wings beating against the bars, veins popping on her neck. Her entire body taut, fingers bent like claws, Cara gasped, helpless within the steel cage, defenceless to the human magic. A moan rasped from the back of her throat—then abruptly, the Goddess stilled.

Swallowing, Erika took a step towards the cage—and then the Goddess looked up. Ice slid down Erika's spine as she saw the grey eyes watching her from behind the bars, the familiar madness swirling in their depths, the rage, the need to rend and tear and destroy...

The light from the queen's gauntlet vanished as the

woman lowered her arm. In the cage, the fight instantly went from Cara and she slumped back to the floor, soft sobs whispering from her throat. Erika's eyes burned as she watched her friend, unable to comprehend the queen's casual cruelty.

"You see, Archivist? The beast lurks within your noble Goddess, waiting to emerge, to betray humanity as the founders of her people once did." The queen spoke in a quiet voice, untouched by emotion. Her eyes did not leave Cara, though Erika thought she glimpsed...something in their emerald depths. "Your treachery denied me for a time, but now I will show my people the truth. In Mildeth, humanity will learn what their Gods truly are."

"You can't do this to her," Erika whispered. "Cara is the best of them, the only one of the Anahera who believed in us, who refused to side with the Tangata." She was pleading now, desperate to dissuade the queen from her plan. "You're right, the others, they have allied themselves with the enemy, submitted to their new ruler, but Cara...she fought *for* us!"

"My dear Archivist, are you truly still so naïve?" the queen said. "I thought you would have learned something of the world by now, after all you have been through."

"I've learned," Erika hissed, clenching her fist, gathering what fragile energy she could muster. "Learned to trust in my friends." She drew in a breath. "To trust in Cara."

At that, she leapt at the cage, light dancing from her fist. Thrusting out her arm, she slammed it against the locking mechanism, and prayed she was strong enough to do what was needed. Red light flashed across her vision, followed by swirling darkness as the last of her strength drained away. Half-blind, she slumped to the floor, ears ringing, the metallic taste of blood on her tongue. Barely able to move, her stomach convulsed and she found herself retching acidic bile to the floor of the cabin.

A moan rasped from Erika's throat as she lay there,

unable to see, to hear, to know whether she had succeeded. In the mountains, the magic of the gauntlet had broken locks easily. Here though, half-starved, she feared the effort might have killed her.

Finally her vision cleared and Erika found herself looking up at the brightly lit cabin.

Her heart sank as she saw that the queen was unmoved, her arms crossed, a smile playing on her lips as she watched Erika. Except…no, she wasn't looking at Erika, but at something behind her. Stomach still convulsing, Erika struggled to push herself to her knees, to look around…

…and saw that the door to Cara's cage had swung open.

Erika felt the darkness rising once more, the call of unconsciousness threatening to swallow her up. She fought it, clinging to her mind, to her sanity. If she lost consciousness, who knew whether she would ever wake again?

Inside the cage, Cara had come to her feet and now stood staring at the queen. Wings spread, face set, she looked ready to spring, and yet…something kept her in place. Erika swallowed the acidic taste in her mouth, struggling to speak.

"Cara," she croaked. "Run, leave me!"

But the Goddess did not flee and as Erika watched, she saw a tremor cross Cara's face. Erika recognised the fear in her friend's eyes, the knowledge that to go against the queen was to risk an agony that could threaten her very sanity.

Laughter came from Amina as she uncrossed her arms and took a step towards them. "It seems my dear Archivist has yet to learn her lesson."

Shaking her head, the queen raised the gauntlet. Cara flinched, but to Erika's surprise, the queen only gripped the artefact with her spare hand. A hiss followed, then the strange metal fibres released their grip on the queen's flesh. Erika inhaled sharply as the gauntlet slipped from the woman's wrist. Tucking it into her belt, she gestured Cara forward.

"Come then, Anahera, let us see your strength."

Standing in the cage, Cara's eyes had widened. Her feathers quivered as she watched the queen for some sign of a trap, but...the woman was only human. She could not face an Anahera, not without her magic. No human came close to matching the Goddess's speed, her strength.

Hesitantly, Cara stepped from her prison. When the queen did not reach for the gauntlet, it seemed to grant her confidence, and spreading her wings, she snarled. Then suddenly she was surging across the cabin, wings beating hard, fingers outstretched. Erika flinched at the violence of the action—in the mountains, she had seen Cara tear a man limb from limb in the grips of one of her rages. Only Romaine's dying pleas had brought the Goddess back from that madness. If she lost control here...

The harsh *thud* of a fist striking flesh reverberated through the cabin, followed by a *crash* as Cara struck the floor. Erika watched, shocked, as the Goddess thrashed, wings entangled, fingers clutching at the boards, unable to stand, to regain her feet. When she finally managed to get her limbs right beneath her, she struggled to rise, to regain her footing...

...only to meet a second blow from the queen. There was a sharp *crack* as Amina's fist connected with the Goddess's brow, then the Anahera went down in a heap. Her wings twitched, and this time she did not rise, did not even move. Instead, Cara's amber eyes slid closed as she slipped into unconsciousness.

🜲 6 🜲

THE SOVEREIGN

L ukys paused in the doorway of their apartments as he caught a glimpse of Sophia within. She stood at the edge of their balcony, looking down into the now empty amphitheatre, the wind tugging at her curly brown hair. From where he stood Lukys could not see her face, but he could sense her mind once more, the grief roiling within.

He swallowed at the depths of his partner's sadness. It came not just from Sophia's own personal loss, but that of all her people, the pain passed on by those who had perished a decade before, when the Calafe had led the invasion of Tangatan territory. Lukys shuddered to think how many lives had been lost on both sides because of that disastrous campaign. The war between their peoples had been born in those dark days.

But the past was fixed, unchangeable. There was nothing he could do for what had already come to pass—he could only hope to change what was yet to come. Drawing in a breath, he moved through the apartment, out onto the balcony where his partner waited.

"Are you okay?" Lukys asked as he came alongside her and leaned against the railing.

Sophia did not look at him, but he could see the tears shining on her cheeks. Drawing in a breath, he looked out over Ashura. The spiral pattern of the citadel spread out before them, its swirling labyrinthine a testament to the arrogance of Sovereigns past—a masterpiece of architecture created only for their eyes. The passages of the outer citadel had no roofing, leaving them exposed to the elements and the eyes of the Sovereigns above. Lukys could see even now the men and women who were their subjects moving about the corridors. Various chambers housed nobles and dignitaries such as King Nguyen, and these formed domed circles amidst the spirals, like the compartments of some giant beehive.

Beyond the citadel, Ashura spread out across the slopes of the hillside, its multitude of marble buildings a stark contrast to the shacks their people had first settled in. At his back, Lukys could feel the icy chill of the mountains above the city, the endless depths of the fir forests. The Perfugians had built their city as a collision between civilisation and wilderness.

They were so like the Calafe, in that way. But there were differences here as well. Where the Calafe left no barrier between themselves and the wilds, living in small villages amidst the trees, the Perfugians built great stone walls around themselves, leaving the wilderness untouched, but separate from their lives.

But what did any of that matter? The Calafe had fallen, their lands taken by the Tangata, ruled over now by the Old One. Lukys wondered whether the creature would remain there, safe on the island of New Nihelm, or if she would march soon against the kingdoms of humanity.

The smarter tactic would be to remain, to consolidate

her power, but Lukys's new knowledge whispered to him. The Old Ones were not patient. She would seek to use her newfound army, to lead the Tangata against her enemies, to strike first, before they had time to organise. Even now, the Old One might be leading a force through Calafe, intent on striking at the Flumeeren border. Unless forewarned, they could not stand against so many.

But if Lukys were to send a message, it would warn Amina of the new leadership in Perfugia, that the Sovereigns had allied themselves with her enemy, King Nguyen.

"I thought we'd left this all behind," Sophia said suddenly. Lukys started, glancing at her from the corner of his eye as she turned towards him. "I wanted to escape the wars, the killing, Lukys," she continued. "Not wage one against my own people."

A pounding began in the back of Lukys's skull as he sensed his partner's uncertainty, and for just a moment he imagined himself standing in her place, facing the choice between the lives of her people, and that of her adopted home. How would he react, had he been asked to fight against Perfugia? Not just Tasha and her guards, but the ordinary men and women of the city? Maya would bring all the Tangata who lived in New Nihelm. Young and old, they would be unable to resist her call, the power of her Voice. Even those such as they had encountered in the seaside village, innocents who had refused to participate in the war against humanity, would be coerced into joining her campaign.

His stomach twisted and he drew her into a gentle hug. Shuddering, Sophia buried her head in his shoulder and began to sob, but Lukys found he could offer his partner no words, no reassurance for the choice they faced. What could he possibly say? That it would be okay, that they would save her people, find a way to kill the Old One while protecting the Tangata she controlled?

It was impossible. Maya was too powerful, too dangerous. Even if they *could* reach her, somehow sneak past her armies and Tangatan guards and confront the creature, not one of them had the strength to face her. Cara was the only being he had seen match blows with the Old Ones, and she had vanished with Erika in the Mountains of the Gods. They may never see her kind again.

Their only hope was to use overwhelming force, to defeat the Old One with sheer weight of numbers. That meant an army, one that must first face the Tangata she controlled.

There was no other choice but war.

So Lukys held Sophia tight and waited for her grief to pass. And as they stood together, his eyes drifted to the fleet of ships upon the harbour, the hundreds flying the colours of Perfugia and Gemaho, more even than they had soldiers to field. Some would remain in Perfugia, they had already decided, to protect the kingdom should their campaign fail. As for the rest...

...the rest would bring fire and sword to the mainland.

And death to Sophia's people.

"I want to live, Lukys," Sophia rasped, lifting her head from his shoulder. Her eyes met his. "I want to laugh and love and grow new life."

Lukys swallowed. There was such longing in her voice, in her eyes. Leaning down, he kissed her, his lips hard against hers, pulling her tight against him, holding her desperately, as though at any moment she might be lost to him. When they finally broke apart, he was panting. A fiery desire burned in his chest, to lift his partner into his arms and carry her to their chambers, to grant her everything she desired.

Instead, he gently brushed a lock of hair from her eyes. "You will have it all," he whispered. "I promise."

A tear spilt from her eye as she watched him, streaking her cheek. Her lip quivered and when she spoke again, her voice was so soft he barely heard her words. "At what cost, Lukys?"

Lukys shivered, but reaching down, he entwined his fingers through hers, then leaning in, he kissed the hot tears from her cheeks. "Don't cry," he whispered. Drawing their hands up between them, he held her tight. "We will find a way, Sophia."

"How can you be so sure?"

Has he ever lied to us?

Lukys looked around as two figures stepped from the shadows. It was still strange to see Keria and Isabella, Sophia's sister Tangata, garbed in armour and equipped with the silver spears of their new position, but their support was welcome. He nodded his thanks as they approached, laying their hands on Sophia's shoulders as she stepped away from him.

A wry smile crossed Sophia's lips as she looked to them. *Are you ganging up on me, sisters?*

Laughter whispered in Lukys's mind before Keria, who had chosen Dale as her partner, turned to him.

No, sister, we stand with our family. We expect our strange brother here to do the same.

Lukys inclined his head at the respect they'd shown him, naming him as family. He and the other Perfugians who had returned from the south felt the same. After all, it had been their fellow Perfugians who had condemned them to a cruel death on the frontlines. Whereas Sophia and the Tangata... they had welcome the Perfugian recruits into their homes, into their lives. It was a kindness none of them would forget.

Yet, Lukys found himself haunted by Nguyen's words,

by the king's insistence they would have to choose, that the lives of his people must come first.

But were the Tangata not his people too? After all, the Perfugians shared common ancestors with Sophia and Keria and the others. There must be a way he could protect both, however impossible it might seem.

Clenching his jaw, Lukys nodded in answer to Keria's words. "We will find a way to free your people," he said softly. "We must, or we do not stand a chance."

He could already hear Nguyen's objections, but the king was wrong. Whether he liked it or not, the fact remained that even united, the forces of humanity could not stand against all the Tangata.

It will not be easy, Isabella said. *You have felt the power of Adonis's Voice—he is only of the third generation. Maya is infinitely more powerful, strong enough to hold captive the will of our people, even over some distance.*

Lukys turned to Sophia. "Ay, but we are no longer just Tangata or human," he said quietly.

As he spoke, he reached with his mind for hers, felt their consciousnesses reunited, the surging, burning force of their collective of minds, the power of a hundred Sovereigns long passed, all the way back to the ancient rule of the Old Ones. Those voices cried out in unison against the rise of Maya, at the threat to their people and Tangata both.

Lukys's mind thrummed with the power of their Voices, the harmony he felt with Sophia. Could they use this strength, these past minds and memories against Maya? Surely there must be a secret, some power, some weakness of the Old Ones they could exploit.

Finally they looked back at their friends and smiled.

We are Sovereigns now, Lukys and Sophia said in unison. *We will find a way.*

❧ 7 ❧

THE TANGATA

Adonis paced among the silent trees, ice crunching beneath his boots, ears still pounding with rage—even a day after the human's insults. Even now, he longed to find her and tear out the creature's throat for her impudence...

Instead, he shuddered, recalling against his will the Tangata who had guarded the old Matriarch, who had turned on her to join Maya's side. They had perished assaulting the city of the Anahera, but they had been of the third generation too. The Old One had spent long hours with them during the journey into the mountains, when Adonis had lingered with his people, helping them through the storm...

He ground his teeth, and clenching his fists, Adonis turned his mind back to the human, the revenge he would have against her. His heart raced at the thought of watching the life flee from her eyes, to see her fear as she realised death came creeping upon her...

...how it pained Adonis that he could not touch her, not yet. For now, all he could do was stalk the forest in search of another target for his rage. It would be a day yet before they reached human territory, and even then, they may need to search for their foes if Maisie's information proved true.

But when they did finally encounter the humans, when they destroyed the enemy armies and took more captives, Maisie would no longer have value.

Then she would learn the true extent of his displeasure.

In truth, only Nyriah had kept Adonis from unleashing his rage against the human. Despite her subservience, the Anahera had stepped between them, protecting the creature's welfare, just as she had been ordered by Maya.

But that had not protected her from Adonis.

Now he paused in his stride, turning to where the Anaheran woman shadowed him. He'd removed her from assignment with the human. She was too close to the cunning creature, it seemed to Adonis, and so he'd made her his own personal guard. To keep an eye on her...

...though looking upon her now, a shiver ran down Adonis's spine. She had defied him to protect the human, and so he had unleashed his rage against her instead. Now bruises covered Nyriah's face and arms, just reward for her obedience. The pale skin typical of the mountainous Anahera seemed to bruise easily, though surely his blows could not have caused great damage to one of their kind. Certainly, Adonis suffered far more with Maya, when the lust took his mate and she threw him down beneath her...

What makes you believe her children are your own?

Adonis's rage returned and he advanced on Nyriah. They were alone in the forest, and he saw the fear in her eyes now, saw her flinch at his approach. Instantly, he regretted his actions. It was the human that deserved his castigation. Not this sorry excuse for a god.

You should not have stopped me, slave, he said harshly, looking up at the woman. He had quickly come to ignore the wings. Far from being a symbol of the Anahera's strength and majesty, he saw them now as a reminder of their cowardice, of the unfulfilled promise of her people.

"I was ordered to watch over her," Nyriah replied meekly.

To keep her from escaping, Adonis spat. He turned away, the anger slipping from him. *She will pay for what she said, one way or another.*

"Yes, master."

He glanced at her. *That's not…necessary.*

The Anahera bowed her head but said nothing. Adonis shook his head. It didn't matter what this creature said, what the human thought. He knew the truth. His future, the future of the Tangata, was bound to Maya. The children she birthed would be his, would give way to a new era for the Tangata. Within a generation the greatness of his people would be restored, while humanity would fail, crushed beneath the boots of the Tangata, reduced to mere servitude…

A shiver ran down his spine as another image flickered into his mind, of bodies in the snow, of the dead children Maya had left in her wake. They too had been weak, too fragile to be worthy of her love, however much they wished to serve the Old One.

She isn't even one of you.

Adonis clenched his fists, hurling the words from him. Maya was harsh, it was true, but everything she did was for the betterment of his people. After all, look what had come of their sacrifice, of the sacrifice of those they'd left behind. His people had conquered the Anahera, a feat unimaginable before her coming. And now…

…now they marched children through the snow. He swallowed, a lump lodging in his throat. The young Anahera were the picture of innocence, with their pale wings and wide eyes. They couldn't understand this cruel world they'd suddenly been plunged into, the hardship and death and pain they faced.

She reminds me of Farhan.

Adonis looked around as Nyriah's words whispered into his mind. The Anahera's eyes widened at his attention, as though she hadn't meant for the silent words to escape. His frown deepened and he advanced on her, watching the fear grow in her eyes, even as she clenched her fists, as her wings lifted in preparation for a fight.

But he knew she would not resist him, not with the threat hanging over the Anaheran fledgelings. She might have lost her own child, but she would not risk the lives of the others.

What did you say? he murmured.

A tremor passed across her face and she dropped her eyes to the ground, wings slumping into the snow.

"Please, forgive me, master. I spoke out of turn."

I asked you what you said, slave.

"I...only that the Old One...she reminds me of my former partner, of Farhan."

The one Maya slew? Adonis frowned. *Explain.*

Nyriah shook her head. He could see that she regretted speaking, could read the terror in the white of her aura. "Only that she is powerful, that she dominates those within her control, just as...just as Farhan did for our own people." She hesitated, still looking away. "But...I would not think to speak for your master."

She is not my master, Adonis hissed.

This time Nyriah did not flinch away. Instead, she faced him, eyes wide with defiance, though her body was tense, awaiting his blows.

She is my mate, Adonis said instead, *my Matriarch. Soon to be the mother of my young. She is more powerful than any other being alive. It is her right to dominate, to control those too weak to decide their own fate.*

"So very like Farhan indeed," the Anaheran woman replied softly.

No, Adonis rumbled. *Your Farhan was weak, trapped in a past long since vanished.*

And it is so different with the Old One?

Enough, Adonis snarled at her words, angered again despite himself. He turned away, struggling to contain himself. Drawing in a breath, he sought to slow the racing of his heart, then faced her once more. *Your words deserve punishment, but you have already suffered enough. I will spare you this once, Anahera. But be warned: you must learn to still your tongue.*

The Anahera bowed her head in submission. *That is kind of you, master.*

You may call me Adonis, he said dismissively.

In another lifetime, you might have called me Nyriah. But now I am naught but a slave, and you my master. She finished there, but he sensed there was more beneath her words, a hint that she thought the same as Maisie, that he was as much a slave as the rest of them.

Be gone, he snapped before he lashed out again. *Return to your duties with the human. I have no more need for you, slave,* he snarled.

As you wish, master, Nyriah replied with a short bow. Turning, she vanished into the trees.

And Adonis was left alone with the ghosts of his doubts.

❧ 8 ❧

THE PRISONER

Anger shone in the queen's eyes as she watched the unconscious Cara. The moment stretched out, until it seemed certain she would strike again, would snuff out the life of the Goddess with a final blow. A cold smile spread across her lips as she looked to Erika.

"I should kill her for that." Lifting her boot, she placed it on the Anahera's throat.

Her eyes never left Erika and a shudder shook the Archivist. Still too exhausted to even pull herself up off the floor, she shook her head, eyes watering.

"Please, don't," she gasped.

The queen's emerald gaze did not flicker, but she removed her boot.

"I should have expected nothing less from my former prodigy," she said finally.

Leaning down, she gripped Cara by one of her wings and dragged the Goddess across the cabin. With a flick of her wrist that revealed again her impossible strength, she tossed the Anahera back into her cage. A clang sounded as the unconscious Goddess struck the bars and slumped to the metallic floor. Erika reached for her friend, but a boot came down on her hand, pinning her to the floor.

"The game is at an end, Archivist," Amina said softly. "All that remains is for you to concede."

Tears blurred Erika's vision as she stared up at her former mentor, the woman she had aspired to become, whose approval she had sought to win for so long.

The same woman that had seen her father murdered, her kingdom cast down, her friend killed.

Who had just defeated one of the Anahera in hand-to-hand combat.

"How?" she rasped, still unable to comprehend the queen's power.

Laughter rumbled from Amina's throat as she removed her boot. Pain shot up Erika's arm as the blood rushed back to her fingers, and the barely mended bones began to ache. She made to sit up, but faster than she thought the queen lashed out, her boot catching Erika in the side. Breath hissed between her teeth as the blow threw her onto her back.

Gasping, unable to inhale through her winded lungs, Erika lay looking up at the queen's rage.

"Stupid bitch," Amina spat. "When will you learn to admit your failures? You're weak, Erika. Unworthy." Shaking her head, she turned away. "You will never understand the burden I carry, the responsibility placed upon my shoulders."

Finally catching her breath, Erika managed a groan as she rolled onto her side. She did not speak or try to rise, fearing the queen's wrath. Amina had not replaced the gauntlet on her hand, but it was obvious that the woman had never needed it, not for one so weak as Erika. What secret had the woman hidden all these years, to possess such power? Her vision swirling, Erika watched the queen cross to the mirror in the corner.

Then lifting her arms, she pulled off her heavy chainmail vest. The rings chimed as they slipped over her shoulders, then struck the ground with a jingling *thud*. The woollen tunic she wore beneath followed, until all she wore were her fine undergarments.

A hiss rasped from Erika's throat when she saw the queen's back. Suddenly blood was hammering in her ears and she found she could not look away, could not tear her gaze from Amina. Crouched on the floor, Erika stared at the scars the queen bore, at the twin circles of twisted tissue marking the skin on either side of her spine.

"Imagine my father's joy when my mother first revealed herself to him," Amina murmured, turning so she could study her back in the mirror. "And imagine his shame when years later she finally revealed the truth about her people." Erika could see the queen's rage in the mirror, furrowing the edges of her eyes, turning down her narrow lips. Abruptly, she spun and advanced on Erika. "He loved her. I know it, though I have no memory of the bitch."

Erika opened her mouth, then closed it again, unable to form a coherent thought—let alone words. How was this possible? How could one of the Anahera have sired a human queen? A murmur came from behind her, as Cara stirred in the cage, and an icy suspicion filled Erika's chest. Could it be?

"Your mother?" she croaked.

The queen looked away. "The creature seduced my father, convinced him he had been blessed by the Divine. Only during my birth did he learn the truth. With his own eyes, father saw my mother change, saw the beast that lurked within, the madness they share with the filthy

Tangata. It broke his heart, but he knew he had to act, before that beast was unleashed upon our world."

"He killed her," Erika whispered.

"Eventually," Amina replied with a sneer. "My father was prudent. He knew there were truths to be uncovered, secrets the false gods had hidden from us. With fifty of his most trusted men, he tricked my mother, imprisoned her deep beneath the citadel in a cell not even her kind could escape." Amina shook her head. "The...creature admitted it all, by the end: the treachery of the Anahera, how they destroyed the cities of our ancestors, ground us into the dust."

Erika shuddered at the cold way Amina talked about her own mother, but already the queen was speaking again.

"They say she begged my father to spare me. Perhaps that is why I still live...why he laid this charge upon me, why he spent his final years preparing me to face the demons that hide in the mountains."

Erika swallowed, horror still clawing at her throat. "He...he took your wings."

"The mark of demons," Amina spat, swinging on her. "My father hoped removing them would spare me their darkness, though he was prepared..." She trailed off, glaring down at Erika. "He took a terrible gamble, but he hoped I would have the strength to stand against them, to do what was necessary. Every moment of my life has been spent in preparation for these days."

"He created a monster," Erika whispered, slumping to the floor. Shaking her head, she looked up at the woman. "But why would you kill my father, when he fought against the Tangata?"

A cold smile crossed Amina's lips. "Your father served his purpose well," she replied. "Peace had made humanity weak, unprepared for the coming threat. The Calafe king was a fiery man, quick to anger, easily manipulated. He began the war that would forge humanity anew, but I could not allow one so flawed to lead us. When he fell, humanity was to unite beneath my leadership. Together, the four kingdoms would have crushed the Tangatan threat." She hesitated, eyes narrowing. "But King Nguyen ruined everything when he abandoned the alliance. I had to find other ways to bring about unity." She gestured back in the direction of Gemaho, as though in explanation.

Listening to Amina's words, Erika felt something die within her, the last remnants of her defiance. Her eyes slid closed, despair withering her soul. All along, this woman had been a step ahead of the other monarchs. Amina was right. Erika could not defeat this woman. She was too weak, her strength sapped, her last hope lying crumpled in the cage, defeated.

Abruptly, Erika's world spun as the queen grasped her by the shirt and hauled her up. Crying out, she struggled against the queen's impossible strength—until she glimpsed the fiery light of the gauntlet. Amina wore its silver threads on her hand again. Now its glow bathed the cabin, red and threatening, promising pain.

Watching that light, Erika found herself unable to look away, to fight back, to do anything but slump in her captor's grip and wait for the pain to find her, for the agony to sweep her mind away on a sea of madness...

...but that pain did not come, as instead the queen suddenly turned from Erika, her eyes drawn to the wooden walls of the cabin. A frown creased the woman's forehead.

"What?" she murmured. Before Erika could understand what was happening, her eyes widened. "So they have come. It is earlier than I'd hoped, but I am not unprepared."

Erika cried out as the queen hurled her backwards. The back of the open cage brought her to an abrupt halt and she crumpled atop her friend, drawing a moan from Cara. Before Erika could even roll off the Goddess's wings, the door to the cage slammed shut with a harsh *click*, the locking mechanism reengaging. Smouldering emerald eyes glared down at them.

"I will leave you to contemplate your fate, Archivist. If you still have the strength to use your gauntlet, I dare you try and escape. You will not make it far." She held up her fist, a flash of light sending tremors down Erika's spine. "And I promise, the attempt will make your end all the longer."

With that she turned away, disappearing up the stairs to the upper deck of her ship.

9

THE SOVEREIGN

Wind whipped at Lukys's cheeks as the ocean surged around the ship, sending water hissing over the bow to strike at his flesh like knives. He ignored the stinging, eyes fixed on the distant walls that rose from the swirling blue.

Mildeth.

He could still recall his last journey to the city, a brief stop at the end of a short voyage across the narrow sea. The crossing had taken only hours and the Perfugian recruits had not lingered within the city before beginning their march south.

This time, Lukys intended to make an extended visit.

The defensive walls facing the harbour were taller than those in Ashura, raised in centuries past to defend against pirates that had once plagued the coast. The rise of Perfugia had put end to those outlaws, as their fleet hunted them down one by one. But the Flumeeren walls remained, and now they barred the soldiers of Perfugia from an easy victory.

But Lukys had hopes it would not come to battle. Their intelligence was that Queen Amina remained in the south with the majority of the Flumeeren army. That suited Lukys's purposes. Their own fleet followed a half-day behind with Nguyen, but if things went to plan, they would not need the king's forces to take the city.

It was a risk, sailing ahead with but one ship. If those in control of Mildeth suspected a trick, they might bar the gates. Forewarned, the city would mass defenders atop those giant walls, making it difficult for the invaders to gain a foothold. They might extend the siege for weeks—long enough for the queen to bring reinforcements.

That was why Nguyen had wanted to attack immediately, using overwhelming force so the city would fall quickly. But Lukys couldn't bring himself to throw away the chance for a peaceful resolution.

After all, the Flumeerens had no reason to believe Perfugia came for conquest. The Sovereigns rarely left the shores of the island, but it would not be the first time they had ventured to the mainland in times of strife. He remembered when they'd come to the assembly called by King Micah of Calafe…

…Lukys shook his head, trying to separate himself from the consciousness of the Sovereigns who had come before, who had stood with the other kingdoms and set out to make war against the Tangata. Such a strange sensation, to know he had played no part in those events, and yet…

…he could picture the noble Micah perfectly as he called on their aid, could recall his righteous fury as he demanded support of Queen Amina, as he swayed the young King Nguyen to his side.

Lukys found himself turning in search of Sophia. Finding her alone at the railings, he wondered if she too had found that memory. How must it feel, to recall making a decision that had condemned so many of her people to death?

Even for himself, that memory was a knife twisting in his gut. The Sovereigns before them had been so cold, so calculating in their decisions, the product of a hundred lifetimes placed into the minds of children. Their predecessors had never had a chance to live their own lives, to develop a consciousness beyond that which they inherited.

Struggling with those memories, Lukys wondered whether he too would succumb to the tide, if one day he and Sophia would become as those Sovereigns before them, removed from the lives of mere mortals, incapable of measuring the value of a single life.

Would Lukys one day come to understand the logic of sending untrained recruits to die for the simple crime of failing an examination?

The thought made him shiver, but he shook off such dark contemplations and crossed to where Travis stood at the tiller. His friend wore a broad grin as he directed the ship towards the safety of the harbour, though he offered a quick salute at Lukys's approach.

"My Sovereign," the man said in an overly dramatic fashion. "A million thanks for this ship you have provided. Much better than the last one."

Lukys snorted. "You mean the holey fishing boat you sailed across half an ocean?"

"I remember her fondly," Travis remarked. "A shame this journey is so short. I would have liked to see how this beauty did against a storm."

Lukys shuddered at the memory his words conjured. This one he had lived himself. "Let's just give thanks for the sunny skies," he replied with feeling.

Silence fell as they turned their eyes to the city. Two smaller vessels had detached themselves from the docks to escort them in, and Lukys couldn't help but feel his tension growing.

"I'll leave you and Isabella onboard with a skeleton crew," Lukys said. "If we don't return…"

"Don't be so grim, Lukys," Travis said with a laugh. "It's a few bureaucrats and those in their army who were too old or green to march south. After facing Tasha and her rebellion, the pair of you should have no problem with this lot."

Lukys sighed. He wished he could feel Travis's confidence, that everything would work out as they intended. But whatever his jovial friend said, things had a habit of spiralling out of control when it came to Lukys's plans. Ever since he'd first picked up a spear and lead them in defence of Fogmore's walls all those months ago, nothing had gone as he'd intended.

But he would press on regardless. There was no other choice.

As the Flumeeren vessels pulled up on either side of their flag ship, Lukys was relieved to see only a few soldiers aboard. He hoped that meant the Flumeerens remained unaware of their alliance with Nguyen. Even so, he watched the gates of the city as they approached, seeking signs of some trap.

But as they drifted into the port, no soldiers came rushing from the gates to attack them, nor arrows from the sky to strike them down, and Lukys finally let out a breath and moved to join Sophia at the bow. She wore a cloak with the hood pulled up, a veil drawn across her face. He quickly lowered his own to complete their illusion. The mystique of the Sovereigns was well-known across the human kingdoms, and he prayed the Flumeerens would not question the concealment of their faces. One glimpse of Sophia's grey eyes, and all his careful planning would fall apart.

"Peace, My Lady," Lukys said softly, reaching out to take Sophia's hand. "I promise you. Now, let's go trick some Flumeerens."

They were met on the docks by two dignitaries and their guards. Lukys had rarely seen such an odd assortment of nobles, although his experience with their kind was rather limited. An overweight man in a bright orange robe led the way, his face damp with sweat, as though their arrival had forced him to run through half the city to reach the docks in time. Behind him followed an elderly man with more wrinkles than even the most ancient of Lukys's history professors back in his academy. Supported by a cane, the man arrived a few steps behind the big man.

The two fell into a steep bow as Lukys and Sophia descended the ramp from their ship, and Lukys was struck by the difference a few weeks made. It seemed like only yesterday that their arrival on the shores of Perfugia had been met with armed soldiers and threats of violence.

Then again, if the Flumeerens realised that a party of Tangata stood amongst them, it might yet come to violence. After all, this kingdom had been at the forefront of the war with Sophia's people for ten long years.

"Exalted Sovereigns!" the large man wheezed, clearly still trying to catch his breath. "Please, I am Wallace, steward of the royal citadel. I must apologise for my queen's absence, but she is occupied by grave matters in the south. I welcome you to Mildeth in her absence."

"It is an honour to witness your arrival on our humble shores, your dignities," the elderly man added, his voice soft. "I am called Zayaan, chief advisor to the queen. As the good steward says, your visit is welcome—if unexpected. I fear you have come to Flumeer at a time of ill fortune."

"So we understand," Lukys replied, doing his best to adopt the haughty tones of the nobility. "Some trouble with Gemaho?"

"Yes," Wallace replied, his eyes flickering to the open sea. "We are on high alert for the Gemaho king. His fleet has not been seen since the coward fled down the Illmoor, escaping our majesty's righteous wrath. Your ships have not caught a glimpse of his presence, perhaps?"

"I'm sure the noble Sovereigns of Perfugia would have alerted us immediately had they encountered the coward king," Zayaan interrupted, hands clasped at his back as he shot the steward an irritated look. "As I am sure they would prefer to discuss such delicate matters within the protection of the city walls."

Lukys blinked, taken by surprise at the speed at which they had been invited into Mildeth. Despite their outward confidence, it was clear both men were nervous about the prospect of an attack on the city by Nguyen. If only they knew how close they were to the truth. Thankfully though, Lukys's veil concealed any emotion that might have given him away, and he only inclined his head in agreement.

"We thank you for your hospitality, Zayaan," he replied. "Shall we proceed to the citadel then?"

The men nodded quickly, but as they made to turn away, something behind Lukys and Sophia caught the steward's attention and he hesitated. Glancing over his shoulder, Lukys saw that Dale and the other royal guards were marching down the ramp onto the docks.

"Oh!" Lukys turned back as Wallace let out an exclamation. "You brought soldiers, I see. Excellent, excellent, every sword is welcome in the war against the traitor. Only..." He hesitated, glancing at the elderly Zayaan, then back to Lukys. "We have orders from our queen prohibiting the entry of foreign soldiers into the city, regardless of their allegiance."

Lukys's heart began to race as he saw all his carefully laid plans unrolling before him. They had hoped to gather the leaders of the city in an assembly and take them hostage with their own guard, preventing them from commanding their forces to defend the city. But without Dale and the others, Lukys and Sophia would be alone in the citadel. They risked becoming hostages themselves when Nguyen arrived with the bulk of their forces.

"My dear steward," Sophia spoke before Lukys could announce his displeasure. "It would be a difficult task for our soldiers to defend the city if they are forced to remain outside its walls."

Lukys glanced sharply at his partner, surprised not only by her words, but how they had been spoken. Gone was the singsong accent she'd adopted since receiving the gift of the Sovereigns—in its place was a perfect imitation of a Perfugian noble. For a moment, he was left questioning whether it was truly Sophia who spoke, or if another of those minds within her had taken control of her voice.

"I..." The steward wrung his hands, clenching and unclenching his fists as sweat dripped from his brow. "I am sorry, good Sovereign, but I...perhaps a message...the queen."

"Surely your queen could not have thought to apply such restrictions to the Sovereigns of Perfugia, her last remaining ally in this terrible war? To think we would enter a foreign city alone..." Sophia shook her head, glancing to Lukys. "It seems we were wrong to think our aid would be welcomed, my dear. Perhaps we should return—"

"No!" Wallace interrupted. "Please," he continued, lowering his voice, "our forces are badly depleted here. Should Nguyen appear, we could not hold the walls against him for even a day."

Sophia said nothing, only stared at the man from beneath her veil, waiting...

"I am sure we can come to some arrangement," Zayaan said finally, shifting alongside the steward. He had named himself the queen's advisor—perhaps that meant he had some authority to supersede her orders. "Perhaps we could permit…two of your guards to enter alongside your noble personage," he offered finally.

Lukys grimaced beneath his veil. His plan didn't require defeating the Flumeeren army, only that they took enough of their leaders hostage to prevent the organisation of the city's defences. Would four of them be enough?

It would have to be.

"Very well," he said abruptly. "Dale, Keria, you will accompany us into the city." Their helmets would conceal Keria's Tangatan eyes, and her Tangatan strength would be an added advantage. He inclined his head to the pair of nobles. "If you would permit our remaining soldiers to disembark, perhaps they could take refreshments outside the walls. That way they might be of some aid outside the gates, should the Gemaho fleet happen to make an appearance."

Zayaan nodded his agreement, and Wallace sighed his relief. "Excellent, excellent," he exclaimed, offering another short bow before spreading his hands in the direction of the city gates. "Then may I again bid you welcome to the glorious city of Mildeth."

Lukys sucked in a breath as he looked to the gates of the city, wondering whether they were making a terrible mistake. A glance back at their ship showed their soldiers beginning to disembark. He clenched his jaw, considering one last time the wisdom of this decision, before turning again to the two men. If things went wrong and this was all some elaborate trap, at least he would be able to communicate with the Tangata outside. That was an advantage the Flumeerens would not suspect.

And so he exhaled, and nodded for Wallace to lead them into the stronghold of their enemy.

✤ 10 ✤

THE TANGATA

The dark waters swirled as Adonis struck out through the racing currents. The river fought him, sought to drag him down into its murky depths, to steal away his warmth. But on the quiet spring night, it would not succeed.

His heart pounded with the thrill of what was to come, his mind thrumming to the beat of war, the Voice of his mate. The time had finally come for them to strike against the true enemy, to destroy the humans who had dared venture so close to his people's territory.

The ships had anchored themselves only a few hundred yards from the shore. Truly, the humans had grown bold while the Tangata had been occupied in the south. Now they would suffer for their arrogance.

The sight of the ships had driven Maya into a rage. Her hatred had swept over the ranks of her Tangata, their numbers swollen by the journey north, until all who stood upon the banks of the great river had yearned for the blood of their foes. With night already fallen, the distant lanterns burning upon the waters had become beacons, drawing the Tangata like moths to the flame.

Adonis led the attack, an assault that would finally break the impasse upon the great river. United, the Tangata would sweep the humans back from their barricades, shatter their defences. Without the natural advantages of the river to bolster their defences, it would only be a matter of time before the armies of humanity crumbled, before their cities fell, before their so-called civilisation was reduced to ashes.

His stomach churned strangely at that thought, and he found himself thinking back to New Nihelm, the human city the Tangata had conquered, that they had made their home. Though he loathed the creatures who had built the city, Adonis couldn't deny that there had been a beauty about the place. Those who had first raised the wooden buildings had long since passed, but their descendants continued their work, caring for the city, adding to it, until succeeding generations had built something grand.

Swimming through the racing waters, Adonis found himself wondering if one day his children might build such a city, if they might raise wonders from the stones of this earth…

…or if they too would bring destruction.

He shook off the thought as the shadow of a ship rose above him, the curve of its hull illuminated by a lantern hung from its rigging. Pausing, Adonis sought the Voices of his brethren, their rage, the thrill of their excitement for the battle to come. His own heart responded, his anger stirring, though he could not muster the same emotion he had felt at Maya's side.

A rope ran from the ship into the waters, taut with the weight of the anchor. Quiet now in the swirling currents, Adonis directed himself towards the rope, catching the coarse fibres in strong hands. As the others in the water grew close, he began to climb.

The night greeted him with a cold breeze that cut

through his thin clothing. Water poured from him to splash upon the river, loud enough that he feared the humans might hear. But the creatures' senses were blessedly poor, and no shouts carried through the night to alert the sleeping soldiers.

A smile touched Adonis's lips as he continued his climb. He had missed the battle with the Anahera, being one of the few Maya had trusted to hunt the fledgelings instead. Now he once again had the honour of leading his people in battle. This was what he lived for, what he had been born to do. The third generation had been great warriors, the last of the true Tangata, possessed of the strength to run all day and battle all night.

The stench of humanity struck Adonis as he pulled himself over the railings, the reek of dozens of bodies crushed together in filthy conditions. He couldn't imagine how the creatures stood to live in such cramped confines. Even now he could hear them below, the whisper of voices, the snoring and the grunts. The ship must have held a hundred of the creatures, yet it could not have been larger than the villa he had occupied in New Nihelm.

Dropping to the deck of the ship, Adonis examined his surroundings, waiting for his brethren to join him. Most of the soldiers slept below and at first he saw no one. A small cabin was lit by a lantern at the stern, a pile of barrels stacked nearby. This was the largest of the dozen ships anchored on the river. Maisie had claimed it was the flagship of the Flumeeren kingdom, that it might belong to the queen herself.

That thought made Adonis's heart clench with anticipation. If the Flumeeren queen fell this night, the kingdom would not be long in following. That was the way of these creatures. Led by the right man or woman, they fought like demons, refusing to lie down and die when they had no right to fight on. But when that leader fell, her followers fell with her.

Adonis tensed as he sensed movement, and a human armed with a spear emerged from behind the cabin. He must have been making his rounds, for he continued along the railings, eyes on the water below. Adonis watched the man, wondering if the humans were truly so arrogant to post only a single guard. Surely this close to Tangatan territory, there must be another…

The squeak of a board was the only warning Adonis had. Spinning, he flung up an arm as the soldier creeping up behind him thrust out with a spear. Adonis wore no armour and the blow would have driven the blade straight through his back—if not for his inhuman speed. Instead, he twisted, wrist slamming against the haft of the weapon and deflecting it into the wooden boards at his feet.

The soldier's eyes widened as his attack failed, and snarling, Adonis leapt at him, seeking to silence the threat before it could alert others. But the soldier recovered his wits quickly, and a scream escaped his lips a second before Adonis tore out his throat.

Adonis stilled as the body struck the deck, fists clenched, praying that none had heard the cry, that the foolish humans would put it down to a trick of the wind, of the river…

Whoooorl!

Adonis cursed as a bugle horn came from the other side of the ship, the second soldier sounding the alarm. The note rose above the silence of the night, carrying to the soldiers below—and the other ships as well—alerting them to the danger that stalked them this night.

But it alerted the Tangata too, and the battlecry of Adonis's brethren rang out across the river.

Adonis's body reacted before his mind. Surging across

the deck, he caught the human before it could blow another warning note. The horn struck the deck with a heavy *thump* as Adonis sucked in a breath, fighting off the call of the Tangatan rage. He could not afford the madness now, not if he was to lead his people.

Movement came from nearby, followed by shouts and a sharp *twang* as something fired in the darkness. Adonis spun and something *hissed* through the space he had occupied. A clacking sound followed that Adonis recognised as the reloading of a human crossbow.

Roaring, he charged towards the noise. From behind, he sensed his brethren as the first reached the top of the rope. Adonis needed to keep the enemy occupied for only a few moments longer.

The human with the crossbow saw him coming and tossed their weapon aside, its wire still only half loaded. He fumbled for his spear, but Adonis caught the wooden haft before the man could bring it to bear. Fear showed in the human's eyes as Adonis tore the weapon from his hands, but to his credit, the man did not flee. He was reaching for the dagger on his belt when Adonis's fist struck his skull. Despite the metal helmet worn by the human, he dropped without a sound, and Adonis turned in search of his next victim.

The first of his brethren had reached the deck now, but as Adonis watched, a door at the rear of ship burst open and humans half-dressed in armour poured from the darkness below. In moments, a dozen of the creatures stood against him, weapons held high, dull eyes scanning the darkness for hint of the creatures that had come upon them. The few lanterns burning were not enough for the pitiful humans to spy the Tangata in the shadows. Adonis might have laughed.

Instead, he roared and charged the group of humans.

The soldiers reacted instantly, swinging towards the

sound. A dozen was too many for Adonis, even in the dark, but his charge drew their attention away from where his brethren still emerged from the dark waters.

Then Adonis was amongst them, slicing through their ranks like a dagger, fists flashing, leaping and dancing between their blows, striking soft flesh and hard steel wherever his foes lowered their guards. Cries of pain filled the night and in those first seconds several of the humans crumpled, clutching at broken ribs or shattered kneecaps.

Still roaring, Adonis ducked and weaved, narrowly avoiding the desperate thrusts of steel weapons. The humans found their spears almost useless in such close proximity, and several of the more intelligent tossed the weapons aside and drew short swords.

It was one of these that spilt the first of Adonis's blood that night. He cursed as the blade sliced his cheek and leapt back, twisting away from an awkward spear thrust in the process. Heart racing, he felt some of the rage leave him, reason returning. The human's blow had been just inches from his throat. It had almost ended him, snuffed out his life and left his children alone, with only Maya to raise them.

For some reason, that thought chilled Adonis and he took another step back from the humans, allowing them a moment to regroup—and for his brethren to finally join the battle. Their silent cries echoed through the night, unheard by the humans, so that they did not turn as the Tangata charged.

Adonis smiled, satisfied as his brethren fell upon the humans from behind. Of the fourth and fifth generations, human bones still shattered beneath their blows. Despite their resilience thus far, the humans crumpled before the surprise attack. Screams rent the night as they scattered—and one by one were hunted down by their Tangatan foes.

His victory achieved, Adonis was about to join in the

hunt, when a figure stepped from the nearby cabin. Garbed all in steel and wearing a helmet engraved with a golden crown, the figure raised a sword high and charged a group of Tangata. Distracted by the human soldier they had been tormenting, Adonis's brethren scattered at the sudden assault, though not before one had fallen to the newcomer's blade. Spinning to face the others Tangata, the human raised its blade to the sky.

"Soldiers of Flumeer!" The woman's voice lifted above the chaos, calm, determined. "To me!"

❧ 11 ❧

THE PRISONER

E rika sat up in the cage as a scream carried down from above. Her vision swam at the sudden movement and she would have thrown up if there had been anything left in her stomach. The long days without food had more than taken their toll and now she barely had the strength to keep her eyes open. How she wished that they'd never left the mountains. Maybe she and Cara might have found peace somewhere amidst the endless peaks, far from the queen's darkness, from the rage of the Old One and her Tangata.

But no, instead Erika had brought them to a land torn by war, following the futile hope that she might help her people, might find a way to save the very kingdom that had turned its back on her as a child.

She had doomed not only herself, but Cara too.

Erika shook herself as another scream came from the ceiling, followed by the ring of weapons. Erika struggled to concentrate through her exhaustion. The ship was under attack, but who in the kingdoms of humanity still had the power to threaten the Flumeerens? Had King Nguyen escaped after all?

A chill touched Erika as she recalled the queen's words.

So they have come. It is earlier than I'd hoped, but I am not unprepared.

No, not the Gemaho at all. The Old One and her Tangata. Erika must have been locked in the hold longer than she'd imagined, if the creatures were already here, though it was a shorter route to cut through the fallen lands of the Calafe than the roundabout way she and Cara had taken through Gemaho.

Her stomach twisted at the memory of the Old One, at how the Anahera had bowed to her will, the way she had looked at Erika. The creature loathed humanity above all else. No matter what preparations Amina had made, whatever strength she had inherited from her mother, the queen could not possibly be prepared for that.

Another scream sounded, high pitched and unending, as of some soldier horribly disfigured. Heart pounding in her chest, Erika turned to Cara. Somehow, they had to escape this cage. She didn't want to be trapped here when the Old One finally came.

"Cara, she's here, isn't she? The Old One?"

The young Goddess did not stir, only sat with her knees drawn up to her chest, eyes on the steel floor of the cage. Erika swallowed, then gently reached out and clutched Cara's shoulder.

"Cara, come on, I need you. We have to find a way out of here."

Still Cara did not stir and Erika feared she'd lost her friend to madness. But then the Anahera's head lifted, her amber eyes meeting Erika's. A tear streaked her cheek as she blinked and began to shake.

"I never gave up," she croaked. "Never stopped hoping she was out there somewhere. That one day I'd be flying over the plains, and she would find me."

Another tremor shook the Goddess. The tears were flowing freely now. Grief contorted her face and Erika felt her friend was about to shatter, to crumble beneath the weight of her pain. But Erika said nothing, only crouched beside her, waiting.

"After all these years of searching…" Cara's voice broke as words gave way to sobs.

Despite their danger, despite the screams of dying men from above, Erika hugged her friend tight. What else could she do? At the end of her strength, Erika could no more will the cage away than she could defeat the queen in single combat.

Amina, the queen of Flumeer.

And Cara's unknown half-sister.

Only one Anahera had left the city in the past decades —Cara's mother. The creatures had said little of the woman, only that she had vanished. Not even Cara had known her fate. Until now.

"She abandoned me." It was a moment before Erika heard the words in Cara's sobs. Suddenly the Goddess stilled. "Left me all alone with *Farhan*. All so she could be with one of *you*." She looked up then, and Erika could see the rage in her eyes now, fed by the depth of her grief. "And what did it get her in the end? Only more pain, only death. Maybe my father was right to hate your kind."

Erika swallowed, but she could find no words to reply, no argument for the grieving young woman beside her. It was difficult sometimes, to recall that Cara was in fact fifty years of age. Due to the slow development of the Anahera, she appeared no older than a teenager. Human blood from Amina's father must have aged the queen faster than her sister, yet looking at the Goddess now, Erika finally saw the similarities—the sharp cheekbones and scarlet shades of their hair, the large eyes that seemed to pierce you to the soul.

"I don't know what to say, Cara," Erika said at last, her own vision blurring, though she kept the tears from falling. "It's a cruel place, this world our ancestors left for us. Humanity is what the fires of the Fall made us—harsh and merciless. I know it cannot bring your mother back, but I am sorry for what we did to her."

The Goddess looked away at that, though every so often a tremor would shake her wings, the feathers standing on end. The sounds of battle were growing louder now, fiercer. Erika glanced at Cara, but there was no signs of life in the Goddess. The anger had died from her eyes, leaving only despair, only the darkness of the defeated.

She clenched her fist, wishing for the strength to summon the magic. She only achieved another bout of dizziness. A gasp slipped from her lips as she slid sideways, slumping against the bars. Cara frowned as she watched her, seeming confused.

"Why are you still fighting?" she said, her voice almost angry, as though Erika's lack of despair were an insult to her. "It's over, Erika. The Old One and her Tangata are here, some of my people too. I can hear their Voices—they're all around us. Not even my bitch sister can fight them. It's over. Maya has won."

"No," Erika hissed, forcing herself to sit up. "No, I won't let them." She gripped Cara by the shoulder and forced the Goddess to look at her. "I'm sorry about your mother, Cara. I know what it feels like to lose a parent to evil. But you're not alone."

"Of course I'm alone," Cara snapped, tearing herself from Erika. "My brother, my mother, my father, they're all dead now. My own people bow to the darkness of the Old One. I'm the only one left."

"No," Erika hissed. Gently she cupped Cara by the cheek. "No," she repeated, softly this time, looking into Cara's amber eyes. "You still have me, Cara, always. We're family now, you and I." Gently she pressed her forehead to the Goddess's. "I won't let her hurt you anymore. I won't let them take you."

She thought Cara would pull away, but after a moment the Goddess's eyes slid closed and she began to tremble. Silently she shook her head, fingers pulling at her torn leggings.

"I don't know what I'm doing, Erika," she croaked. "It's all wrong, all of this, what Father did for me, what happened to Hugo...there was so much blood." She was sobbing now, hugging Erika tight, clutching at her back. "I should have done something else, should have been able to save him. He was so young...never had a life...and now Mother...I can't..." Her words became unintelligible as she tumbled from one loss to another.

Erika squeezed her tight then drew back, carefully wiping the tears from the Goddess's cheeks. Cara fell silent, blinking at Erika in the gloom of the cabin, amber eyes reflecting the fading candlelight.

"You did your best, Cara," she said softly, "but no one could have saved Hugo. You said so yourself—he was under Maya's control. She's too strong for any one of your people. And your father chose to save you, to do right by his daughter. You cannot blame yourself for the choices of others. All you can do is honour their sacrifices."

The tears still slid down Cara's face as she hiccupped softly, shivering in the confines of their cage, feathers trembling. But finally she closed her eyes and nodded. Angrily she wiped away the last of her tears, then rose abruptly, eyes on the ceiling.

"Maya's close," she said sharply. "There isn't much—"

AARON HODGES

Boom!

❧ 12 ❧

THE SOVEREIGN

Standing at a window looking out over the harbour, Lukys struggled to contain the pounding in his chest. At any moment, he expected the alarm to sound, for soldiers to come rushing into the room and take them hostage, or worse. Wallace and Zayaan sat at a table behind him with a growing number of nobles, but the most important of their number had yet to join them—the officer in charge of their defences.

"This has been the strangest of times," Wallace was saying to Sophia who sat with them at the table. "Hidden Gods and traitorous kings and all."

He doesn't know the half of it. Lukys sent the silent words to his partner, and sensed a ripple of her mirth in response.

Earlier, Wallace and Zayaan had led them through the streets of Mildeth. The queen might have left with most of their army, but Lukys couldn't help but notice the frosty manner of the populace, the suspicious glances they cast at the strange group moving through their midst. Most relaxed when they noticed Zayaan, but Lukys still sensed their distrust in the sickly green of their aura.

Thinking of their reception, Lukys couldn't help but question his plan, whether the four of them would be enough. Even if they took hostage the members of this room, would the people on the streets submit willingly? Or would they rise up against the invaders?

"A strange time indeed," he said finally, moving from the window to join those gathered at the table. "Though I am glad to find that Flumeeren hospitality has not changed."

Taking the seat alongside his partner, he allowed his eyes to roam over the gathering. Wallace and Zayaan had been joined by half a dozen others, minor officers and nobles from the south that had fled the Tangatan threat. Most of those with higher ranks would have marched with the queen, but Amina must have trusted at least a few of these men and women, to have left them in command of her capital.

"Indeed," Zayaan replied. "Though I admit, I had not thought them strange enough to merit your noble presence in our city, Sovereigns."

Lukys narrowed his eyes as the queen's advisor spoke, sensing the man's suspicion. Zayaan was seated at Lukys's side, while Wallace took the spare seat alongside Sophia. It was clear these two carried some measure of authority over the others, though neither were military men. He glanced at the door, but there was still no sign of the officer in command of the city guard.

"It has been some time, has it not, since your last visit?" Zayaan continued.

Sensing the question in the man's words, Lukys allowed himself a smile beneath the veil. It took a moment to find the memory he needed—those more recent seemed easier to uncover.

"Ten years," he confirmed. "Not since the gathering of kings have we stepped foot on the mainland."

Zayaan smiled at that. "I must say, I find your attire… puzzling. The veils must be quite the advantage during negotiations. I can hardly tell which of you is the man and which the woman, let alone the thoughts behind your words."

Sophia and Lukys turned their eyes upon the man. Though neither spoke, Lukys could sense his partner's unease. They both recalled the near disaster of their arrival in Perfugia, when Tasha had torn the blindfold from Sophia's eyes, revealing her true lineage.

Thankfully, Wallace came to their rescue, as his face grew red and he spluttered something unintelligible at the elderly Zayaan.

"My apologies!" he said finally, turning to them, "I am sure Zayaan meant no offence with his words."

Lukys proffered an exaggerated sigh beneath his veil. "It is a tradition of our people, you understand," he replied. "Only our own—and royalty, of course—may look upon the likeness of the Sovereigns."

That was only partly true. The memories he held recalled many occasions when the Sovereigns had revealed themselves, but there was no need to make exceptions here. At least, not yet. Not until all had gathered in place.

"Fear not, good Sovereigns, we in Flumeer respect the traditions of the ancients," Wallace proclaimed, flashing Zayaan a glare as he spoke. "Why, the good queen has often remarked to me the loyalty of your kingdom. Perfugia has never missed a tribute to the alliance."

Lukys's heart twisted at the man's words. He knew all too well what Wallace was referring to—the recruits like Lukys that Perfugia had sent each year to fight on the frontline. Only…

"It is a welcome arrangement for us all." Lukys forced out the words, though they made his intestines squirm.

"Your generals receive more fodder to slow the Tangatan advance, and we...rid ourselves of wasted mouths."

Lukys, you know that is not true, Sophia's concern sounded in his mind, a wave a warmth accompanying her reassurance.

He smiled beneath his veil and sent back his silent agreement. Outwardly, he said nothing, though he saw shock in the expressions of some around the table.

"You are surprised at our candour," Sophia offered, picking up the conversation. "We believe one should always talk openly amongst allies—lest distrust be allowed to enter relations." She lifted her drink to offer a toast.

Lukys raised an eyebrow at her words, but the others were already following Sophia's lead and toasting her back. With a sigh he did the same, though it was difficult to pass the cup of liquor beneath his veil.

But as he sipped the burning whiskey, an idea came to him. Looking at those seated around the table, he realised they didn't seem so different from the Flumeerens he'd once fought with in Fogmore. Richer, certainly, but not the greedy nobles he had expected of those who followed Amina. Rather, their loyalty seemed...misdirected, abused by a woman who had abandoned them here, helpless to defend themselves against their enemies. No wonder they had welcomed their arrival so readily.

Lukys rose to his feet before he could doubt himself, drawing the attention of the others at the table.

"On that sentiment, my good lords and ladies—" he started, but as he spoke the door to the chamber banged open, and a man garbed in the red uniform of the Flumeeren army entered, a sword hanging from his belt.

Lukys tensed, but he spied the golden lieutenant's badge a second before Wallace leapt to his feet. "Finally! Lieutenant Ewan, what kept you?"

The lieutenant frowned as he crossed the room. "The safety of the city?" he said shortly, irritation in his voice. "You do realise we're at war, steward? I cannot attend every dalliance you decide to host on a whim. There was another protest amongst the Calafe camps that needed dealing with…" He trailed off, eyes noting the presence of Sophia and Lukys at the table.

"Yes, well, as you can see, Lieutenant, we have important guests," Wallace replied shortly. "My dear Sovereigns, may I introduce Lieutenant Ewan, the man in charge of our defences in the queen's absence." He paused, belatedly remembering that Lukys was on his feet and clearing his throat. "Er, Sovereign, you were saying something?"

Lukys hesitated, needles prickling at his brow as the attention of the room returned to him. This was their chance. With the members of this room captured, the city would be left without leaders. He cast his gaze to the back of the room, where Dale and Keria lurked. The Flumeerens had guards of their own of course, but none possessed the strength of the Tangata. With Sophia and Keria on their side, it wouldn't be difficult to take control…

…but what if violence was not the answer here?

"Thank you, Wallace, for your kindness," he said softly. "It is welcome after the difficulties we have suffered these last months." He drew in a breath as a frown crossed the steward's lips, then continued before the questions could begin. "In truth, we are new to our roles as Sovereigns. Word would not yet have reached you here on the mainland, but there has been a change in leadership in Perfugia. The old Sovereigns were killed…unexpectedly."

"Killed?" Wallace exclaimed. Seated nearby, the elderly Zayaan only frowned, lips pressed in a line, eyes fixed on Lukys.

"Slain by their own guards," Lukys confirmed grimly,

gesturing for Sophia to rise. He sensed the tension in his partner as she came to her feet, felt it too from Dale and Keria as they edged towards the other guards. "We do not intend to make the same mistakes."

"I should hope not," Zayaan responded calmly. "Treachery must be quashed wherever it is found."

"That was not their mistake," Lukys said. "Their mistake was filling the hearts of their people with hatred, in clinging to the past."

Even as he spoke, images flickered in Lukys's mind, of a people exiled, of the former Tangata as they landed on a barren shore, of men and women coming together to create a new kingdom. But always those memories were clouded, distorted by the hatred of his predecessors, by their anger towards those who had seen them banished.

Lukys closed his eyes, exhaling. He knew what he had to do.

"We must find a new way," Lukys continued. "One of peace, of respect amongst equals. We can no longer blindly follow your queen."

❦ 13 ❦

THE TANGATA

A donis shivered as he looked upon the human queen. Seeing her standing calm amongst the chaos, Adonis realised he knew this creature. He had glimpsed her from afar, at the height of the human invasion so many years before, when the Tangata had trapped the human army between their forces. The enemy might have been crushed that day, had it not been for a calvary charge that had forced the Tangata back, giving the humans time to retreat.

This woman had led that charge against his people, had saved the humans from disaster so long ago. If not for her, the war might have ended that day, with the strength of humanity destroyed in one terrible battle.

Adonis would not allow her to save them again. Now, on this night, she would finally fall. And the last resistance of humanity with her.

Brothers, sisters, on me.

Standing in the shadows, he gathered his Tangata. Already the humans were responding to their queen, retreating from the Tangata-inspired chaos and raising their

97

weapons in a defensive formation. His people would need to change their tactics too, if they were to destroy this creature.

Thankfully, the Tangata had already taken a heavy toll upon the human forces. There couldn't be more than twenty left to stand against an equal number of Adonis's brethren. Impossible odds, even for this queen.

Kill them all, Adonis said softly when the last of his Tangata joined him.

As one, they surged forward, charging across the blood-slicked deck, silhouettes in the night. The humans roared in answer and hefted weapons. But most had lost their spears earlier, the one advantage they might have had against the Tangatan charge. Instead, the humans met their foes with swords in hand.

And died screaming.

Ducking beneath a wild swing, Adonis shattered the ribs of the human before him, then leapt over the falling body, eyes on the woman who stood at their centre. Dressed in chainmail armour with a greatsword in hand, she alone amongst the humans stood her ground. Indeed, as Adonis watched, one of his sisters leapt at her and the queen spun, her blade slashing out to catch the Tangata in the neck. The blow almost decapitated the Tangata, and she fell amongst the other bodies littering the deck.

A growl rumbled from the back of his throat and fists clenched, he pushed aside one of his brethren.

Focus on the followers, he hissed. *The queen is mine.*

Encased in her armour, it would be difficult for one of his lesser brethren to pierce her defences, but one blow from Adonis would crush the metal like a hammer. This was the moment he had waited for, the foe he had been created to face.

The other Tangata stepped aside, splitting the ranks of human soldiers and allowing Adonis to pass. They were falling quickly, the queen's human guards, overwhelmed by the sheer power of the Tangata. The queen realised it too, for her helmet flickered left and right, and he heard her voice carrying over the clash of weapons. Her followers, though, could not hear her over the cacophony of battle.

Then the woman's eyes fell upon Adonis. The queen seemed to realise his intent as he started towards her, but to her credit, she did not try to flee. Rather, she squared her shoulders and took her greatsword in a two-handed grip. Adonis smiled at her courage, but it mattered not. This night would see her end. No human could stand against a Tangata of the third generation.

Crying his rage, Adonis charged, closing the gap with his foe in an instant. Her sword came up, reacting with the speed she had demonstrated with the others, but Adonis was confident in his strength, and his arm swept out to slam against the flat of her blade to turn it aside…

…except the blow felt as though Adonis had struck something hard and unyielding, as though the greatsword were fixed in some vice rather than held by a mere human. For a second, he felt bewilderment, confusion—then the point of the sword slammed into his shoulder, tearing through flesh and bringing his charge to a sudden halt.

A cry burst from his lips at the impact, and stunned, Adonis twisted, tearing the sword from his flesh. His cry turned to a growl as he regained his balance, swinging again at the human woman. She raised her blade, face hidden by her helmet, but Adonis saw the mirth in the ripples of the woman's aura.

A frown touched his lips. How had she held the sword against his blow? How could she move so quickly, keeping pace with even his own supernatural speed?

Baring his teeth, Adonis reached a hand to his shoulder, feeling the hot blood gushing from the wound. His right arm had lost some of its strength, but it should still be enough to defeat a human, even one dressed in steel.

Snarling, he clenched his fists and attacked again. This time the queen dropped into one of the strange stances practiced by the humans, sword extended, iron fist held across her chest. Adonis ignored the blade this time, trusting his speed to evade her next blow. All he needed was to land a strike, one with the force to crush her bones, to tear her flesh, and it would all be over.

But as he came at her again, far from awaiting his attack, the queen leapt forward to meet him. For half a moment, Adonis was left frozen. This human dared to attack *him?* Only the hiss of approaching steel snapped him from his stupor, and gasping, Adonis hurled himself aside…

…and again found himself too slow. Pain erupted from his side as the greatsword slammed against his ribs. Fortunately his retreat took most of the impetus from the blow, but even so, he felt something go *crack* as he staggered back.

Gasping, he stared at the woman, hot blood running from his side as well as his shoulder now. For the first time that night, fear touched him. This should not be possible. A human could not stand against him, not unless…

…his eyes widened as a suspicion touched him, and without thinking, he reached out with his mind.

What are you?

Laughter rattled from behind the iron visor, lifting above the screams of the dying. Reaching up, the queen tore the helmet from her head, revealing great eyes of emerald and flaming red hair.

"I am the saviour of humanity," she shouted into the night.

A roar came from nearby as one of Adonis's brethren, caught in the grips of the Tangatan rage, crushed his foe's skull—then caught sight of the queen standing nearby. Before anyone could react, he charged at her.

The queen didn't bother with the sword this time. Instead, she lifted her empty hand, and only now did Adonis notice how it rippled, how it was different from the rest of her armour. A burning light lit the night, and his brother fell to the ground, writhing against the wooden boards.

"I am the death of gods," the queen continued, even as Adonis's brother died in agony.

Adonis shook his head, staring at the human in disbelief. She *was* human, that he sensed, smelt, but…somehow she had Heard him, had matched him blow for blow, had injured him.

Abruptly, the queen raised her sword and shouted into the night. Too late, Adonis realised his danger as she charged. His brethren were engaged with the last of the humans, leaving him to stand alone against the queen, against whatever creature she was, and the human magic she wielded.

Watching her charge, Adonis realised his death was upon him. Even so, he clenched his fists and readied himself for battle, though its end seemed already written in the night sky.

A sharp *crack* came from overhead, then a shadow fell over them, black-feathered wings flashing out to slam against the queen's blade, finally tearing it from her impossibly strong grasp. Adonis barely had time to recognise Nyriah before the Anahera launched herself at the queen, fist and boot and wings lashing out, driving the woman back, leaving her no opening to use the magic of the gauntlet.

The queen roared as she matched the Anahera's blows, revealing a strength beyond anything Adonis knew to be possible for a human, for even a Tangata. His heart hammered hard in his chest as he watched the two battle amidst the flickering lanternlight. This queen could not be human nor even a descendant of his people. She was too powerful, her strength too pure for that.

No, this creature had come from the Anahera themselves.

But the false gods had their limits, and as the last human soldier fell, Adonis's brethren formed up around him. This was their chance. With Nyriah's aid, they could still win a victory. He could still salvage his injured pride. The creature could not fight them all.

With me, Tangata, he called. *The human queen falls this night.*

Across the deck, he saw the pale face of the queen swing in his direction and he cursed silently. She had heard him, knew they were coming for her. But what did it matter? The Anahera had the woman pinned against the bow where Adonis had first climbed aboard. She had placed a pile of barrels to her back to keep from being surrounded, but even that would not help against so many. There would be no escape for the human queen.

Grinning, he started across the deck with his Tangata.

An all-too-human curse slipped from the creature's lips and she leapt back from Nyriah, finally managing to bring up her gauntlet. Light flashed as its magic lit the night and Adonis rushed forward, his Tangata with him. He knew this weapon, its magic. The queen could not strike them all with its power.

Nyriah's wings swept down, hurtling her into the sky as the queen unleashed the magic. Adonis and the other Tangata charged into the gap the Anahera had left and one of his brethren went down, caught in the gauntlet's awful power. But not Adonis, and teeth bared, he leapt at the queen...

...but she was already turning from him, her magic vanished, reaching instead for a...lantern. The sight gave Adonis pause and he hesitated, watching as the queen wrenched the flaming light from a hook and raised it high. The whisper of wings from above announced Nyriah's return, but the queen paid no mind to her. With a shout, the queen hurled her lantern at the pile of barrels.

The *crash* of breaking glass followed as it smashed upon the wood, spilling burning oil across the barrels in a *whoosh* of heat. Even as Adonis stared, she swung on one of his brothers, bringing the Tangata down with a terrible blow to the face.

Then the queen was charging through the gap the fallen Tangata left. Reaching the railings of the ship, she hurled herself over the side before any could catch her.

Adonis had just a second to stare at the point where the queen had disappeared, pondering her plan, before—

Boom.

The night erupted in an inferno.

❧ 14 ❧

THE PRISONER

Erika cried out as a wave of light and sound burst through the cabin, followed by such heat that she feared they had been engulfed by flames. Smoke seared her lungs as she drew in a breath to scream, and instead found herself choking. Her ears rang and stars danced across her vision, but the heat vanished as quickly as it had appeared, and she found herself lying again in the iron cage.

Except the cage was no longer standing upright, but rather lying twisted on its side. Groaning, Erika struggled to push herself up, even as her vision cleared and the first sound returned to her ears. Somewhere nearby she heard the roaring of flames and screams of men in agony, before a whisper from nearby drew her attention, desperate, urgent. A hand grasped her by the shoulder and shook her.

"Erika, are you okay? Please, I can't—" Cara's voice broke, as though she were already imagining the possibility of Erika's death.

Erika let out a moan, hoping it would reassure the Goddess, though truthfully she wasn't sure what condition she was in. She was already so weak...and now she could hear a roaring from above, of...flames, growing closer.

What had happened? That explosion...it had to have been the black powder Amina had mentioned earlier, when speaking of the fall of Fort Illmoor. She couldn't help but feel some small measure of satisfaction at that. It seemed only fair that the woman's stolen weapon had been turned against her. The Archivists knew the perils of the black powder well, and never stored great quantities in one place.

Deciding she was still in one piece, Erika managed to push herself upright. "I'm okay," she said softly, placing a hand on Cara's arm as she looked around. The walls of the cabin had been torn apart by the force of the explosion, but they hadn't been so lucky with the cage. Some of the bars had twisted, but otherwise it remained in one piece.

Fear touched her as she saw the fire flickering beyond the broken ceiling. Orange lit the night, illuminating the silhouettes of men and women still struggling on the decks of the galley. Erika didn't know whether to scream for their help or hope they didn't notice them. The queen did not appear and Erika could only pray she had been consumed by the explosion.

Swallowing her fear, she turned to Cara. They would get no better chance than this—if only they could free themselves of the cage. The Goddess seemed to have realised the same thing, for some of the life had returned to her. Seeing that Erika was unharmed, the Anahera turned her attention to the bars of their prison. Pale fingers closed around the steel and veins appeared on Cara's neck as she exerted her incredible strength. Erika held her breath; Cara obviously hadn't been able to escape this way before, but if the explosion had weakened one of the bars...

...but even as the Goddess strained, the steel bars

resisted. They would not give an inch, not even to a Goddess made flesh.

Warmth touched Erika's cheeks, a dry, searing heat that swept through the broken cabin. The silhouettes beyond the shattered walls had vanished, the ship apparently abandoned, but the light of the flames only grew, creeping closer. She could feel the ship rocking sharply beneath them too, the floor pitching as the vessel sunk lower on the river.

Idly, Erika found herself wondering which would reach them first—the flames or the water. Whichever took them, at least they would be free of the queen and her torturous magic. Perhaps she had even perished in the explosion. The thought was cold comfort to Erika. She didn't want to die, not yet, not when there was still so much for her to do. Even after the agony she had suffered these past days, it was the hope for a new life that had given her strength to resist. Watching Cara strain to save them, seeing her own fear reflected in her friend's eyes, Erika found herself clenching her fist, wishing for a final whisper of power, enough to crack the lock again…

The power did not come, but looking at the silver chains she wore, an idea came to Erika. Starved and beaten, she had no strength left to summon her gauntlet's power.

But there was another option, a choice someone like Amina would never consider.

Reaching down, Erika squeezed the gauntlet around her wrist the way the queen had earlier. A soft *hiss* followed, then a tingling in her skin as the wires separated from her flesh, like a thousand tiny needles withdrawing from her arm. Finally, the gauntlet slid free and fell into her lap, its intricate threads shimmering in the fiery light.

"Cara," she whispered.

Her concentration still on the bars of their cage, it was a moment before the Goddess looked back. When she did,

Erika saw again the terror in her eyes, the fear they would both be consumed by the flames.

"Take it," Erika said, holding out the gauntlet to the Goddess. "I...don't have the strength to use it, but you do. Break the lock, save us."

Cara's eyes widened at the sight of the gauntlet. Erika had fought so hard to keep this artefact, had feared and yearned for it in equal parts these past months. Now she offered it freely to the Goddess.

"It's forbidden for us to use human magic," Cara whispered, still staring at Erika's offering.

"Add it to the list of our crimes," Erika retorted. "At least we'll be alive."

The Goddess swallowed visibly, hesitation written across her face, but finally she reached out and took the gauntlet from Erika. Holding it in her hands, Cara paused, looking from the artefact to the broken walls. Fear turned Erika's innards to ice as she saw that the fire had reached the cabin. The air was hot to breathe now, and tainted with smoke, it seared her lungs. As she watched, another wall went up in flames with a *whoosh*.

"Quickly," she wheezed, swinging back to the Goddess.

Clenching her jaw, Cara slipped the gauntlet over her hand.

A burst of light flashed from the artefact, forcing Erika to turn away, but Cara did not hesitate now. A low buzzing filled the cage as she thrust out her palm, slamming it against the lock. The shriek of twisting metal followed as the Goddess drew on her strength, far greater than Erika's dwindling energies. But another scream echoed the breaking steel, torn from Cara herself, as though something within her were breaking, reacting to the artefact's power...

The light cut off again as a sharp *crack* came from the

lock—then the door to the cage was falling open, crashing sideways to the wooden floor.

A moan came from Cara as she swayed on her knees, and Erika was shocked to see a trail of blood running from her friend's nose. The magic had cost the Goddess something, but there was no time to consider the price of their freedom. Grasping her friend beneath the arm, she pushed Cara through the opening, then scrambled out after her.

The heat swelled as they stood, Erika still supporting the Goddess. Smoke swirled about them, blinding, burning as they struggled to breathe. Dizzy from the darkness and her own weakness, Erika swung in one direction, then another, unable to find the direction of the door, of freedom.

"Erika!" Cara's voice rose above the inferno as the Goddess straightened. It seemed all the world was aflame now, the pair of them standing in a tiny oasis amidst the firestorm. "*Do you trust me?*"

There was no time to consider the answer. "Yes!" Erika screamed.

The breath hissed from Erika's lungs as Cara tackled her, picking her up, hugging her tight. Then they were hurtling towards the flames, towards the burning walls, towards the searing heat—

Dark wings enclosed them both, cutting off the brilliant light, the burning. A *crash* followed as they struck something solid, but whatever it was did not halt the Goddess's momentum and they tumbled on, swirling, falling, tumbling...*burning*.

Erika opened her mouth to scream her agony—and the icy waters of the Illmoor rose to claim them.

15

THE SOVEREIGN

"We can no longer blindly follow your queen."

A collective intake of breath came from around the room at Lukys's words. Men and women rose to their feet, some banging fists against the table, others demanding an explanation for the insult. A spluttering came from Wallace and he rocked back in his chair as though Lukys had struck him.

"No!" the steward gasped. "You cannot betray her! You're Amina's closest ally."

"Amina has had other allies—all of them are dead now, their kingdoms broken," Lukys said harshly. Reaching up, he pulled off his veil and swept his eyes over the room. "I will not allow the same to happen to Perfugia."

To his surprise, the room fell silent at his words, those gathered momentarily shocked by the removal of his veil. Even so, not everyone was frozen. The guards in the corner had hands on their weapons, and Ewan was on his feet. His stomach tied in a knot, Lukys sent a silent message to Sophia and Keria.

Be ready.

Abruptly, Zayaan pushed himself to his feet. Around the table, eyes flickered, turning to the old man. A frown wrinkled his face as he studied the pair of Sovereigns, as though he already knew what lay beneath Sophia's veil. His frown deepened as Wallace continued to splutter, clutching at his chest as though in pain.

"Oh, calm yourself, Wallace," Zayaan snapped. Wallace's gasps cut off as he stared up at the queen's advisor, while Zayaan returned his focus to Lukys. "The good Sovereigns obviously did not come to conquer, or we would already be dead."

Lukys frowned at the elderly man. He'd expected Zayaan to lead the resistance against them, being the queen's personal advisor. Indeed, it seemed others in the room had thought the same, for with his words came an uncertain calm as the other nobles looked from Lukys to the elderly advisor.

Lukys drew in a breath. "We have received…word of a new threat to the south, of a creature beyond even the powers of the Gods. The ancient enemy of legend has returned—and your queen plays politics while the world burns." He shook his head. "Her tyranny has gone too far. You speak of the renegade King Nguyen, but the man did not start this war with your kingdom."

"Nguyen broke the alliance," Zayaan said matter-of-factly, as though he held no opinion about the events of which he spoke. Alongside him, Wallace whimpered. "Amina's invasion was retribution for that betrayal."

"You can't do this!" Wallace interrupted, pushing himself to his feet. Puffing, he swung on Zayaan. "You don't understand, it's impossible to resist her! We must remain loyal, she'll—"

"*Nothing* is impossible," Lukys cut the man off, leaning forward and pressing his hands to the table, eyes still on

Zayaan. He sensed this was the man he needed to convince if they were to take this room without bloodshed. "If my presence here proves anything, it is the truth of those words. In just a few short months, I have witnessed Gods come to life, seen lost magics and the rise of creatures long thought to be extinct. I have…" He hesitated, glancing at Sophia before drawing fresh breath.

"If all that can be possible, if the Gods themselves still live, then we humans can find a better way. If we can stand together, as one, we have a chance for peace, for unity amongst the kingdoms. Can you imagine a world without war, without needless death? A world of peace." He drew in a breath. "Even with the Tangata themselves."

Finally the old man's face showed a change in emotion, as he frowned at Lukys's last words. Lukys could sense the tension building in the room, the doubt in the eyes of the men and women at the table. Peace with Gemaho and Perfugia was one thing, but these people still saw the Tangata as monsters, the enemy they had fought for ten long years to subdue.

But Perfugia *was* the Tangata now.

Lukys, are you sure? Sophia's words whispered into his mind, drenched with doubt, with fear.

Fists clenched, eyes still locked on Zayaan, Lukys nodded. He sensed movement alongside him as Sophia reached for her veil, but he did not take his eyes from the queen's advisor, did not so much as blink. If the man signalled for the guards to intervene, Lukys would be ready.

Slowly, Sophia lifted the veil, her grey eyes blinking in the lanternlight. Gasps came from around the room, and Lukys watched the colour drain from Wallace's face. Only the queen's advisor remained steadfast, though his eyes did flicker in Sophia's direction, widening a fraction as he registered the grey eyes of the Tangata.

"I thought it odd," Zayaan said at last, a quiver in his elderly voice despite his mask of calm. "The creature's accent...changed from sentence...to sentence." He hesitated, eyes flicking momentarily to Sophia before returning to Lukys. "Might I ask how you tamed it?"

"I needed no taming, *sir*," Sophia snapped, reverting fully to her singsong accent. "I grow weary of saying it, but my people are not the monsters you think us."

"One can be uncivilised without being a monster," the queen's advisor said softly.

This time a growl came from Sophia's throat, and Lukys sensed the anger building in his partner at the old man's words. Quickly he reached for her hand, seeking to calm her. There would be time enough for repudiation later. For now, they needed the people in this room on their side.

Probably shouldn't have brought us along if you wanted that, Keria's Voice carried from where she stood across the room.

They would have realised the truth sooner or later, Lukys replied, before focusing his attention back on the queen's advisor.

"Sir, I would advise you to remember with whom you speak," he admonished. "Tangata or no, Sophia and I *are* the new Sovereigns of Perfugia. We will not hear you insult our people."

To Lukys's surprise, Zayaan chuckled. "In that case, might I assume you slew your predecessors yourselves? Is Perfugia burning even now, Ashura lying in ruins?"

"No," Lukys shot back, looking from the man to the others at the table. He noticed several of those on their feet edging towards the door, but Dale had thankfully already moved to bar their exit. "The rest of our people are on their way here, in fact, with King Nguyen."

"I see." Clasping his hands behind his back, Zayaan stepped out from behind the table.

Lukys tensed and the man paused, one grey eyebrow lifting towards the fringe of his failing hair, as if to ask, *May I?* After a brief delay, Lukys nodded, allowing the advisor to move around the table. As he did so, Lukys sensed a distant call, as though one of the Tangata were reaching out to warn him of something. The horns began to sound from the city a few seconds later.

"I suppose that would be your fleet then?" Zayaan asked as he crossed to the window and looked out over the harbour.

Heart hammering in his chest, Lukys joined the old man and saw the blue and yellow sails marking the horizon. On the streets below the citadel, men and women scurried like ants, a steady flow making for the walls. Fists clenched, he looked to Wallace and Ewan and the others at the table, but none of them made any move to act. They all looked to Zayaan.

"It's not too late," Lukys said softly, his heart pounding. This was their chance, the moment they had been waiting for. If they could convince this man to turn against his master... "There doesn't have to be bloodshed, Zayaan. Call off the guards, surrender the city, and we will face Amina and the Old Ones together."

Unclasping his hands, Zayaan turned from the window, and for a second Lukys thought they would scream for the guards to attack, for the Flumeerens to resist at all costs. Then the queen's advisor met his eyes.

"No harm will come to our people?" he murmured. "Our city will remain undisturbed?"

"*None,*" Lukys said, his Voice ringing silently in emphasis of his words.

A grim smile appeared on the old man's face. "Very well, Sovereign," he said softly. "It seems Amina's reign over Mildeth has come to an end."

"*No!*"

A scream from the table was followed by a *crash* as Wallace attempted to leap across the wooden boards. He tripped and fell, but moving with a speed that belied his size, he scrambled up again. Steel flashed as he charged at Lukys, but Sophia was faster still. Though the steward was four times her size, a blow to his sternum sent him crashing to the floor.

Lukys's gut churned as he approached the man. "Wallace, there is no need for this," he said, even as the steward struggled against Sophia's impossible strength. She was forced to push him face-first against the ground and pin an arm behind his back, but he still continued to scream and whimper, sobbing into the wooden floors.

A frown touched Lukys's forehead as he knelt beside the man, trying to make sense of his words.

"Please!" Wallace cried. "You don't understand, you don't know what she *is!* Amina, she does not forget. She'll kill us all if you cross her!"

❧ 16 ❧

THE TANGATA

The water was the only thing that saved Adonis.

Even as the fire licked at his flesh, he felt the force of the explosion lift him up and hurl him backwards, sending him tumbling through the air, over and over until he struck the river with a harsh *thump*.

The icy waters extinguished the flames instantly, though the pain remained, the lingering agony of burns to his face and chest, a shrieking from his flesh that he knew would only grow.

For the moment though, he had more pressing concerns than his pain. Submerged beneath the water, his lungs screamed and he kicked out, struggling in the depths, unable to tell up from down, to find the surface. Caught in the currents, he slammed into something hard—and moving. Another of his brethren, or the queen?

Regardless, he caught hold of the unknown figure, fingers latching onto rough fabric—not the queen in her iron suit, then—before he kicked out again, finally glimpsing the light of the flames. They would mark the surface.

He broke free of the depths with a gasp, sucking in great

lungfuls of air. Strength rushed back to his failing limbs as he looked around at a world turned to chaos. The screams of the dying and the roar of the burning ship thundered across the river. Gritting his teeth, he struggled to drag his burden up from the depths. Something weighed the figure down, and it took all his strength to pull them above the surface. Only then did he see why they had been so heavy.

Nyriah coughed and spluttered as her head broke the surface, her water-logged wings churning the river as she struggled to keep above the water. It was clear she had no idea how to swim—and that with her heavy wings, she was in danger of dragging them both back into the depths.

Cursing, Adonis struck the Anahera across the face.

Calm yourself! he growled, his rage pressing upon her mind.

It did nothing to calm her panic though, and gritting his teeth, Adonis reached out again. This time he sought peace, to rid himself of the rage that had driven him for so long. Slowly the Anahera calmed as he sought to share some measure of tranquillity with her, until finally she stilled in his grip.

Lie on your back, he ordered. *Tuck away your wings, if you can.*

Adonis offered nothing more, but after a moment Nyriah obeyed. Cursing his own weakness and the growing pain of his burns, Adonis gripped her beneath the arm and kicked out towards the distant shore.

Behind them, flames lit the night as the human flagship burned. Adonis watched as it sank beneath the waters, and cursed the queen with all his being. How had she caused such an explosion? It had not been the magic of her gauntlet, but some other power, born of fire. Something the Tangata had never seen before.

For the first time in his life, Adonis felt a tremor of fear for the humans. This night, he had witnessed the threat Maya had predicted. Finally, he understood the danger these creatures posed. Worse, he knew now they were not led by a fragile mortal, but one of Anaheran descent, a creature that could stand against any of the Tangata, perhaps even Maya.

Lying in his arms, Nyriah said nothing as they swam, though she was shivering by the time Adonis's found ground beneath them.

We are safe, Nyriah, he said softly. *You can stand.*

Her overly large eyes blinked in her pale face. Unlike himself, it seemed she had escaped the worst of the flames, though the force of the explosion must have been enough to knock her from the sky. Her water-soaked wings would have dragged her straight to the bottom if he had not encountered her in those swirling currents.

"You saved me," she murmured, standing in the muddy shallows. Her wings spread wide and a tremor shook them, spraying water into the air. A frown touched her forehead when she looked at him, clothes clinging to her body in an…unseemly manner. "Why…master?"

Adonis gritted his teeth and quickly looked away. *Your aid proved vital to our cause,* he said vaguely. *And I needed information.* He looked at her sharply, recalling his earlier suspicions. *The creature we fought, the woman who led the enemy, she is not entirely human.*

"No…" Nyriah murmured, quickly glancing away.

He was on her in a second, catching her by the wrist, squeezing. Despite his burns, he was still strong, still needed to know.

What is she? he hissed. *Who is she?*

The Anahera lowered her eyes. "Only one of our kind has left the mountains in generations," she said softly. "Cara's mother, Farhan's partner before me. She disap-

AARON HODGES

peared one day. Though no one knew what had become of her, Farhan always suspected…she had a great interest in the humans."

Adonis narrowed his eyes. "But that was not her?"

Nyriah shook her head. "That creature was not full-blooded Anahera. But perhaps…a daughter."

Adonis nodded, his thoughts turning to the human Maisie. Had she known this? Was that why she'd sent him against the flagship, knowing the queen would be there?

Anger touched him and suddenly Adonis was striding from the water, leaving the Anaheran woman behind him. Could Maisie have been manipulating them all this time, using their anger and hatred, their excitement to destroy the humans against them? It seemed unlikely—Maisie had been isolated from her people for weeks. But the humans were manipulative, cunning creatures. After this night, who knew what else they might be capable of?

The sound of footsteps on mud came from behind Adonis as Nyriah followed, but even with his injuries, she struggled to keep up, her wings still heavy with water. Adonis clenched his fists, casting a glance over his shoulder at the river. At least two other ships were burning—had they taken inspiration from the queen, or had this all been a trap from the start?

He bared his teeth, wondering at the weapon the queen had unleashed. Was this the extent of the new power, or was there more? How long did the Tangata have before the humans created other such weapons? In just the last few months they had uncovered magic gauntlets and explosives. But even before that, their war manoeuvres had advanced, as they learned to use their shields and spears as a unit against their stronger foes.

Maya was right. The humans had to be eliminated before they grew to threaten the entire world.

Movement came from the waters of the river and Adonis was thankful to see that others had escaped the inferno. He could sense the fear of his brethren for what the enemy had revealed. The queen had been within their grasp, but in an instant she had turned the battle, decimating the Tangata and escaping into the night. It was a humiliating defeat for Adonis.

A soft pounding came to his mind as he climbed the bank, a tremor of rage, a warning of what awaited him. Reaching the borders of their camp, he moved towards the source, towards Maya's fury. Her rage swept out across his people, stirring them from their shock, calling upon their emotions…

Calling them to war.

Adonis found his mate standing atop a small hill. Her golden hair shone in the light of the distant flames, her stomach straining against the simple Tangatan clothing she wore. Her grey eyes fixed upon the burning waters, she did not seem to notice his approach at first.

You have failed me, my mate.

Adonis flinched as Maya's Voice roared into his mind, so loud he staggered back from her, his entire being trembling. Looking up at her, he tried to meet the grey eyes of his partner—and failed. Bowing his head, he tried to retreat—only for her to surge forward. Before he could resist, her hand caught him by the throat.

Maya bared her teeth as she hauled him into the air, and in that moment Adonis finally realised his peril—for in Maya's eyes he saw not her usual calm, but the insanity he had glimpsed the first time he had woken her, the madness that had been passed down to her descendants, the rage of the Tangata.

Maya! he shrieked, reaching out with his mind in a desperate attempt to calm her. But he sensed only chaos from his partner now, only the terrible rage. *Please! They are led by one of the Anahera!*

Somehow, his words must have pierced the haze of her madness, for suddenly Maya blinked. The glow in her eyes softened, giving way to confusion. They narrowed then, and she lifted him higher, as though suspecting him not just of failure now, but treachery.

What is this? she hissed. *The Anahera are* mine! *There are none left to oppose me.*

One left their city long before our arrival! Adonis gasped desperately. *The ex-mate of their leader. Nyriah believes the queen who leads the humans could be her daughter.*

Impossible, Maya growled, and Adonis's gasp was choked off as her fingers tightened. *You* lie *to protect your own humiliation—*

"No," a voice interrupted.

Adonis's heart twisted as he glimpsed movement from the corner of his eye, then Nyriah stepped into view. Before Maya could react, the Anahera surged forward, slamming into the Old One's arm and tearing Adonis from her grip. He cried out as he crashed to the mud, while above Maya snarled, turning her fury against the Anaheran woman.

Adonis's vision swam as he lay in the dirt, as he struggled to catch glimpses of the battle between his partner and Nyriah. The Anahera's black wings hung limp against her back, still heavy with water, and she clearly was still suffering from the earlier explosion. Adonis tried to raise a hand, to call for them to stop, but he found Maya's mind was closed to him now, her power focused on the Anahera that dared oppose her.

And with all the strength of an Old One, she struck the Anaheran woman down.

Crying out, Nyriah slammed into the ground with a *thud*, her wings fluttering weakly, trying uselessly to carry her to safety. Bones crunched as Maya stomped her boot down on one, followed by a ghastly scream as Nyriah thrashed in the mud. The colour drained from the Anahera's face as she struggled to rise, to flee, but there was no escaping the Old One's wrath.

I warned you what would happen if one of your kind betrayed me, Maya hissed, boot grinding down, shattering the bones of Nyriah's wing. Her Voice pounded against Adonis's skull, rending at his mind, threatening to summon the madness within. *Tell me, Anahera, which of the fledgelings is yours, that I might exact a just punishment?*

"*None!*" Nyriah screamed. Tears appeared in her eyes as she slumped against the ground, suddenly limp. "None," she whispered, scrunching her eyes closed. "If there is punishment to be had, let it fall on me."

No, Adonis grated, struggling to rise, to force Maya to hear his words.

Her mind remained closed to him, but he saw her eyes flicker in his direction. A frown creased her forehead as she looked from him to the Anaheran woman.

*So this is the source of your trea*chery, she whispered, tilting her head as she examined Nyriah. *I am disappointed, my mate.*

No! Adonis tried again. *No, I told it true. There is a half-blood who leads the humans, one of Anaheran and human descent.*

This time, finally, his words penetrated the barrier Maya had erected around her mind. Her frown deepened as she paused, seeming to consider his words.

If this is true, she said finally, *then the humans pose a greater danger than even I had thought. My plans must be advanced immediately.*

Still crouched in the mud, Adonis bowed his head. *As you will, my Matriarch,* he murmured. *My people will follow where you lead us.*

Silence answered his words—followed by a mad laughter. His head jerked up at the sound, only to find Maya leering down at him.

Your people? she murmured. *Oh my dear, Adonis, after this failure, what makes you think yourself worthy to stand at my side, let alone lead this army?* She shook her head. *No, after this, all will know of your humiliation at the hands of the human. They will spurn your authority.* The smile faded from her lips as she turned to regard Nyriah, still lying motionless beneath her boot. *You are as worthless to me as an Anahera who refuses to bow.*

With those words, Maya surged forward. Adonis lifted a hand to cry out a warning—but he was far too slow. With all the strength of her kind, Maya brought her boot down on Nyriah's neck.

A terrible *crack* echoed through the night.

Followed by a haunting silence.

And Nyriah lay still upon the mud.

No! A scream tore from Adonis as the rage finally split within him, shoving aside sanity, lifting him from the dirt to stand against his partner.

But she was still an Old One, and her power was greater than any he could imagine. With a backhanded blow, she sent Adonis crumbling back to the dirt. A groan hissed from his lips as his anger slipped away, despair replacing it, leaving him alone with the pain, with the guilt of another life lost.

I SHOULD KILL YOU, MAYA'S VOICE WHISPERED IN HIS MIND, taunting, terrible. *But your blood flows in the runts I carry. For that, I shall spare your life, though from this day forth your people will curse the name of the cowardly Adonis.*

With that, the Old One turned and walked away.

THE PRISONER

Crouching in the long grass, Erika eyed the horse standing several yards away. It hadn't noticed her yet, though its soft snorts in the night revealed its nerves. Flames had scorched its saddle, probably the same ones still burning along the banks of the Illmoor behind her, but there was no sign of its rider.

She held her breath, watching the darkness, waiting to see if this was some trick, a trap set by Amina to ensnare her missing Archivist. It had to be. Surely it could not be that Erika's luck had finally changed. Fate had long ago decided it would not favour her. She couldn't believe she would be so fortunate now, to find a horse here on this burning night.

As the minutes passed and no movement came from the long grass, Erika finally allowed herself to hope. But still she waited, watching, shivering as the cold wind cut through her damp clothes. Though…at least she had not been burned in their flight.

Slumped beside her in the grass, the Goddess had not been so fortunate. Erika could not tell the extent of Cara's burns without daylight, but half the Anahera's hair had been devoured before they'd struck the water. Flames had kissed her auburn feathers too and Erika felt a pang of guilt—it had been Cara's wings that had protected her from the fires, and her friend suffered the brunt of the inferno.

The gauntlet still glinted on the Goddess's arm, and Erika felt a stirring of jealousy, that another wielded her power. She shoved it down—they were both too exhausted to even consider its magic now. They needed to get clear of the river, where even now the distant screams of men told of the battle being waged between the Tangata and Amina's land-based forces.

Whatever the outcome of that battle, the victor would soon turn north towards Mildeth. They needed to be long gone by then, and the horse was their only hope.

Swallowing the last of her doubts, Erika rose from the grass, taking care not to startle the gelding. Cara remained on the ground, the last of her strength consumed by their escape. She'd barely managed to pull them from the river before collapsing on the muddy shore.

The horse swung in Erika's direction at her appearance, nickering nervously in the dark.

"Hey there, greatness," she murmured, extending an empty hand, praying to the Gods she'd long ago discovered to be false that it would not flee. "Are you alone? Do you need a rider?"

The horse nickered again and for one horrible moment Erika thought it would bolt. Heart in her throat, she stood frozen in place as the gelding hooved the ground, but finally it seemed to settle. Abruptly it stepped forward and pressed its nose into her outstretched palm.

Erika stood, stunned, as the wet of its tongue licked her palm, blinking in the moonlight. Soft laughter came from behind her and she turned to see Cara sitting up, her amber eyes aglow in the moonlight.

"I didn't know you were a horse whisperer," she rasped, her voice sounding raw.

Erika found herself smiling back as she stroked the horse's brow, then gently reached up and took its reins in hand. Stroking its neck, she leaned closer to inspect the animal. The metallic tang of blood touched her nostrils and her hand found a wet patch on the hard leather saddle. At least that explained what had become of the horse's rider. She wondered if there would be anything left of Amina's army come morning. Recalling the terrible eyes of the Old One, Erika wasn't sure which side she preferred to win.

At least Amina fights for humanity, an inner voice reminded her.

"Erika," Cara's voice interrupted her thoughts. She turned to find the Goddess standing alongside her. "Are you okay?"

Erika nodded quickly, though as a distant scream carried to her ears, she knew it was a lie. Amina was the last hope humanity had of defeating the Old One and her Tangata. By fleeing this fight, was Erika placing her own life above her people yet again, against humanity itself? But no… surely Amina could not be the future for her people.

"Come on," Erika said softly, pushing aside her doubts.

Even if she'd wanted to, Erika could do nothing for the queen now. Not unless…her eyes drifted to the gauntlet Cara wore. Wielding her Anaheran strength and the twin magics of their human ancestors…could Amina have won this night?

It was too late for second thoughts now. Turning to the horse, Erika swung herself into the saddle then reached down and offered Cara a hand. The Goddess hesitated, eyeing the horse, but after a moment Cara accepted her aid.

Warm hands wrapped around Erika's waist as the Goddess clutched her tight, before she felt her friend's head upon her shoulders.

"So tired," a whisper came in her ears. "So *hungry.*"

Erika's stomach rumbled in agreement but there was no time to check the saddlebags for food. That would have to wait. Starved as she was, first they needed to put distance between themselves and the battle.

"Hold on tight," Erika said.

Then, praying she still had the strength to guide them, she kicked the gelding into a canter.

———

MORNING FOUND THE PAIR STILL ON HORSEBACK, BUT AS THE sun's glow turned the mountains a deep red, Erika knew they had best find shelter. She was swaying in the saddle by then, kept in place by sheer desperation and Cara's arms around her waist. Responsibility for the young Goddess sat heavy on her shoulders. The knowledge that Cara was also at the end of her strength forced her on.

They had ridden north through a passageway that cut through the rolling hills of Flumeer, but now as the daylight lit the open ground, Erika began to search for shelter. There were few trees left in Flumeer these days, with most cut down to create the ships and forts that had guarded the Illmoor, while the rest had been burned for farmland.

There were no farmers now though. Word of the armies amassing to the south must have driven them out, sending them north to shelter behind city walls. Directing their gelding along a goat track leading up into the hills, Erika wondered which would come for them. Would it be Amina, with her gauntlet? Or would it be the Old One with those terrible grey eyes?

A shiver passed down Erika's spine at the thought of the Tangata stalking their trail, following their scent from the waters of the Illmoor.

No, better that Amina emerged victorious. At least they might have a chance to escape human pursuers.

Erika drew her horse to a stop before a remnant of forest nestled in a small vale. Its steep slopes must have made it unsuitable for livestock, for these were the only trees she could see for miles. Their shelter would conceal them from sight of their pursuers, whether they came by land or air…

…but the trees would also be an obvious hiding place. Her eyes slid closed, exhaustion weighing heavy on her shoulders, but Erika's instincts whispered that they could not stop here. It would be the first place their hunters looked.

Skirting the treeline, she led the horse up towards the crest of the hill. There Erika took stock of their surroundings. Pasture and young crops of corn stretched out for miles around them, while flocks of sheep and cattle moved in the distance. She wondered what would become of all this should the farmers not return in time for the harvest. Did the Tangata know how to harvest crops or care for livestock?

Her eyes caught on a distant shadow—a farmhouse, she thought by the size of it. The hour was still early and a chill breeze blew off the snowcapped peaks to the east, but there was no sign of smoke around the chimney. Praying that meant it had been abandoned, she kicked the gelding into a trot.

A half hour later, Erika could hardly bring herself to believe they were safe within stone walls. She'd taken the time to lead the gelding into a small stall attached to the house, then had half-carried, half-dragged Cara inside. Still in a daze and murmuring softly with her eyes closed, the

Goddess had hardly stirred. She was far heavier than she looked, and it had taken the last of Erika's strength to lower the young Anahera onto the down bed in the corner of the great chamber that was the interior of the farmhouse.

Darkness swirled at the edges of her vision and she could feel unconsciousness calling, but even then, Erika knew she could not rest. Their enemies might come for them while they were unawares, and besides, her hunger had only grown more urgent through the night, until it felt as though her insides were consuming themselves in their quest for sustenance.

Returning to the horse, she found some salted beef and dried fish, even some cheese wrapped in a wax cloth in the saddlebags. A quick scout about the farmhouse revealed an abandoned hen coop, its door left open by the departed farmers. The birds squawked and fled at her appearance, already feral from the absence of their owners, but inside she found several eggs. There was also an overgrown vegetable patch out back.

Returning to the house, Erika laid her prizes on the kitchen bench, her stomach rumbling with renewed desperation. There was enough to cook a stew or broth, but the smoke from a fire would be seen for miles during the day. If only a storm would sweep down from the mountains, she might risk a flame. The owners had even left a stack of wood in the hearth for when they returned.

Perhaps when night fell, if they were not discovered before then. In the meantime, she grabbed a piece of the salted beef and took a bite—and groaned as flavour filled her mouth. Her stomach rumbled in anticipation, but she chewed slowly, aware that after so long without eating she didn't want to overdo it. Finally she approached the feathered bed where she had laid her friend.

Cara still slept, though it was a fitful rest, her breath

coming in ragged gasps, as though even in her dreams the demons pursued her still. Her feathers stood on end and Erika shivered as the light coming through the shuttered windows revealed the damage the flames had done. Her wings, so recently healed from their crash in the mountains, had been blackened along their edges, the auburn feathers scorched by the flames. There was a smell about her too, the stench of burnt hair, though at least her skin had been spared the worst of the flames.

Another moan came from the Goddess and she twisted violently atop the covers. Erika swallowed the last of her scant meal, clenching and unclenching her fists. It pained her to see Cara this way, and without thinking she climbed onto the bed. Taking the cover Cara had kicked off, she drew it over them both, then curled up beside the young Anahera, pulling her head to her chest, holding her tight. For a while, the Goddess lay tense in her arms, breath still coming in ragged gasps, hissing between clenched teeth.

After a time though, the tension leached from Cara's muscles and her breathing eased, her groans and twitching easing. Erika closed her eyes, still holding Cara safe in her arms. The fiery warmth of the Goddess soon drove back the chill of the day, the woollen covers weighing down on them both. She listened with relief as her friend's breathing grew regular. After all Cara had done for her, saving her, protecting her, this was the least Erika could do.

She just wished she could do more, that she could bring back Cara's mother, that she could have made Farhan see the truth about his daughter. Far from deserving punishment, Cara was an incredible, caring, loving young woman, deserving of pride, of love. If only she could have convinced the Anahera to see that truth, to abandon the folly of their own ancient ways, maybe then the world would have hope.

But instead, Erika had failed yet again, had returned

from the Mountains of the Gods empty-handed. She knew now she would never change things, could do nothing to save her people.

All she could do was lie in an abandoned farmhouse and hold her friend tight, banishing the cold and the nightmares for a time.

Erika prayed it would be enough.

✤ 18 ✤

THE FALLEN

Adonis lay in the dirt, rain falling softly about him, cradling the head of Nyriah in his lap. Hours had passed, slipping away like autumn leaves caught in the winter storm.

Adonis didn't care. He knelt there holding the fallen Anahera in his arms. She had saved him. Adonis struggled to comprehend what had happened, why she would have done such a thing. What had he been to her? Why would she try to stop Maya, put herself in harm's way for him? After everything he'd done to her, how he had treated her people, how was it that Nyriah had found the strength to defy the Old One on his behalf?

More hours passed and night turned slowly to day. The light found Adonis alone in the mud, lost, forgotten. Silence hung over the riverbanks, over his mind, the muddy field abandoned. His fellow Tangata had left, abandoning him to exile, gone with the creature he had delivered them to, the Old One that carried their future.

His future.

A shudder swept through Adonis and finally the dam

broke, and he felt at last the rejection of his entire people, of the woman he had sworn himself to—and the loss of the Anahera in his arms too, the slave he had so hated, who had stood proud against Maya's Voice, even as all around her bowed in subservience.

A hiss escaped Adonis's throat and he doubled up, holding the cold body tight, wishing he could give her his warmth. He didn't deserve to live, to continue after his failures, when this noble creature lay dead. Nyriah had possessed more courage than he ever had. She could have left this darkness and forged another path had she wanted, despite Maya's powers, despite the fledgelings—but she didn't.

The human found him like that, knelt in the dirt holding Nyriah, his body broken by Maya's beating, barely conscious, barely sane from his grief. He sensed her before she crouched nearby, *smelt* her, even through the stench of smoke that drifted from the river. Immersed in his pain, at first Adonis ignored the creature, lying still, hoping her cursed presence would move on. But this human never could leave well enough alone.

"Are you alive?" Maisie's voice came finally, then when he did not move, "Adonis, is *she* alive?"

His head jerked up at that, and he fixed his eyes on the human. The grey eyes of the Tangata, enough to send one of her kind scurrying in their weakness. But this human did not so much as flinch as she crouched beside him, brown eyes meeting grey.

Instead, it was Adonis that looked away first.

"I see." Sadness crept into the human's tone, and when he looked at her again, a tear streaked her cheek.

Maisie sat back on her haunches, still eyeing him, watching closely. "I should kill you, you know," she said softly, and for the first time Adonis noticed the knife she held. Where had she gotten that? How was she free, in fact? "For everything you've done, you deserve it."

Swallowing his pain, Adonis gently laid Nyriah down, her black wings falling limp in the mud, then turned to face the human. She rose quickly at the movement, knife raised before her, and he felt a brief satisfaction. At least his injured presence was still enough to generate fear in the human.

But as he pushed himself slowly to his feet, it became obvious that Adonis could not defend himself. Pain ate at his leg where it had twisted in the fall, strong enough to cripple him. It would be days before the torn muscles repaired themselves. Based on the look in Maisie's eyes, he didn't have days, or even hours.

So instead he slumped back in the mud and stared up at her, lips pursed. For the first time in his life, he wished he could speak the language of humans, if only to demand she do it quickly, that she end his shame, his suffering, his... grief. He watched her with wide eyes, arms limp at his side, as though to say he was ready.

But the human did not act, only stared back at him, knife gripped at her side. "I won't though," she said abruptly. Shaking her head, she turned away, her gaze falling on the fallen Anahera. "I don't know why she saved you, but...I won't undo what she did." She flashed him a glare. "So you don't need to worry about me."

Adonis hesitated at her words, heart twisting in his chest. For a second, he felt the urge to throw himself at the human, to *force* her to kill him, to end his suffering. The Anahera's wings, so glorious, so beautiful, lay in the mud, dirt treaded into her soft feathers. Dead. Dead because of his foolishness. Because of what he'd done to her people.

He wiped away a tear of his own, then looked around. The grounds before the great river had been churned to mud by the passage of his people, but the Tangata were long gone now. They had crossed the river in darkness, following the eager drumbeats of their master's Voice, driven into a frenzy, into the madness his people had long sought to suppress.

Commanded by Maya.

"You're wondering where your beloved Old One has gone?" Adonis looked at the human sharply as she spoke, eyes narrowing, but Maisie's gaze was also on the river. "Afraid I have some bad news for you," she continued. "She's ditched you, bud. Gone off with that army you helped her win." She looked at him then, and he saw the accusation in her eyes. "You know, the thousands of Tangatan villagers and Anaheran slaves you recruited. Pretty sure they'll make short work of anyone standing in their way on the other side." She shrugged. "On the bright side, they were all in such a frenzy when they left, they seemed to forget all about little old me."

The queen, Adonis thought, reaching out to Speak without thinking, *the half-blood. Maya fears her.*

He trailed off when the human did not react, then belatedly remembered that Maisie could not hear his Voice. Adonis cursed softly in his mind. How could so many of his brethren stand to bond with these coarse creatures, when they could not even communicate with one another? His eyes fell again on the knife, wondering...

"I know, I know," the human mused, seeming to notice the direction of his stare. "I really should kill you. Only, I'm pretty sure you're my only hope of reaching civilisation." She gestured at her leg, and while the human stood now without aid, when she took a step, it was clear she couldn't put much weight on the injured limb. "I'm not in any condition to walk unaided. Looks like you're pretty beaten up yourself. Must have really pissed off that Old One of yours.

Still, I'm hoping you're a faster healer than this old body of mine."

She hesitated, looking at Adonis as though waiting for something. He nodded hesitantly, and she cracked a smile.

"So you *can* understand me. I was beginning to think I was raving to myself."

Adonis offered a scowl, then ignoring her, he pressed his hands to the ground and forced himself up. Agony sliced through his left leg, the torn muscles screaming their outrage. Gritting his teeth, Adonis fought the pain, until finally he found himself standing. He looked at Maisie, teeth bared to show his strength, though in truth he wasn't in any better shape than the human.

At least the rain had ceased during the night and the morning fog was lifting, revealing the broad expanse of water—and in the distance, the flames of Maya's conquest.

The burning ships had long since sunk beneath the brown surface, but on the far distant banks, something else was aflame. A building, or perhaps an entire town, had already fallen to the fury of Maya's rage.

Even after her rejection, Adonis's heart lurched at the thought of his mate out there alone, carrying his children without him...

"I know." He flinched as Maisie spoke into the silence. "Sucks to be rejected, doesn't it? Let's face it though, she was out of your league, bud. Made the same mistake myself once, if it makes you feel any better. What is it about monarchs and all that bloodline business?"

Adonis clenched his jaw and flicked the human a look. Already her coarse voice was grating on him, but there was little he could do about it. If only she could Hear, he might make her understand her crudeness. Once he recovered his strength, he would be able to influence her emotions to a point, but for now he did not even have the energy for that.

Beside him, Maisie sighed. "I know, I'm talking too much." Adonis looked at her sharply, as her words reflected his own thoughts. "I don't...normally. Haven't in a long time. Part of being a spy, all that going unnoticed and what-not." She chuckled. "I guess I'm...reverting. It's the fear, you know? Haven't been this helpless since...well that's another story." She glanced at the fallen Anahera. "She was going to be my ticket out of here, once we figured out how to rescue the fledgelings. But that Old One of yours..." She shuddered visibly. "She's insane, you know. Surely you know that?"

The human fell silent then, though her eyes remained unnervingly fixed upon Adonis, as though waiting for a response. As if he could. He bared his teeth at her words. Despite his fall, he remained loyal to Maya's cause, to the destruction of humanity, the elevation of his people above all others...didn't he?

Maisie's eyes drifted past Adonis, to the distant burning. "She'll destroy them all, you know," she whispered finally. "Humanity, the Anahera...even your Tangata. That thing, she doesn't care about any of us. You know that, right? Surely you have to see it."

Something deep in Adonis's soul responded to the human's words. Instinctively he reached for the warmth of Maya's mind, seeking reassurance from her presence, that the path she had set them on was righteous...

...and found only silence. Only emptiness. Since her departure across the river, Maya's mind no longer touched him, no longer spoke to his consciousness.

No longer influenced him.

In that moment, Adonis finally saw the last months for what they had been. Saw the grief of his fellow Tangata as they slaughtered their human partners in New Nihelm, helpless to resist Maya's commands. Saw again his brothers and sisters lying in the snow, the dead face of a child staring at him in accusation. He witnessed the conquest of the Anaheran city, heard the pain of the fledgeling as she fought against him, saw the anguish in the eyes of Farhan as he bowed before the Old One, and Nyriah's pain at her son's death.

And through it all, he recalled the pressure of Maya's Voice on his mind, her silent whisperings, her influence upon his people—and upon himself.

Finally he turned to Maisie, and nodded.

A smile touched the human's face. "Then what are we going to do about it?"

❧ 19 ❧

THE FUGITIVE

E rika awoke with a start, aware that darkness had claimed the world. For a moment she thought she was back in the hold of the ship, that the flames, their escape, even the queen's true identity, had all been but a dream.

Then the darkness resolved into shadows and she felt the weight of the covers atop her, the softness of the mattress beneath. Except...the bed was cold, empty.

She sat up abruptly, looking around in search of the Goddess. She had been right about the darkness—sunlight no longer streamed through the shutters. How long had she slept? So much for keeping watch for the enemy. Anyone could have come upon them while they'd been unawares. A chill spread down her spine—they could be creeping up on the house even now, surrounding them with soldiers, or worse, with Tangata.

Throwing off the covers, Erika swung herself out of the bed and scrambled for her boots. At least she'd left her clothes on, but in the dark the holes of her shoes evaded her, until with a curse she let them fall and raced to the nearest window. Placing an eye to the blinds, she searched the ground outside, but clouds must have come across the sky as she slept, for there was no moon to light the world outside.

The sound of a foot scuffing the dirt floor came from behind Erika and she turned, raising her fist as a matter of habit, though she had not recovered the gauntlet from Cara.

A soft glow lit the room, but instead of coming from Erika's hand, it came from Cara's as she ignited the gauntlet. A smile crossed the Goddess's lips as she raised an eyebrow.

"Don't worry, there's no one out there. I already checked," she said with laughter in her voice.

"Oh," Erika replied, then glanced over the Goddess's shoulders at her wings. "Are they okay…"

Erika trailed off as the smile fell from her friend's face.

"No," Cara said softly. Her wings twitched at the pronouncement, as though they too longed for the freedom of flight. "Another week now, I think…"

Erika's stomach twisted at the sadness in her friend's voice, and she drew the Anahera into a hug.

"A week then," she said, and gently she stroked her hand over the Anahera's feathers. She knew how sensitive they could be, and the soft murmur from Cara showed her appreciation. "We're free, Cara, a week is nothing."

The Goddess remained silent at first, but finally Erika felt her nod and draw back. "You're right," Cara said, looking away. "It's just…everything. The Old One, my mother, this queen of yours. How do you humans handle so much chaos?"

"To be fair, this all only started when you appeared, Cara."

Cara snorted at that. "All this started when you went digging in things that were best left buried," she replied, raising the gauntlet. She reached up and squeezed her wrist.

The artefact gave a hiss as it separated from her hand. Cara held it out with a hesitant smile. "Here, you had better take this. I'd rather not be caught breaking any more of my people's prohibitions."

"Thank you," Erika said, swallowing back a wave of desire.

Whatever the Goddess had said in the mountains about the gauntlet's magic being harmless to its user, the power had a hold on her. The rush, the exhilaration she felt when she activated its power, it was addictive. The gauntlet may not have been responsible for the terrible things she'd done with it, but there remained a selfish part of her that did not want to see another use it. She slipped it onto her wrist and shivered as its silver threads melded with her flesh.

Light leapt from the mesh as Erika squeezed her fist, her strength at least partially restored by the earlier meal and sleep. Her stomach gave another rumble though, and she looked beyond Cara to where she'd left the food.

"Have you eaten?" she asked.

Cara's stomach gave an audible growl as a sheepish look crossed her face. "A few of the eggs," she said, wrinkling her nose. "I wasn't sure whether it was safe to light a fire," she added, glancing at the hearth.

Erika nodded. "It should be now, so long as we keep the windows shuttered. Come, let's see what we can cook up."

An hour later the pair sat back on the earthen floor with a warm bowl of stew in their laps. Inhaling the rich aroma of the broth, Erika began to salivate. But if Erika was hungry, Cara must have been moments from starvation, for the Goddess was practically inhaling her bowl.

Chuckling to herself, Erika ate more slowly, taking care not to burn her mouth. It was a shame they had no bread to give the broth substance, but the tubers she'd dug from the vegetable patch with her bare hands helped. The remnants of the salted beef added flavour too, and by the time she was finished Erika felt better than she had in…who knew how long. She hadn't had a proper meal since leaving the City of the Gods.

They helped themselves to seconds, then Erika let Cara finish the remnants from the beaten pot. The Anahera needed more sustenance to thrive than the average human, and it was obvious the past weeks had taken their toll on her friend. The flesh had sunken on Cara's face, revealing sharp cheekbones. Even the slim muscle of her shoulders and arms had withered. No wonder the queen had beaten her so easily, despite only being half-Anahera.

Turning her eyes to the gauntlet, Erika studied its shimmering links, feeling its innate warmth. They would both need to rebuild their strength if they were to stand a chance against Amina. This house would not be safe for long, regardless who won the battle for the Illmoor. But where *would* be safe for them? Gemaho had fallen and all of Flumeer was aligned against them. Perfugia was far and away, impossible to reach without a ship—and besides, they too were allies of Amina. The Sovereigns would turn the pair over the moment they appeared on those distant shores.

"You look worried."

Erika's head jerked up at the interruption. She frowned at the Goddess. Light from the gauntlet bathed Cara's face, adding a glow to her amber eyes as she leaned closer, as though to inspect Erika. Blinking, Erika considered her words, and struggled to contain a mad bout of laughter.

"Me, worried? Why would I be worried?" she asked wryly. "I mean, there's an insane creature and her legion of Tangata hunting us. And the only ally I had left is dead, his entire kingdom burned to the ground." Her voice grew in pitch as she spoke, tears welling in her eyes as the weight of what they faced fell upon her shoulders. "Then there's the

Flumeeren queen, your half-sister, the woman I served for years, the same woman who killed my father. A woman with the powers of the Anahera and an army at her back, who would love nothing more than to torture me until the end of my days."

A tear streaked Erika's cheek and she turned away from the Goddess, fixing her eyes on the fire. She felt just like a vase that had been heated by the glass blower for too long, filled to bursting, ready to shatter into a thousand pieces at the slightest touch.

Then strong hands were wrapping around her, holding her close. A sob burst from Erika's lips as she turned to Cara, the pressure within bursting, and all her pain and despair and anger came gushing out. Gasping, she buried her head in the Goddess's shoulder.

"Whatdamigonnado?" The words rushed from her between sobs. Fists clenched, she clutched Cara as though she were a true Goddess, as though she possessed the power to lift her burden, to free her from their danger.

"You'll find a way, Erika," Cara's whisper came through the darkness. "I believe in you."

A hiccup burst from Erika's lips as she finally pulled away, eyes still hot with tears, cheeks wet. The Goddess offered a hesitant smile as they drew apart.

"What if I can't?" Erika whispered. "What if it's beyond me?"

"You will," Cara replied firmly. "It's what makes you special, what made me—" She cut off abruptly, and it seemed her face brightened in the flickering firelight.

Erika frowned. "What?"

The Anahera shook her head, her feathers rustling as she turned towards the fire. Silence fell, before Cara breached it with a new topic. "Maybe it was because of how different you all are from us," she murmured.

"Huh?" Erika asked, her confusion deepening at the Goddess's cryptic speech.

"That made my mother fall in love with your people, with the queen's father."

"Oh..." Erika exhaled. She couldn't help but shudder at the memory of Amina's naked back, the terrible scars left from her amputated wings. "What are you saying?" she added at last.

"There is so much *life* in humanity," Cara said, eyes still on the flames. "The clothing, the art, the music, in everything you do. It's like you fit a dozen of our lifespans into every year of your own existence, every moment. Each of you are so different, so unique, even the Tangata must wonder at it." She looked up, eyes locking with Erika's. "When I first saw you, I thought you must have been a different species than the others—Romaine and Lukys and the Perfugians. They were warriors, rugged and unkept, their hair and beards so tangled and...*filthy*. The other villagers in that place too."

She drew in a breath. "Then you appeared. Dressed in silk, with your hair kept long, tied back for riding, clean and tidy and elegant...I was entranced."

Erika felt her cheeks grew warm and she shook her head. "I was an arrogant fool," she said, recalling the day she'd arrived in Fogmore. "I thought I was better than everyone in that place, even Romaine, a man with ten times my courage."

"A man who believed in you," Cara insisted. "You might not be a warrior, but you have just as much courage as Romaine. You've proven it every day since we stepped into my mountains, in the way you faced my father and the Anahera, the way you stood against the Old One and her Tangata. Even on the ship with Amina. You are elegant and glorious and strong, Erika, everything your people need."

"My people are dead," Erika whispered. "I failed them long ago."

"Your people are every human who does not wish to be enslaved by Maya or my sister, every man and woman who resists their tyranny. Forget your petty kingdoms—they don't matter, they have never mattered. Even the differences between human and Tangata and Anahera are nothing. In this world, there are only the free and the enslaved now, Erika."

Swallowing, Erika looked at the Goddess, wondering at the change in her friend. Just a short time ago, Cara had been in despair, defeated by her sister, crushed by the death of her brother and father, the enslavement of her people. Something had given her hope…but surely it could not have been Erika?

She shivered, unable to meet the Anahera's eyes. Looking at her hands again, she clenched her fists, watched the shimmer that lit the gauntlet. It was the artefact's magic that had gotten her this far, that allowed her to do the impossible things Cara spoke of. She was no leader, no princess as she had once claimed to Romaine. That wasn't why he'd followed her. It was not her own reputation, but her dead father the king that Romaine had believed in. Her father had led Calafe to glory, before betrayal had cast him down.

She could not be that leader, could she?

A shiver shook Erika as she recalled the vow she had sworn the day Romaine had fallen. She had promised to return to Flumeer and help her people, the Calafe refugees that had been condemned by the queen's cruelty. An impossible task, surely, and yet…

…on her last visit to Mildeth, there had been thousands camped outside the city walls. Her people all, the last remnants of the fallen Calafe. Impoverished and homeless they might have been, but they were Calafe still, proud and unbroken, trained as youth to survive, to fend for themselves, even to wield a blade. Could they form the beginnings of a resistance against the mad queen?

A shiver ran down Erika's spine as she stood suddenly, looking at Cara. A grin spread across the Anahera's lips as she rose beside her.

"You have a plan?"

Erika swallowed. "The beginnings of one."

❧ 20 ❧

THE SOVEREIGN

L ukys paced the floor of the royal chamber, his footsteps echoing up through the overlooking rows of empty chairs. The nobles of Mildeth had mostly marched south with the queen, and those few who remained had been imprisoned once the Perfugian forces had entered the citadel. Zayaan had been helpful in identifying those likely to keep their loyalty to Amina and those who might be persuaded to the Perfugian cause.

For now though, Lukys had other concerns on his mind.

How many days will it take for your people to reach the city? he asked, glancing at Sophia.

She stood fixed in place while he paced, but Lukys could sense the same fear within her, the same doubts. Everything had changed with the news from the south, and now it seemed the weight of the world fell upon their shoulders. Neither had been prepared for such a burden, not yet. Abruptly he crossed to where Sophia waited and drew her into a hug.

A shudder wracked them as they stood alone on the floor of the giant chamber. Less than a week had passed since their bloodless conquest of the city, and they'd hardly had a moment of peace since. Their time had been consumed organising the city's defences, with their first act inviting the Calafe refugees into the city.

Zayaan had argued against it, claiming that the presence of the so-called barbarians would disturb the fragile peace in Mildeth and turn the people against them, but Lukys had not forgotten his old mentor Romaine. The last warrior of the Calafe had been the only who had believed in him back in Fogmore. No one had heard a word of Romaine in weeks, but Lukys would not abandon the man's people when the Tangata came.

And come they would.

Word had reached the city in the night, carried on the lips of the first refugees—the Tangata had crossed the Illmoor. Amina's forces had waged a great battle for the river, but in the end her fleet had been destroyed and they had been forced to retreat. General Curtis, the man who had commanded the southern defensive for nigh on a decade, was said to have fallen defending the walls of Fogmore, and a sizeable chunk of the Flumeeren army with him.

For the first time in living memory, the Tangata had gained a foothold north of the Illmoor. And it did not look like they would stop there.

Somehow, Queen Amina had survived the conflict. Riding a white stallion, she had led a charge against the enemy in a replica of her efforts so many years before. This time though, the charge had failed, faltering as the winged Anahera came against her forces. Witnessing the Gods themselves turn against humanity had sown chaos amongst the Flumeeren ranks, and the last resistance had finally crumbled, turning the battle into a full-blown rout.

The news of the Gods' betrayal had turned Lukys's

blood cold, and he could feel a memory stirring within, a whisper of a truth long forgotten. The last Sovereign had warned them not to trust the Anahera, that they had failed humanity once before, but the memory of that failure still escaped him.

Days. No longer.

He shivered as Sophia finally responded to his question. Meeting her gaze, he saw the pain shining in her grey eyes and hugged her tighter, wishing he could make this all easier, that he had the answers. But they possessed the same memories, the same knowledge and power. They both knew what marched towards them, the death that followed in the footsteps of the Old Ones.

We will find a way, was all he said, though he knew Sophia saw through his words. Their minds grew closer each day, and he could feel her thoughts fluttering against his own. *What if…we tried to speak with them, with your people?*

Sophia let out a sigh as they drew apart. *If even the Anahera have bowed to Maya…* She shook her head. *What chance do my brothers and sisters have against the power of her Voice?* She hesitated, and he saw her doubt. *We are not a people used to questioning, Lukys. It is a part of our fabric, obedience, subservience to our Matriarch, to the most powerful amongst us.*

Lukys shivered, reaching out to lift her chin so that they stood eye to eye.

"I don't believe that," he whispered, gently kissing her lips. "If that were true, you and Keria and the others would have killed us back in New Nihelm, when Adonis commanded it of you. If that were true, you would not be with me now, doing everything in your power to stop her."

"Maybe," Sophia replied. She looked across the debating chamber towards the south, as though her Tangatan eyes might pierce the stone and distance, might allow her to look upon the darkness that came for them.

"Maybe that is what we had been striving for, what our Matriarch wanted for us—the freedom to choose our own fate. But..." She sighed. "Lukys, I fear she died too soon. This Old One, she cares not for the weak, whether Tangata or human. She wants only to dominate."

Lukys sighed, reaching out to squeeze her fingers. "We will find a way to free them."

"We'd better," a new voice spoke from the side of the chamber. They looked around as Nguyen entered. Isabella and Travis followed, looking apologetic for the interruption. They'd been posted outside as guards, but the Gemaho king was a difficult man to deny. "If you can't find a way to bring at least some of your brothers and sisters to our side, this war will be over before it even begins."

"Thanks, Nguyen," Sophia said, adapting a wry tone. Lukys was impressed by how quickly she had learned to adjust to the inflections of spoken voice. "As though the fate of my own people wasn't enough pressure, let's just add the existence of humanity to the burden as well."

The king chuckled and his gaze lifted to the rows of seats that ringed the chamber floor, a hundred in the first tier, another two hundred in the second for minor nobles. The only piece of furniture on the floor of the chamber was a golden throne. Zayaan had explained how the queen held her court here, seated beneath the gaze of her nobles, allowing them to participate in debates over the kingdom's future, as well as witness her judgement against those brought before the throne.

The size of the chamber was but a fraction of the Sovereign amphitheatre back in Ashura, but that theatre had been kept empty, all semblance of the public excluded from the presence of their rulers. They intended to do away with that tradition upon their return. Perhaps they would draw on the queen's custom, though with true citizens of Perfugia, rather than a few privileged nobles.

A part of him cried out against that idea, a dozen minds deep within that resisted such an indulgence of the public, but he pushed them aside. They were the voices of the past —it was time Perfugia had new ideas.

First, though, they had to survive. He looked again at Nguyen, who had seated himself in the golden throne and now lounged with his legs draped over one of the arms.

Lukys raised an eyebrow. "How do you think Amina would react, knowing you sat in her chair?"

"It's our chair now," the king replied with a wave of his hand. "Amina will behave, once she realises we have her city. She knows she cannot face the Old One alone. If she wants to have any chance of survival, she will have to accede to our conditions."

Lukys frowned at that. "You would let her through the gates?"

The king shrugged. "I don't see any alternatives."

Lukys sensed a stirring of anger as Sophia stepped forward, eyes burning. "That woman is responsible for the genocide of my people," she hissed. "For starting a war that has slain thousands on either side. You would greet her as a friend?"

"I would greet her as the enemy of my enemy," Nguyen said softly, unflinching from the rage in Sophia's eyes. He grimaced, glancing around the room. "This is her city, Sophia. She will know best how to defend it. And she still has an army. Better them on our side, rather than fighting against us." He sighed. "I don't like it any more than you do, believe me. But it is as I said back in Perfugia—a ruler must set aside his own principles and do what is best for his people. Justice will come for Amina one day. For now, we must stand together, or risk annihilation."

Sophia said nothing at that, only stared the king down, her aura a burning red. But it was clear that Nguyen had won the argument. Lukys shivered. The man was right. Whatever her crimes, they needed Amina now, needed her army. Though he feared she would sooner see them all dead than stand alongside them.

Is there not another way? a new voice said, and Lukys looked around at Isabella. The Tangata rarely spoke in these meetings, and he nodded for her to continue.

She hesitated, placing a hand on Travis's arm, as though it granted her courage.

It seems to me, she said, and Sophia translated for Nguyen and Travis, *that ever since we encountered your people, you have been able to do the impossible.* She hesitated. *Or rather…find a way to make the impossible possible. When faced with an immovable barrier, instead of giving up, you simply find another way.*

"What are you saying, Isabella?" Travis asked, entwining his fingers with hers.

A smile touched her face as she looked at him, then back at the room. *We have been trying to find a way to defeat Maya's army, to match her power, but however we look at it, the task seems impossible. She is too powerful, our brothers and sisters too numerous.*

"And what would you suggest?" Nguyen asked.

That we look at our problem another way, Isabella replied. *There is much we do not know about the Old One, but it seems to me there is a question we have not yet asked.*

And what is that? Sophia said hesitantly.

What does she want? Isabella responded.

Something stirred within Lukys at the Tangata's words, a memory buried deep. He shuddered as he sensed Sophia alongside him, realising she felt the same stirring. They stood together in silence, concentrating on that lost past, on secrets hidden inside their own minds. Images emerged slowly from the depths, and Lukys held his breath, waiting, watching with Sophia as faces took shape from the shadows…

Ten pairs of grey eyes stared around the circle of those gathered, but Lukys sensed that these beings were not Tangata, that this memory was older even than the arrival of his ancestors in Perfugia, before the kingdoms of man had risen, from a time when the old world had Fallen.

These were the first of their kind, the Old Ones in flesh.

A shiver ran down his spine as he recognised Maya's face amongst those who had gathered.

"How many years have passed now, brothers, sisters?" The speaker stood with Maya, and Lukys realised from their closeness that they were partners. "How long since we unleashed the doom upon this land? Since we last birthed a new generation?"

"It has not been so long," another replied. He shifted nervously on his feet, reaching for the female who stood with him, clutching her hand. "Only a few years. The children will come."

"No." It was Maya who spoke now, her voice touched by anger. "The winged ones have betrayed us, betrayed the sacrifice of my sires." She bared her teeth. "There are those who speak of sightings in the mountains. We should go to them, take our vengeance, before the end comes."

"It was your own father who brokered the peace," the first speaker argued. "I will not break it now, not when our strength wanes."

"You would rather a slow death?" Maya's

partner replied. "To see the noble Chead fade away, lost to the annals of history?"

"It has not come to that, not yet," came the reply. The Old One hesitated, and Lukys could see the doubt on his face. "And...there are still the humans. We know from the past—"

"A false hope!" Maya snarled. "You would see us debased, our powers corrupted by those creatures? No, I say it must be war. If not against the cursed winged ones, then with humanity itself. You know the danger they pose. Pockets of their civilisation remain, hidden beneath the earth, protected from the darkness we unleashed. We should seek them out, destroy them once and for all, before they rise again. And...perhaps they might hold the key to our survival, some secret in our creation that could save us."

Many of those who stood with Maya stirred at that, and Lukys sensed their agreement. Even then, hundreds of years before the Sovereigns and the war started by the queen, it seemed there had been hatred between their peoples. But he noticed that others dissented, and now the male who argued against Maya and her partner stepped forward.

"We are tired of war," he said softly, shaking his head, "of death. For years we have dwindled. I will see no more of my people's blood spilt in senseless violence."

"You would rather waste away, the glory of our people lost to time?" Maya's mate questioned.

"I would rather live to face whatever glory,

whatever doom fate has dictated for the Chead," came the reply.

"So be it," Maya spat. Shaking her head, she turned her gaze on the rest of the circle. "Follow Tangata and Chiara if you must, but I will not go quietly into the night. Raxion and I will live as did my sires when they saved us from humanity's wrath. Any who wish to see the Chead rise again, follow me, and I will lead you to glory."

There was a pause around the circle, but as Maya and her partner turned to leave, several broke ranks and followed. Lukys watched them go, realising belatedly that he recognised some of those who left. Their faces were etched into his memory, terrible and twisted, maddened as they sought to slaughter him. These were the creatures they had unearthed in the hidden chambers so many months before, the ones the Archivist had uncovered, and Cara had slain.

Slowly the memory faded and Lukys found himself standing again in the debating chamber. Beside him, Sophia slumped against him, her eyes wide, entire being trembling. He held her close, feeling the same shock at what they had seen, though it was impossible now to know whether it was his own, or hers. The sight of Maya in that ring of Old Ones, of her disdain as she regarded those who would not follow…

"She will kill them all," Sophia whispered to the room.

The hairs on Lukys's neck stood on end at her words. Sophia was right. Maya loathed humanity. She cared nothing for the creatures that had become the Tangata, who had mixed their blood with her enemy. They were beneath her, unworthy. All that mattered to this creature was the survival of her own people.

The survival of the Old Ones, the *Chead*.

And Lukys knew now what she wanted.

A true mate, another of her kind that had lain sleeping through the centuries, one that might restore her race to its former glory.

He opened his mouth to speak, but before the words could leave his lips, a *boom* came from the entrance to the chamber. Lukys stumbled, still struggling to return his mind to the present, to the grand chamber in which they stood, as the queen's former advisor burst inside. Eyes wide, Zayaan's gaze swept the room until it settled finally on Lukys and Sophia.

"Your Majesties!" the elderly man cried. "Please, you must come quickly. The Calafe refugees, there's been an uprising. They're marching on the citadel!"

21

THE FUGITIVE

Erika struggled to make headway as the crowd pressed against her, the dense bodies threatening to swallow her up. Refugees from all across southern Flumeer had converged on Mildeth, fleeing before the retreating army and the Tangata surging across the kingdom. The chaos had made it easy to enter the city unnoticed by Amina's guards, but it complicated her plans. The unwanted Calafe, after more than a year spent camped outside of the walls, had finally been allowed into the city. If she could not find them, she would fail.

Alongside her, Cara struggled with the crowd even more than Erika. While she had healed enough to fly on their journey, she now wore a jacket they had taken from the farmhouse to cover her wings. Rumours of the winged creatures that harried the queen's army had raced ahead of the battle, and now instead of looking upon the Anahera in awe, the Flumeerens spoke of them in the same breath as the monstrous Tangata.

But it was the crowd itself that was causing Cara problems. She had coped fine in Fogmore, but that had been a backwater village compared to the population of Mildeth. Thousands surged around them, more people than the young Anahera had ever seen before, and Erika could see the anxiety in her friend's eyes, could feel it in the strength of Cara's grip around her hand. She was pretty sure that grip was the only thing keeping the Goddess from fleeing into the sky.

Thankfully, Cara kept her feet on the ground, at least for now. They were chasing a rumour that the Calafe refugees had taken up residence in a plaza not far from the citadel itself. She wondered what Amina would think of that, should the woman survive long enough to return. Erika still prayed the Tangata would strike the queen down, but given her Anaheran strength and the human magic she wielded, the odds seemed stacked in Amina's favour.

A princess could dream, though.

Finally the crowd began to shift. The girls went with the flow rather than trying to force themselves in a particular direction. All roads in Mildeth led towards the citadel—it was only once you reached the mountain on which the citadel perched that the way would be barred.

Still, the crowd thinned as they approached the citadel, as the refugees were taken in by those households and taverns willing to help, or more often found a spot on the sidewalks, plazas or parks—wherever they could find space not already occupied by another lost soul. Compared to the tranquil city she had last left just months before, Erika could hardly believe the difference now.

But then, the Tangata were coming.

They found the plaza crowded like all the others, but it was difficult to tell immediately whether the rumours had been true, that the Calafe were the ones who occupied this space. Certainly, the plaza seemed better organised than others, with makeshift tents set up in long lines, creating avenues through which foot traffic could pass.

Still clutching Cara's hand, Erika led them into the square. It wasn't long before she heard the rough southern accent of the Calafe amongst those camped there. Her heart quickened at the sound, and she found herself studying the faces of the men and women they passed, noting their differences from the average Flumeeren. While the locals generally preferred spears and swords, these refugees carried axes, clubs and maces. The weapons were older too, their handles worn with use, though Erika saw not a speck of rust upon the blades.

The final confirmation came when she noticed that the women carried weapons too. The warrior queen of Flumeer was an exception to the norm in Flumeer, where most women went unarmed.

Which meant Erika had found the Calafe, her people.

As though summoned by the thought, a rough hand grabbed Erika by the wrist, jarring her to a halt and spinning her in the direction of her assailant. Heart lurching, Erika raised her fist, but the man spoke before she could summon her power.

"Who are you?" he growled, spittle from his swollen lips flying between them, such that Erika took a quick step back. The man released her, but advanced after her retreat. "This is Calafe territory," he continued. "Outsiders are not welcome."

Erika struggled to contain her surprise—she hadn't expected her presence to be noted so quickly, let alone confronted. Now she found herself staring up at the gruff stranger, dwarfed by his size, by the bulk of his massive barrel chest. The hilt of a greatsword rose from between his shoulders and he wore an old chainmail vest, its links polished so they shone. Such was his size, it was a long moment before Erika noticed his missing arm, the empty sleeve where his left hand should have been.

Her heart lurched at the sight and she remembered Romaine, how he had lost his arm protecting her in the caverns. But the man had not been alone in his loss—amongst the Calafe, many had suffered similar injuries in the decade long war against the Tangata. Though...most had not continued the fight as Romaine had.

Remembering his courage that day in the mountains, so long ago now, when Romaine had fallen, Erika drew herself up. "I am no outsider," she snarled at her accoster. "Who are you to question me?"

The man raised a bushy eyebrow. "I am Darien of the Calafe," he rumbled. "And I know all of my people in Mildeth, those who survived the death of our kingdom. And I don't know you."

"And yet I am Calafe."

"Did you come from the south then?" Darien asked, his voice taking on a mocking tone. "Perhaps you've lived amongst the Tangata all this time, sharing their beds, breaking your fast with them." He snorted and waved a hand. "Begone, women, look for shelter elsewhere."

Movement came from behind Darien as two others stepped from the crowd with clubs in hand. One sported a missing eye, the other a nasty scar that started at his exposed shoulder and disappeared beneath his shirt. Erika shivered again at the evidence of their lost war. Most of the Calafe had refused to flee from the Tangata. Only those too injured to fight, or with families to protect, had fled willingly. Even Romaine had only survived because of a head knock that had incapacitated him during the final battle.

Alongside her, Cara shifted at the sight of the men and Erika sensed her friend's tension. Quickly she stepped between them. She didn't want to see what would happen if the people of this city witnessed the Goddess in all her glory. After the rumours that had spread ahead of the fleeing army, they were unlikely to be friendly…

"Ay, I came from the frontier," she said softly, allowing the accent she had worked so hard to squash the past decade to slip back into her words. She kept her eyes locked with Darien. It was obvious he enjoyed some degree of status amongst the refugees. "I stood with Romaine of Calafe when he marched south against the Tangata." She hesitated then, knowing she carried news the world had not yet heard. "And I was at his side when he died."

"Romaine is dead?" the man asked, shock showing in his eyes. He lowered his hand, the tension going from his body. "It cannot be true."

Cara stirred at his words. "It is," she said softly. "He died saving me, protecting me from a terrible man."

For the first time, Darien took note of Cara. His eyes narrowed as he looked her up and down and Erika's heart clenched, fearing Cara would be recognised as the Goddess that had revealed herself on the Illmoor. This man could not have been there, but rumours would have spread…

"It is said that Romaine journeyed into the mountains to protect a…woman with fiery hair and eyes of amber," he said softly, and Erika realised this man knew the truth. But he only inclined his head to Cara. "I am glad to hear his passing was not in vain. Long did our champion seek the release of death."

The Goddess swallowed at his words, her eyes shining in the afternoon sun. Erika felt a sting in her own eyes, but she clenched her teeth and forced the grief aside. How much easier this would have been, if Romaine had lived to stand at her side. They could have worked together to reunite their fallen kingdom…

…but there was no use wishing to change the past.

There was only the present now, only her. Drawing herself up, Erika nodded to the Calafe.

"He died fighting for his kingdom," she added.

A frown touched the man's face, and he looked at her, perturbed. "Who *are* you, girl?"

"I am no girl," Erika said, inserting every inch of authority she possessed into her voice. These men must not view her as a child, and so she drew about her the practiced air of the Flumeeren court, the skills she had acquired in her years training beneath the queen. "My name is Erika, daughter to King Micah, and the rightful Queen of the Calafe."

The man stared at her, eyes wide, brows lifted into his ragged mop of black hair. Then abruptly, he threw back his head and let out a booming laugh. Erika jumped at the sound, flinching back from him, before a scowl crossed her face. Instinctively, she clenched her fist.

The sound of Darien's laughter drew the attention of the nearby crowd, and as his laughter faded, Erika and Cara found themselves surrounded now by onlookers. Embarrassment rose within Erika as she felt the weight of their gazes and her cheeks grew warm.

But they fell silent as the heat grew in her hand, their eyes drawn to the light seeping from her fingers. Swallowing her doubt, Erika raised her fist, the gauntlet aglow, its magic bursting out to bathe the faces of the onlookers. Even Darien's eyes widened at the sight and unconsciously he took a step back.

"What sorcery is this?" he whispered.

Erika ignored him. Instead, she scanned her surroundings, settling finally on an appropriate place to stand. Crossing to a nearby fountain, she climbed up onto the rim. The water within had long since dried up, probably one of the first luxuries to be halted with the approaching war.

There was a statue within of a man upon a horse, probably queen Amina's father, Erika guessed, though she could not have said for certain.

Ignoring the now silent crowd, Erika crossed the barren fountain and pulled herself up onto the statue, climbing higher, leaving behind those below, until she stood upon the back of the horse and looked out across the plaza.

A thousand faces stared back at her, mouths wide, eyes fixed upon the glowing gauntlet. Erika grimaced as she looked at them, at their pain, their poverty, the cruelty the world had dealt them. Once, she had condemned these people for their misfortune, but now she saw more. A mother who wore a sword upon her belt as she supervised a group of children. Warriors like Darien and his friends amidst the crowd, eyes alert for troublemakers. The orderly placement of the tents, though they had only been in the plaza a few days.

The Calafe might have lost their home, but they had not lost their pride.

"Hear me, people of Calafe," Erika called, speaking in a soft voice, though such was the silence now, that her words did not fail to reach the ears of a single watcher. "My name is Erika. You do not know me, but my father was Micah, our fallen king. My mother and I were driven from New Nihelm upon his death. Perhaps you know the story." She hesitated at that, memories flickering into her mind, of a life lost, of suffering and hardship, of her heartbroken mother doing her best to raise an ungrateful child. Then she exhaled, and let go of that pain. "In truth, I have lived much of my life hating the Calafe for what was done to me." She drew in a breath. "But that time has passed. I have learned much these last weeks, the truth about my father, about our kingdom."

Erika paused, eyeing the crowd, knowing that what she

said next would change everything. Revealing the truth would set the Calafe against Queen Amina, and all who stood with her. But there was no choice. However she justified her treachery, the woman must pay for the crimes she had committed against the Calafe.

"It is time I shared that truth. It was not the Tangata who killed my father, our king, but an assassin. Sent by Queen Amina, he slew Micah at the height of the southern campaign, when our forces were committed to battle, so that the Calafe would collapse, leaving our lands unprotected. All so Queen Amina could play the hero, so the other kingdoms would turn to her in fear."

A rumble rose from the crowd and she sensed their disbelief, their anger. She had felt that same doubt herself. How could anyone be so selfish, so cold-hearted, to commit such an atrocity against her fellow man? And yet her words were truth. She caught sight of the man that had accosted her as he pushed his way to the edge of the fountain.

"Is it true?" Darien called up to her, his face twisted, anger shining from his eyes. Cara hovered at his side, looking from Erika to the Calafe man.

Erika clenched her fist and light burst from the gauntlet. "Every word I have spoken is truth," she proclaimed. "I served beneath the woman for years, trusted her, loved her. But I cannot allow her treachery to stand. No longer."

Darien stared at her for a long moment. "And what would you do about it, Erika of the Calafe?" came the question.

Erika clenched her jaw. "I would lead my people against the one who betrayed us."

Darien nodded, then dropped to one knee. "Then I will follow you, My Queen."

Erika eyes widened at the man's abrupt change of heart. But his gesture was already spreading around the plaza, whispers passing through the crowd as they looked upon Darien. In that moment, Erika realised she'd been correct in her assessment, that Darien was someone important amongst the Calafe.

Standing atop the statue, Erika watched in disbelief as one by one, the Calafe gathered below fell to their knees and pledged their loyalty. In that moment, looking out over her people, Erika's worries evaporated, and she felt a warmth within, a quiet confidence. If she could do this, then nothing was beyond her. Not with her people united behind her.

Her eyes flickered towards the mountain that rose from the centre of the city, the walls of the citadel twisting up to enclose it. Amina was still marching north, the bulk of her forces with her. Most of the Mildeth's remaining defences would be committed to the city walls, leaving the citadel relatively unprotected. But if the queen was allowed to retake the city, that would change.

There was no time to hesitate.

"People of Calafe," she called, lifting her arm to point the way. "Let us take our vengeance upon the home of our enemy!"

⚜ 22 ⚜

THE SOVEREIGN

L ukys stumbled to a halt as he turned a corner and was greeted by the roar of raised voices. Sophia stopped beside him, even as Nguyen and their guards fanned out around them. For a second, all Lukys could do was stare at the Calafe as they advanced up the street. Weapons glistened in their hands and a burning red aura rolled out ahead of the crowd, thrumming with their rage.

Instinctively, he reached out with his mind and felt Sophia moving with him, seeking to cool the heat of their emotion, to restore calm to the approaching mob. For once, though, they resisted, and Lukys sensed a flickering of images from their minds, of a man with wild black hair cut down, of burning villages and the fall of New Nihelm, and...

...he started as a woman's face emerged from the images, one he knew, that of the queen's Archivist he had known once, though it seemed a lifetime since he'd ridden south with Erika...

"Lukys!"

His head jerked up as someone shouted his name over

the roaring of the crowd. His heart lurched and his mouth fell open as a figure leapt into the air, wings snapping open, beating down, sending their owner hurtling upwards. Screams sounded from the crowd as the Anahera soared higher, and curses came from his guards as they raised spears and shields to protect the Sovereigns and the king.

Lukys hardly noticed their actions. His eyes were fixed on the winged woman, on the figure spiralling down towards him, taking in the brilliant auburn wings and copper hair, the ringing voice calling his name, the joy upon the face of the Anahera.

Only when he heard the clacking of crossbows did he take note of his guards.

"*Stop!*" he shouted desperately, using his inner Voice too. The crossbow winches fell silent as Travis and the others looked at Lukys, eyes wide, and in the air, even the Anahera seemed to falter at the power of his Command.

With a soft *thump*, the Anahera landed on the cobbled streets a few yards from where their party stood. As one, Dale, Travis and the other guards spun towards her. Only then did recognition bloom in the eyes of Lukys's fellow Perfugians.

The Anahera standing before them was Cara, their long-lost friend from Fogmore.

"Lukys?" Cara said his name again, but this time he sensed her hesitation, the doubt in her mind.

Lukys couldn't blame her. As far as she and most of the world had known, he and his friends had died south of the Illmoor. For Lukys to be standing there alive, let alone in the garb of a Sovereign…well, even he had trouble believing it at times.

"Cara?"

Another voice spoke before Lukys could greet the

Anahera, as Travis stepped from the line of guards, tearing off his helmet.

"By the...well, you, I guess, it is you!" he exclaimed, a sudden grin stretching across his lips.

Then he was racing forward to drag Cara into an embrace, lifting her from the ground and spinning her around, wings and all. A chuckle whispered in Lukys's mind at the sight and he glanced at Sophia, seeing the grin on his partner's lips.

So this is the Anahera you're all so fond of.

So it would seem, Lukys said quietly, then hesitated, wondering if he should reveal more. But...Sophia would sense the truth from him anyway—there were no secrets between them now. *Travis in particular...*

He trailed off as Isabella stepped hesitantly after her partner, lifting the helmet from her own head. Still embracing Cara, Travis noticed her approach and turned from the Anahera, still wearing his grin.

"Cara, there's someone I want you to meet!" he said with his usual enthusiasm. Releasing the Anahera, he stepped up to Isabella and kissed her quickly, before looking back at Cara. "This is Isabella, my partner!"

Lukys's heart twisted as he watched the smile fall from Cara's lips and she took an abrupt step backwards, eyes wide, suddenly shining. There was no missing the shock on her face, even if he had not seen her aura change from pink to white. Her mouth opened and closed, but the surprise of seeing her former...crush with another had obviously robbed her of words.

"You must be the Anahera who protected my favourite human from the Old Ones," Sophia interjected quickly, stepping forward to offer Cara a hug. The Anahera had regained a little of her composure by the time Sophia stepped back, and Lukys smiled at his partner's quick thinking. "It's a welcome sight to see one of your kind on our side," she continued, though Cara was still staring at her in surprise, no doubt wondering at her Tangatan nature. "We have heard terrible rumours of the Anahera fighting along-side the Old One."

"I'm afraid that much is true," a new voice interjected, and Lukys's heart clenched as the face he'd glimpsed in the minds of the crowd approached. So Erika *was* here. Behind her, the Calafe lingered, apparently shocked to a standstill by Cara's appearance. "I thought you were dead, recruit."

An audible groan came from somewhere behind Lukys at the Archivist's appearance. He cast a sharp glance over his shoulder, catching Dale's eye, but the guard only shrugged. Erika wasn't exactly their favourite person, after she'd forced them all to join her on her mad quest south. Regardless, Lukys shook off his hesitation and stepped forward to greet the woman.

"Archivist," he said, keeping his tone pleasant regardless of his true feelings about her. "It is good to see that you have endured these past months." He did not offer any explanations for his own survival.

"I have a new title now," she replied somewhat hesi-tantly, glancing over her shoulder. Several men of the Calafe moved to join her and Lukys thought he glimpsed what might have been a nod from one missing an arm. Appar-ently reassured by their presence, Erika faced Lukys and Sophia again, though only for a moment, as her eyes regis-tered another presence.

"King Nguyen," she greeted, arching an eyebrow. "I am surprised to find you here. Don't tell me you've allied your-self with Amina after all?"

Nguyen chuckled at that. "The Sovereigns and I decided we liked the look of Mildeth, so we took the city for ourselves."

A frown creased Erika's brow at his words. "Sovereigns?" Her eyes flicked back to the pair of them and widened. "I see…" She hesitated, then made to offer her hand. "It seems we have all moved up—"

Before she could come any closer, the one-armed Calafe man leapt forward, grabbing her by the shoulder and dragging her back. "Beware!" he cried, a blade appearing in his hand as he placed himself between the former Archivist and the Sovereigns.

"Darien!" Erika gasped, struggling to retain her balance as she staggered. "What in the—?"

"A Tangata stands with these kings," the Calafe man hissed. "See the eyes of the two women?" he added, gesturing to Sophia and Isabella, neither of whom were concealing their faces now.

Blood began to pound in Lukys's ears as he watched the colour drain from Erika's face. Light burst from the familiar gauntlet she wore, even as the Calafe warriors raised their weapons. Her head whipped around, focusing on Sophia as the glow of her gauntlet grew brighter.

"*Stop!*" Lukys bellowed, unleashing his Voice for the second time in as many minutes.

Erika stopped dead, hand half raised, that strange glow dancing around the metallic links. But she did not—could not—bring herself to open her fist and unleash her power. Drawing in a breath for calm, Lukys placed himself between the new queen and his Sovereign mate.

"Peace, Erika," he said softly, hands raised. "Wait a minute, before you make a mistake you will regret. Sophia and her brethren are on our side."

Rage shone in Erika's eyes and her face twitched. Abruptly, Lukys's spell broke and letting out a sharp exhalation, she retreated from him, gauntlet still raised in readiness for an attack.

"What was *that?*" she hissed, looking from Lukys to Sophia, then back at Cara. "It…it was like he was in my mind."

"The Voice of the Tangata," Cara replied, still frowning. "Lukys has it, though it has become far more powerful since I knew him in Fogmore." She looked to Sophia. "And it should not be able to have such an effect on a human."

Erika watched the Anahera a moment, then shaking herself, she swung on Lukys once more. "How can you say they're on our side?" she hissed. Flinging out a hand, she pointed to the south, in the direction of the approaching armies. "Don't you know what's happening out there, the danger that marches upon this city? Their kind are slaughtering people all across Flumeer."

"I know," Lukys replied, refusing to retreat from the rage in her eyes, nor the fear behind it. "And the Anahera too, if the rumours are true." He looked pointedly at Cara. "But it is not the Anahera, nor the Tangata, who are our true enemy." He swallowed, staring at Erika, recalling the darkness of the tunnels they had uncovered, the stench of rot and death thick on the air. The creatures that had stalked them in that darkness. "Do you remember what we found…that day beneath the earth?"

Erika started at his words, her eyes widening, revealing her shock. For a moment, he thought she would deny his words. She had been knocked unconscious during that conflict, had only caught a glimpse of the Old Ones before Cara had slain them.

Then the former Archivist lowered her fist, the light dying from her gauntlet, and she nodded.

"So you have seen her too," Erika whispered.

❧ 23 ❧

THE FALLEN

For days, Adonis and Maisie followed behind the Tangatan army, trailing in the shadow of their conquest, surviving off the scraps they left behind, watching, waiting. There was nothing else for them to do, no alternative path either could take. After all, where else could they go? The lands behind them belonged to the Tangata, but they were mostly empty now, their inhabitants swept up in Maya's power.

And so Adonis followed in the wake of his former mate, tracking her passage through the human lands. Maisie's people had retreated before the might of Maya's army, avoiding a pitched battle and forcing the Old One to give chase if she wished to bring the half-blood queen to heel.

Even so, they still found bodies scattered across the hilly landscape, the remains of skirmishes between the Tangata and the enemy, only…it was strange how Adonis had never noticed before how difficult it was to distinguish between the two in death, how similar his people looked to the humans, lying side by side with them.

A week after his fallout with Maya, Adonis's wounds had

at least partially mended. The same could not be said for Maisie with her human frailty, and after a few hours walking each day, she often resorted to her makeshift crutch for support. Or failing that, his shoulder.

Despite his own improvement, it would be obvious to any they crossed that neither was up for a fight. Thankfully, the attention of Adonis's brethren remained focused on the human army. Whenever they drew near the fringes of the Tangatan camp, he could sense their rage, like the distant pounding of drums, sounding to the beat of their conductor, to the Voice of Maya.

Even at the edges of her influence, Adonis found his own emotions stirring, his fists clenching tighter, his anger rising at the human's incessant chatting. Fortunately, Maisie tended to grow quiet at those times too. She might not hear the Voice of Maya, but that did not entirely spare her from the Old One's influence. Adonis couldn't help but wonder if it was that power which had broken the human army. If Maya could stoke the rage of so many Tangata, might she also be capable of influencing the humans, of fuelling their fears until they fled?

Such a use of the Voice had long been forbidden amongst his people, even on the smaller scales capable of by the Tangata. Adonis had argued against such restrictions, but their former Matriarch had denied him, enforcing the principles of ancestors long since perished.

Now, watching the madness that had consumed his people, Adonis at last saw her wisdom. His people might have won the battle for the river, might have driven the humans back, might even soon claim a final victory...but what had they lost in doing so, in bowing to the greater power of Maya? What remained of his people now but a mindless mob, thirsty for the blood of their enemies?

No, this victory had cost his people their souls.

Standing atop a hill at the top of the valley, Adonis looked upon the Tangatan horde—and the walls of the city that towered beyond. Mildeth, Maisie called it, the capital of the Flumeeren kingdom. The humans and their half-blood queen had finally run out of places to hide.

Instead, they had readied fortifications beneath the great walls and turned to face the Tangata. Perhaps suspecting another of the queen's traps, Maya had not yet attacked, but Adonis was sure the Old One would not wait long. Above, he caught glimpses of shadows in the sky, the winged Anahera scouting out the enemy formations, no doubt.

Shivering, Adonis tore his eyes from the mass of Tangata and looked to the human, Maisie. Even after three days, he was still not sure what to make of her. Half the time they'd spent together, he found himself regretting sparing her life. She spoke constantly now, her voice grating on his nerves day and night, and her presence only slowed him now that his wounds were healing. Perhaps he should put the creature out of her misery. After all, there would be nothing left for her kind after Maya's inevitable victory. Death would be a mercy, rather than the enslavement that waited when the new dawn rose.

But with a sigh, Adonis dismissed the thought. The human could have slain him as he lay injured from Maya's beating, but she hadn't. He would not harm her now. He had at least that much honour. Though...

...they were close enough to the Tangatan camp that he could feel *her*, could sense the darkness of her Voice upon his mind, upon the minds of all who resided in the valley. Despite that dark touch—or perhaps because of it—Adonis found himself confused when his thoughts turned to Maya.

Even far from her presence, he found himself longing for her touch. The pain of her rejection had not healed with his other wounds, remaining instead a gaping hole in his soul, a nightmare from which he could not wake. His vision blurred as he recalled the promises she had made him, the children she carried, the future he had envisioned at her side.

Adonis clenched his fists, his entire being trembling. If only...

An image flashed into his mind, the memory of Nyriah, of her body lying cold in the mud, her feathers twisted and broken, empty eyes staring...

Gasping, Adonis tore his gaze from the distant army and staggered back from the crest of the hill. The human made some sounds of concern, but he ignored her. How had it come to this? The great Adonis, third generation Tangata, strongest of his people, now trailed after the woman that had spurned him, yearning like a lost puppy for a second chance. Why did he want her still, when all she had ever done was cause him pain?

A shudder racked him and Adonis squeezed his eyes closed. He'd been wrong to come here, to follow. The human thought Adonis planned to help her, but...he did not have the strength for that, did he? No, he had come to hand Maisie over to his mate, to earn the Old One's praise, to restore himself in her eyes, to...to...

"You still want her back, don't you?" Maisie's voice came from behind him, soft, yet firm. She snorted. "Why not, I suppose? Maybe you can present me to her on a platter, a human that has completely outlived her usefulness. I'm sure it will *entirely* make up for the queen you failed to kill back on the Illmoor."

She laughed, the sound harsh, bitter. Her eyes remained on the army and the city beyond, but as he looked in her direction, they narrowed. "Well, isn't that something?"

Adonis followed her gaze, expecting to see some disturbance amongst the opposing armies, but there was nothing.

He turned back to Maisie and raised an eyebrow in question.

"That wily bastard," she muttered by way of reply. When Adonis only raised his other eyebrow, she sighed. "Seems you're not the only one with an ex-lover on this battlefield. See those flags above the city gates? That one means King Nguyen is in residence." She pointed at another flag, and then another. "The Sovereigns of Perfugia too, and…what's this, the Calafe?" She blinked, glancing at Adonis in disbelief. "Haven't seen that one in a long time. I wonder…"

She trailed off, still looking at Adonis, as though waiting for him to say something. He shrugged and glanced at the flags she'd indicated, but they were only flapping pieces of fabric to Adonis. Humans were so strange, the way they divided themselves, pretending that differences of geography meant something. No wonder they had warred so readily against the Tangata, when they could not even keep the peace amongst themselves.

"You know, Adonis, you're terrible at small talk."

Adonis glanced sharply at Maisie but the human did not elaborate. After a long moment, he snorted at her, a stubborn smile touching her lips. Again, he found himself wishing he could respond in her coarse language.

"It's true, you know," she said, smiling herself.

Retreating from the edge of the hill, Maisie seated herself on a boulder. Her face was pale and she was puffing by the time she sat. Concerned, Adonis followed her, gesturing silently to her leg.

She shrugged. "It's fine," she said, though her expression betrayed the lie. Reaching out with his mind, Adonis glimpsed the swirling grey-black of her agony. "It just needs to rest."

Adonis hesitated before nodding. Dark lines of pain still

radiated from the woman, mingling with her usual rainbow of fear, anger and sadness. After a long moment, he knelt beside the boulder and reached for her leg.

Maisie flinched away from him, her hand dropping to the knife she wore at her belt. He paused, looking up at her brown eyes, but did not move away. Eyes narrowed, Maisie stared back. Despite their days together and her incessant chatting, she clearly still did not trust him. That was smart, considering his earlier thoughts. But finally she seemed to relax, removing her hand from the dagger.

Adonis took that as a sign he could continue. Carefully, he lifted her calf and gently rolled up the cuff of her pant leg. Her skin beneath was pale and the uneven line of her shin revealed where the bones had knitted poorly from her injury. Adonis could do nothing for that, but the muscles of her calf had locked tight, swelling as they cramped from the long journey.

Slowly, gently, he trailed his fingers along her calf, his touch turning to gentle prods, senses extending in search of knots. Maisie flinched again at his touch, her entire body taut, but this time it seemed less due to mistrust, more the pain of her injury itself. Adonis continued, taking care not to press too hard, though he did slowly increase the pressure, seeking the deeper knots, the twisted fibres that had built through the long weeks of disuse.

Seated on her boulder, Maisie gritted her teeth against the pain but did not try to stop him, nor reach again for her knife. Instead, she turned her gaze again to the city.

"It's terrible, isn't it?" she whispered.

Adonis paused, but when he looked at her, he realised she wasn't talking about him. He frowned, then decided she was just trying to distract herself from the pain. He continued the massage in silence, and Maisie went on.

"When I first realised Nguyen was manipulating me…

well, I knew he was a king. What else should I have expected? We're all just pawns to their kind." She sighed. "Still felt terrible though, to be used by someone I loved. At least with me...well, I think it was for a good cause. But you..." She gestured in the direction of the Tangatan army. "You think she cares about them? Your Tangata? She certainly doesn't care about the Anahera. Those kids you helped her capture, they'll be dead before this ends, mark my words. They'll live as long as the adults prove useful, but the moment the Anahera fail..."

She trailed off as Adonis stood abruptly, his task with her injured muscles forgotten. His heart beat faster as he returned to the crest of the hill and looked down on the Tangatan camp. Even as he scanned the distant campfires, his mind filled with images, of the Tangatan children lying in the snow, of Nyriah's pain as she collapsed to the mud, defending him. Adonis owed the Anahera a debt he could never hope to repay. Not unless...

"Oh, that *is* a bold thought," Maisie said softly, as though she had read his mind. Rising, she moved to stand alongside him, following his gaze to the distant camp. "But do you have the guts to pull it off, Adonis?"

❧ 24 ❧

THE QUEEN

Sitting in the parlour of her former chambers, Erika struggled to piece together the warring revelations of the past few days—and the insane political situation she had found in Mildeth. She had arrived in the city expecting a battle, to lead her people in an uprising against the tyrannical Queen Amina, to take back what had been stolen from them.

Instead, she had found that someone had beaten her to the punch, that the city had already been conquered—and by no less than the once-incompetent Perfugian recruit she had thought long dead.

No, not just him, she reminded herself.

There was the Tangata as well, the creature that had partnered with the man, who shared with him the title of Sovereign. Erika clenched her fists, heart racing just at the memory of her unveiling. She should have noticed it sooner, likely would have, if not for the sheer shock of seeing the Perfugian recruits alive. Or…perhaps not. Even after learning of the creatures' intelligence, who would have expected to see one garbed in the fine silks of a Sovereign?

When Darien had shouted his warning, Erika had thought for sure they'd stumbled into a trap, that somehow Maya and her Tangata had infiltrated the city and her followers were about to come swarming from the shadows. The truth, if anything, had been stranger still...

It seemed not all of the Tangata followed the Old One. Lukys's...friends might be few enough, but their presence threw fresh complications into the war between their species. Sophia claimed many amongst the Tangata had only ever wanted peace with humanity. Only her own father's invasion of their land had changed things, forcing them to defend themselves, to fight back.

A shiver ran down Erika's spine. Could it be true? Could her father have led a genocide? He had called for war in response to raids along the Tangatan frontier, to the slaughter of Calafe innocents. But if Sophia was to be believed, the Tangata had not been responsible for those attacks.

It wasn't difficult for Erika to guess who that might have been.

Recalling Amina's words on the ship, her resolve to prepare humanity for war against the false gods, Erika felt the truth in her very bones.

Amina was behind it all.

But the Sovereigns were not the only ones who carried grave news. It had saddened Erika to tell Lukys and the other Perfugians of Romaine's death, to see their pain as they heard how their mentor had fallen, protecting Cara from the queen's assassin.

But Romaine's death still paled in comparison to what else Erika had discovered, the truth about the Anahera, how they had worked together with the Tangata long ago to bring about the Fall of humanity. She had told only Nguyen and the Sovereigns, though she still struggled to think of

Lukys as anything but an inexperienced recruit—and the Tangata as anything but the monsters that had stolen her kingdom.

Erika had left them to contemplate her news—and to ponder their revelations herself. Now she could only shake her head as she considered the past, the secrets upon secrets their ancestors had kept from the world.

With a sigh, Erika forced her mind back to the present. The past would have to wait—she was an Archivist no longer, and had responsibilities of her own now, people that looked to her for answers. Glancing across the room, she noticed Cara slumped on the velvet sofa, her wings drawn around herself in a feathery shroud.

Erika's frown deepened, sensing the change in the young Goddess. The Anahera had been delighted at the sight of Lukys and his little band of Perfugians, but her mood had darkened since. Rising from her armchair, Erika crossed the room and sank onto the couch beside the Goddess. Another shiver raised the feathers on Cara's wings and she gave a muffled sob.

"Cara?" Erika murmured. "What's wrong?"

The Goddess slowly lowered her wings to reveal her face, flicking Erika a glance. "Nothing..." she muttered, her eyes drifting sideways, taking on a distant look. "I just...I never thought..." The words faded, leaving Erika no closer to deciphering their meaning.

Hesitantly, she reached out and ran her hand down Cara's wing. "What's the matter?" she tried again. "Clearly something has you upset."

Tears shone in Cara's eyes when she looked at Erika again, and abruptly she rose. Stalking to the window, her wings snapped open, and it seemed she would hurl herself into the sky. But the Goddess paused at the windowsill, and finally her auburn feathers drooped.

Stumbling back to the sofa, she slumped to the floor alongside it and drew her knees up to her chest. "It's stupid," she muttered.

Erika smiled. "We humans are always dealing with stupid things," she replied. "You might say it's our specialty."

A sigh slipped from the Anahera and she looked up from the floor. "One of the Perfugians," she said quietly. "Travis. I...liked him, once." She snorted. "Like I said, it's stupid, I...there was too much happening...I thought he was dead, and with Romaine and Maya and all your luggage...with my long-lost sister..."

Cara's voice cracked. Sliding onto the floor alongside her friend, Erika hugged the Goddess to her chest. She stroked the young Anahera's hair as another shudder shook Cara, cooing softly beneath her breath the way her mother had once, when Erika had still been innocent. Those days seemed a hundred years ago now.

"I thought..." Cara said, then began to truly sob, the tears coming hot and fast. "I thought...for just a second... when I saw him still alive, even after all this time, after everything we've been through, I thought maybe..."

She gave a violent shake of her head, and Erika sensed the girl's anger—not at this Travis or Lukys or anyone else, but at herself.

"I'm so stupid," she croaked, looking up from Erika's shoulder, eyes shot with red. "Of course he found someone else." She hiccupped, then swallowed them down and went on. "I don't know why I was surprised. The Tangatan lady...seems nice. I'm happy for him...really, happy he's alive, but..." She trailed off.

Erika nodded as fresh tears welled in the Goddess's eyes. There were no words for this kind of thing, nothing either of them could say to make it better. So she hugged the young Anahera tighter, letting her sob and cry and curse, safe in the knowledge someone was there, that Erika would not let her go, that she would be there until Cara found the strength to face the world again.

Or until the world came looking for them.

As one, the pair flinched as a distant horn sounded from outside the window. It was followed by another, then another, as others picked up the call. The hairs on the back of Erika's neck stood on end as she recognised the pattern, the message the watchers on the wall were conveying.

One was the signal for an enemy sighted, for the arrival of the Tangata in the valley of Mildeth.

The second was a greeting.

Queen Amina was at the gates.

❧ 25 ❧

THE SOVEREIGN

S tanding atop the walls of Mildeth, Lukys looked out across the valley and wondered what madness had brought him to this place. Sophia and their guard stood with him, and Erika and Cara were nearby, Nguyen and Zayaan too. But in that moment, looking down upon the vast army gathered beneath the walls of Mildeth, Lukys had never felt so alone.

I am here, Lukys.

He smiled as Sophia joined her mind with his, but not even her presence could relieve his terror, the sense of inadequacy he felt. Below, a woman sat alone on her horse, garbed all in steel armour, a helm marked by a crown upon her brow.

The rightful Queen of Flumeer had come to claim her city.

Amina sat in silence, without advisors or generals or guards to protect her. She knew her enemies were too noble to strike her down unprovoked. She did not even seem overly concerned to find her city held by enemies.

Beyond the queen, the sprawling mass of her army filled

half the valley. Lukys's heart was divided at the sight. Her forces appeared mostly intact. After the rumours that had spread ahead of her arrival, they had feared little would be left of the Flumeeren army. It meant they might stand a chance against Maya's forces, that humanity might yet survive.

But only if they could avoid a battle between the forces of humanity.

Most of those Amina led were mounted, and Lukys wondered what had become of the others, the soldiers that had manned the forts along the Illmoor River, who for years had guarded the kingdom from Tangatan invasion. Judging from the coldness of Amina's face, Lukys suspected this woman would not have hesitated to leave them behind if it meant her own survival.

"Well, well, well," her voice carried up to them, surprisingly powerful despite the distance, *"it seems the mice came out to play while the cat was away."*

Lukys shivered as he felt an echo in his mind, the reflection of Amina's inner Voice. So it was true. Erika had told them about the queen's heritage, but it was one thing to hear of it, another altogether to witness it for himself.

And it meant Erika's other revelations must be true as well. Lukys swallowed a lump in his throat, memories of Romaine rising to swamp his thoughts. Somehow, a piece of him had known the great warrior had fallen. Otherwise, there would have been word of him somewhere, rumours of his presence. The Calafe warrior wasn't one to run from a fight.

Even so, to learn the truth, to think of his mentor lying alone in the cold Mountains of the Gods...

Amina's heritage might have greater import for the fate of humanity, but somehow, it was Romaine who lingered on Lukys's mind.

Shaking himself, he focused on the queen. Despite her ability, she didn't seem to be using her Voice in a deliberate manner. He prayed that meant she was unschooled in her powers. The last thing they needed was another Melder influencing the battle. And it might prove an advantage they could exploit.

"Amina!" he called finally, shaking himself from his silence. "We have co—"

"My, my, is that Nguyen I see up there?" the queen interrupted. "And unless my eyes betray me, my Archivist has come to greet me as well. I might have guessed you would have survived the inferno, though…you should have left your pet to burn."

A growl came from nearby and Lukys glanced at Cara, but Erika had already raised an arm to bid the Anahera wait. The two seemed to have grown close in their absence.

"Oh dear, and Zayaan, they turned you as well? I had thought you at least would remain loyal to my father's cause." She *tsked* softly, and Lukys leapt at the opportunity.

"*Amina!*" he bellowed, adding his Voice to his words. "*Your treachery has been laid bare. Will you submit yourself to the judgement of the Sovereigns?*"

Below, the queen's eyebrows lifted in surprise. "So it's true then?" she said softly, though the words still carried to those above. "The Sovereigns have finally left the safety of their island. I did not think you had the courage." Then her eyes narrowed, her lips thinning into a cruel smile. "But no, I see the truth, even from here. The eyes betray you, Tangata. It seems I find monsters everywhere I turn, these days." She looked again at Nguyen. "I am disappointed, brother king. I did not think you so cowardly as to ally with the enemy."

"The only enemy I see here waits outside these walls, Amina," Nguyen's reply came from beside Lukys.

"Oh?" Amina asked wryly. "And where was the bold king of Gemaho when the Calafe begged—"

"Don't you *dare* speak about my people as though you care," Erika snarled, stepping up on the crenelations. Light appeared in her hand as she ignited the gauntlet, though Amina must have been far behind its range. "It was *you* who betrayed my father, who provoked him to attack the Tangata. You have been behind every death, every pain and loss my people have suffered this past decade."

"Oh, they're *your* people now, are they, my good Archivist? And where were *you* while the Calafe suffered? While they fought desperately for their survival? When everyone else fled, whose soldiers fought alongside them? Who gave them shelter when their kingdom fell? Where were you, *Archivist?*"

Erika lowered her head, but she did not back down. "I failed the Calafe once," she said softly, then looked up to meet the queen's gaze again. "I will not do so again. I am an Archivist no longer—the Calafe have elected me their queen, at least until this war is done."

"Queen, is it?" Amina's eyes narrowed as she appraised the group atop the walls again. "Bold claims you all make, but I see the truth. You are all little better than common thieves, sneaking into my kingdom, stealing my city. Your treason will not save you from my armies."

"Your people stand with us now, Amina," Lukys said, and Sophia stepped up beside him, granting him her strength.

"And *her* people are behind me," the queen snapped. Lips drawing back in a sneer, she gestured to Erika and Nguyen. "Truly you must be desperate, to ally yourselves with such creatures. Is your hatred for me so great that you would see us all destroyed?

Nguyen stirred at that. "Everything I have done was for the survival of Gemaho."

"And everything *I* have done is for the survival of our species!" Amina snarled. "But your treachery threatens to destroy everything I have worked towards, the union I have built."

"*Your union was built on lies,*" Lukys said, and now Sophia spoke with him in unison, as the Sovereigns of old had done. There they hesitated, and Lukys glanced at his partner, knowing what they said next could tear their fragile alliance asunder. But there was no other choice, and looking again at the Flumeeren queen, they continued: "*Yet it is not too late to negotiate a true union.*"

"*What?*"

Lukys did not look around as the cry came from Erika, instead keeping his gaze fixed on the queen. Amina's eyes narrowed at his words, but for the moment she said nothing. Erika, on the other hand, roiled with a burning rage.

Lukys could hardly blame her after everything the woman had done to the Calafe. But the crimes of the past could not change one, immutable fact.

Queen Amina commanded half the forces of humanity. Without her on their side, Maya and the Tangata would crush their piddling army without breaking a sweat.

"And who are you to speak of these matters, Sovereign?" Amina called from below, her gaze flickering to Nguyen. "Nguyen I can imagine perhaps seeing reason, but the Archivist…" She trailed off as her eyes settled on Erika, and Lukys knew without turning what she saw. He could sense the rage bubbling from the former Archivist, a burning, scorching thing.

"No, the self-styled Queen of Calafe clearly does not consent to your idea," Amina continued, eyes returning to the Sovereigns. "Who are any of you to think you could lead such an alliance? Not my dear Erika, who until yesterday fled all hint of responsibility. Surely not Nguyen, who abandoned the last alliance between our peoples, surrendering an entire kingdom to the enemy." Her eyes settled on Lukys and Sophia. "And surely not the Sovereigns of Perfugia, who have hidden on their island for generations, who shirked their duties to the last alliance, just as bad as the coward king."

She shook her head, as though to dismiss them all. "None of you are worthy. There is only one who has fought for all our peoples, only one who saw the threat that lurked in our mountains, who did what was necessary to unite humanity against the coming threat."

Lukys gritted his teeth at the woman's words. "Do not seek to present yourself as the saviour of humanity, Flumeeren Queen," he growled. "You have never cared for the lives of those beneath you." He shook his head. "And my predecessors might have shirked their responsibilities, but I have not. It wasn't long ago that I served beneath your own general, fought in a war that *you* started, against a people that wanted only peace."

"Monsters," Amina replied coldly, her gaze flickering to Sophia before returning to Lukys. "Creatures from the dark, ruled by base emotion. They possess no civilisation, no civility. Just like our so-called gods, they would have betrayed us in the end. There can be no peace with such creatures."

A growl came from alongside Lukys as Sophia stirred. "Yet in the end, it was not my people who broke the peace," she called back. "It was not the Tangata who sought bloodshed, who oversaw the slaughter of innocents on both sides, was it, Queen of Blood?"

Amina raised her eyebrows at Sophia's speech. "So you taught the beast a trick." She snorted, then glanced behind her, in the direction of the distant hills. "But it matters not if one can speak. Make no mistake, her kind *are* the enemy, along with our cursed false gods. When the battle is joined, only one species will emerge as victors."

"The Tangata and Anahera are controlled by another," Lukys struggled to explain, to fight back against her attacks. "An Old One by the name of Maya. She seeks only destruction—of humanity, of the Anahera, of the Tangata even. All so she might one day restore her own kind to life."

Amina chuckled at that, before abruptly turning her horse, presenting them her back. "Very well." Her voice carried on the breeze. "Then I will make my last stand here. At least my death might give courage to the faithful of Mildeth, that they might cast off your tyranny."

"Amina!" Lukys cried, suddenly panicked, that she might truly lead her army in a suicidal charge against the Tangata.

Below, the queen glanced back, one eyebrow raised.

Lukys swallowed, glancing sidelong at Sophia. He could sense her anger, a reflection of the others, of his own, but there was no choice.

"As I said," he continued, clearing his throat. "We came to negotiate. Humanity cannot stand divided against this threat. Whatever the cost, we must work together, or face annihilation alone."

A stirring came from along the wall but Lukys did not take his eyes from Amina. Instead, he ploughed on, not daring to give the others a chance to object.

"Your people will be permitted into the city, on your agreement there will be peace between them and those inside. What crimes you have committed…" He paused, then finally finished, "will be forgiven, at least until the war has ended." He drew in a breath, guilt weighing heavy on his soul. "I warn you though, do not seek to betray us."

Amina watched him for a long time, and reaching out

with his mind, he struggled to pierce the fog of her thoughts, to sense her mind amidst the swirling colours. Grey doubt flickered, the purple of hope too, but a hundred other hues too, mixing and changing as she considered his words…

…until finally Amina shrugged, as though his offer was of no more consequence than a pebble beneath her horse's hoof.

"So kind of you, Sovereign, to offer me safe passage into my own city," came her reply. Then a smile touched her lips and he saw a flicker of triumph in her eyes. "But very well," she said, gesturing with a hand. "My soldiers are disciplined. They will not break the peace." Her grin spread and her gaze turned on Erika, who seemed barely able to restrain herself. "Just be sure to keep your monsters and the barbarians under control. My soldiers will not hesitate to defend themselves."

Abruptly she raised her hand. Horns trumpeted from the gathered lines of her army, sounding the call to advance, as though she'd known they would allow her entrance all along. As one, the Flumeeren army surged forward, marching in ranks towards the waiting gates.

For a moment, Lukys stood frozen atop the city walls. Terror rose in his chest as he watched the army approach. Had Amina outmanoeuvred him? If they did not open the gates now, chaos would ensue, and anything might happen in the confusion. Sensing Erika's rage, the pain of Sophia and her Tangata, already he found himself regretting his decision. And yet…

…there was no other choice. The weight of humanity's survival—of all their survival—settled on his shoulders.

Turning, Lukys nodded for Dale to signal the attendants below to open the gates for the Flumeeren queen.

❧ 26 ❧

THE FALLEN

Adonis and Maisie slipped into the Tangatan camp beneath the cover of night. Once the Flumeeren army had retreated into the city, they'd waited all day to see whether Maya would attack. But as the sun dipped beneath the horizon, it became obvious the Tangatan army was making no move towards the granite walls. Watching Maya's hesitation after her previous aggression, Adonis couldn't help but wonder whether something had happened, if perhaps the children…

His heart quickened at the thought, but he pushed it aside. He couldn't think of that now, could not allow himself to be distracted. It was difficult enough to concentrate with the thrumming of Maya's Voice in his mind again…

All was quiet as they slipped through the long grass of the hillside, down towards the waiting camp, towards the shimmering bonfires in the Flumeeren night. It wasn't long before movement appeared in the darkness. A Tangatan guard stepped before them, her face creased with confusion.

A...Adonis? her voice whispered into his thoughts, hesitant.

True to Maya's word, knowledge of his exile had obviously reached even the lowliest ranks of his people. Still, Adonis was not without his own strength, his own cunning.

Yes, he replied, reaching out with his Voice. He might not have been a match for Maya, but Adonis still had a power over the lesser generations. *I have been gone on a secret task for Maya, but now I have returned.*

You were...banished, spurned, the guard whispered, struggling against the waves of Adonis's mind.

But she could not have been more than fifth generation, her resistance futile.

You will let us pass. The human has vital information for our Matriarch.

With these words, Adonis felt the last remnants of the guard's resistance crumble. She bowed her head and stepped aside, allowing Adonis to pass. Gripping Maisie tightly with one hand, as though she were his prisoner, he strode into the disorganised camp—though he kept his grip on the guard's mind still, infusing her with confidence, with a joy that she had served her masters well. It would suppress her doubt, for a time at least.

Shadows shifted in the night as they made their way through the camp. With their enhanced vision, the Tangata were bothered little by the dark, though he noticed how Maisie tripped and stumbled. Adonis found himself wondering how it would be to find oneself blind, unable to discern the shadow of an enemy from that of a tree or shrub. Such a terrifying, helpless existence, pitiful, when compared to the greatness of the Tangata...

Adonis gave his mind a mental shake. Maya's voice was growing louder now, seeming to vibrate his entire being, though he steeled himself against it. Her influence would only grow greater the longer they remained in the camp, and carefully he gripped the human's hand tighter. Maisie had not seemed overly affected by the Old One's presence, but neither could she defend herself against its affects. If something caught her anger, Maya's influence might drive her to ruin everything.

For now, all he could do was take them in a broad circle around the centre of the camp, where Maya's Voice was strongest. Even so, he could feel its effects within him, the growing desire to turn towards that centre, to go to his mate, to deliver the human to her judgement...

Teeth bared, Adonis resisted and kept on, though his hold on the human tightened even further. He could sense her glances, the concern swirling in her mind, and wondered how she could bring herself to trust him. She couldn't even begin to understand his kind. He certainly did not trust her...did he?

Adonis paused, glancing at the human, and Maisie raised an eyebrow.

"Hey, stay with me, bud," she whispered, clicking her fingers. "The plan, remember? Where are those kids?"

Adonis hesitated, watching her, wondering, then abruptly he nodded. He turned towards the dense clot of fear, the terror radiating from a group that could only be the Anaheran fledgelings. The poor creatures only wanted to see their parents again, the noble beings he had made into slaves. He wondered how many of the Anahera would fall, never to see their children again, before this was all over.

No more, if we can help it, he told himself.

Yet there was another voice within him, a deeper voice, one that whispered that this was madness, that they would never escape with these innocents. Even should they pass the boundaries of the camp, the city was a mile off and morning was fast approaching.

One step at a time. He tried to suppress the doubts, but it was a struggle now—one Adonis feared he would soon lose.

Maisie took a sharp intake of breath as a pair of shadows moved to bar their path. Adonis drew to a stop, fearing for a second they'd been discovered, but he soon realised the reason for the presence of his brethren here. The knot of terror lay just beyond them—these two were guarding the fledgelings.

Who goes there? the first of the guards hissed.

There's a human— the second started, but he broke off as Adonis quickly invaded their minds.

This was a greater challenge, even for one such as Adonis. No amount of trickery would convince these Tangata to part with their charges, not without approval from Maya herself. And they were stronger too, of the fourth generation. To prevent them from raising the alarm, Adonis pressed his Voice upon them.

Do not move, do not Speak, he ordered, before turning to the first of them. *How many of you are there?*

A tremor shook his brother's face as the Tangata struggled, but there was no resisting Adonis's Voice, and finally the guard broke.

Five! came the gasped cry, even as the Tangata slumped to his knees.

Adonis held up a hand, stilling the human at his side, then reached out with his mind for the other guards. He found them stationed amongst the children, alert for signs of treachery. The fledgelings might have been young and apparently helpless, but they were Anahera still. Thankfully, Adonis's brethren were not alert for treachery from their own.

One by one, he took their minds, swamping their thoughts with his Voice. When he had them all, Adonis ordered them to where he and Maisie waited, until finally all five stood rigid before him. Spasms racked their faces as they strained against his Voice, struggling to break free and sound the alarm, but Adonis held them—at least for now.

Trembling with the strain, he turned to Maisie, and nodded.

The human stood wide-eyed, staring at the guards, as though waiting for them to leap forward and tear her limb from limb. At Adonis's gesture, she looked at him, her features knitting into a frown.

"You're doing this?" she whispered, shaking her head. "Incredible."

Teeth still clenched, Adonis gestured again in the direction of the children. Their time was short—he could not hold these creatures long. They couldn't waste a second if they were to somehow escape with the fledgelings.

The human finally seemed to understand and a look of resolve crossed her face. She disappeared into the darkness, leaving him standing alone with the Tangatan guards. Adonis could sense their eyes on him, their hatred as they fought his mental bindings. Silently he prayed for the human to hurry. Against these five, his strength would eventually fail and they would fall upon him, tearing him to pieces before turning on her…

…Adonis's stomach twisted at the thought and he straightened, determined to see this through, to…to…

Maisie reappeared from the gloom. Adonis had no idea how she'd managed it so quickly and without struggle, but a group of tiny figures followed just a step behind. Their wings tucked close to their sides, the Anaheran fledgelings looked from Adonis to the Tangatan guards with open terror in their eyes.

Adonis's heart swelled at the sight all the same. For the first time that night, he felt that they might actually accomplish their mission. But even as the thought came, he sensed a surge of emotion from the Tangatan guards, a terrible rage as they realised his plan and truly began to fight. A gasp escaped him as they stretched against his restraints. Quickly he refocused his attention on the five figures, commanding them to be still, to silence.

A sound like nails on a chalkboard sounded in his mind as the five consciousnesses fought back, determined to defend the charges the Old One had given them. Sweat dripped from Adonis's forehead as he panted, his entire being focused on his prisoners, struggling to hold them.

"Adonis?"

He flinched as Maisie's voice intruded on his concentration. One of the Tangata leapt at the distraction, throwing his strength against Adonis and almost breaking free...

Kneel! Adonis hissed, putting all his remaining strength behind his Voice, seeking to regain control before it splintered into a thousand pieces.

A tremor shook the Tangata and he thought they would repel him. Then the moment passed, and one by one they fell to their knees.

Releasing his breath, Adonis finally risked a glance at the human. Maisie stood alongside him, her eyes as wide as those of the Anaheran children, though in her case it might have been something her kind did to see better in the darkness. But the way she looked at him, the lines that creased her forehead, he could sense her concern.

"Adonis, I have them," Maisie said quickly, flashing a glance at the kneeling Tangata. "Come on, we have to reach the city before they sound the alarm."

Adonis said nothing. He couldn't. All he could do was stand and stare at her, hands at his sides, hoping she would understand. She had to, surely? The perimeter guard had been easy enough to influence—they had no reason to suspect. But these five? They had witnessed his treachery firsthand. And they were stronger too. No compulsion would last once the force of his presence left. Neither would Adonis kill his own kind, whatever it might cost himself. They were his people still, his brethren. It was his own fault that Maya controlled them.

Maisie stared back at him, lips pursed, fists clenched. He watched as realisation finally came to her, the truth dawn in those dark eyes. In the night, drained of their colour by the silver moon, they could have been as grey as his own. Indeed, her courage, her strength in the face of their enemies…she was as bold as any of his sisters.

"I see," she said at last, looking from Adonis to the guards. "You knew…this was to be a one-way journey." She swallowed. "This better…better not be some convoluted plot to see your lover again, you know…" A shiver shook the human as she turned to him. "She'll kill you, you know. After this, when she learns what you've done…"

Adonis inclined his head in a nod. He knew. Maya's rage had been terrible to behold when he'd failed on the river. Now he plotted openly against her, had freed the Anahera. He could only pray to his ancestors that his death was quick.

Exhaling, Adonis looked towards the distant city, where the dark walls were shadows even to his eyes. It would take Maisie more than an hour to cross the terrain with the fledgelings. Could he hold the guards until the dawn arrived? Even as he considered the prospect, he felt them fighting again, their collective wills pressing against his own.

Quickly he made a gesture, a dismissal in the direction of that distant city. Still the human hesitated, until a whimper from the children caught her attention. She glanced quickly over her shoulder, and in that second, he glimpsed her own fear, the terror she struggled to conceal. A lump lodged in Adonis's throat as he felt his regret. Everything that had happened to this woman, to these children, to his people—it was all his fault. If he had not woken Maya, had not led her back to New Nihelm, had not supported her against the old Matriarch…

…but it was too late for regrets now. With a final nod to the human, he turned to his prisoners, taking a firmer hold of their minds. Stones crunched behind him as Maisie finally led the fledgelings away. Thankfully they were positioned near the edge of the camp and he hoped they could slip away unnoticed.

If not…well, Adonis could do nothing more for the human now. All he could do was hold the Tangatan guards for as long as possible. So gritting his teeth, he stared down at his captives kneeling in the dirt.

Five pairs of eyes stared back at him, hatred burning in their grey depths.

An hour passed and the sun had touched the distant horizon when their collective strength finally broke him. By then Adonis was on his knees as well, gasping for each breath as he threw every ounce of his strength into the battle. But as the sun lit the walls of the distant city, the last of his strength slipped away and he collapsed to the dirt. Abruptly, the flow of power reversed, and the crushing strength of five Voices crashed against his mind.

The cries of those five Voices echoed through the Tangatan camp, sounding the alarm, alerting his brethren to their peril.

Chaos ensued as the Tangata responded, leaping to their feet in preparation for battle. At first their response was one of confusion, their minds fixed on the humans, expecting an army to descend upon them at any moment.

It was long minutes before the Voices of the five guards cut through the chaos. Their panic turned to anger then as realisation spread through the Tangatan ranks.

That one of their own had betrayed them.

Adonis shrunk as the collective will of his people turned in his direction.

But before it could strike, another stirred, a mind beyond all others, a rage that made the thousands around him seem like candles before an inferno.

The Old One came for him.

27

THE QUEEN

E rika had never known such rage. It burned in her veins, filling her with the need to destroy, to unleash the gauntlet against her enemies, to see them writhe and scream and beg for her mercy. How satisfying it would be, to watch the queen fall, to see her die slowly by Erika's hand, in recompense for everything the woman had done?

A tremor shook Erika and the image faded, replaced by one of Queen Amina standing over her, matching gauntlet aglow, whispering for Erika to give up, to surrender. A moan tore from her lips, a sharp, rasping cry in the peaceful darkness of the dawn.

Erika struggled against the urge to flee.

Because the truth was, beneath her anger, a terrible fear held her tight, a terror for what the queen would do now that she had regained her city.

Rising from the pile of straw she had used as a bed, Erika knelt in the gloom of her tent. She had spent the night with the Calafe, in the square still called their own, rather than in the citadel. Just the thought of sleeping under the same roof as the Flumeeren queen made Erika sick with terror.

And if Erika had been enraged by Amina's admission into the city, the Calafe had been livid. It was all Erika could do just to keep them from storming the citadel. She still wasn't sure whether it had been the right decision to stop them, to accept the peace Lukys had brokered. She knew Amina. There was always something more to the woman's actions, some ulterior motive that would see her enemies crushed.

Steeling herself, Erika finally gathered herself and rose from the straw mattress. Leaving Cara to sleep in the corner she had claimed for herself, Erika stepped from the tent. A shiver ran down her spine as the brisk morning air greeted her. A flicker of movement nearby announced Darien's presence. The man had appointed himself her guard and was never far from her side now.

She nodded a greeting that the man returned. "Couldn't sleep, Your Majesty?"

Erika suppressed a frown at the title. She might have asked for this, but it still sounded strange to her ears. Shaking off her own doubts, she shrugged, and her gaze was inevitably drawn to the citadel towering on the hill above. There was to be a meeting of monarchs this morning. She would have to be present, to stand in the same room as the woman who had killed her father and listen to her speak. Just the thought of seeing Amina's smiling face was enough to spark a flicker of light from her gauntlet.

Shivering, Erika forced herself to exhale, then turned to stroll down the lines of the Calafe camp. The refugees were only just beginning to rise, and she watched with interest as they prepared kettles over freshly-lit firepits, as they hugged and waved greetings to one another. Her people. It was still difficult to believe it, that they would welcome her so freely after all these years in exile.

"Why, Damien?" she asked suddenly, turning to the stoic warrior who shadowed her.

"Why what?" he replied, a frown wrinkling his brow.

"Why did you kneel?" Erika elaborated. "Why did you decide to follow me?"

"You mean besides the magic gauntlet?"

Erika didn't respond, only stared him down, knowing there was more. It had been bugging her, how easy it had been, to convince this warrior to kneel, for the Calafe to follow her.

After a moment, Damien offered a shrug, nodding to the surrounding camp. "You know how long we have been here," he said softly. "For more than a year we have been camped outside the city walls, refugees without a home, without a leader. Without hope." He shook his head. "Maybe that's why I chose to accept your claim. Your stories could have been fabrications for all I knew. But... at least you offered us change, a chance for vengeance, maybe even fresh hope. Figured that was worth taking a risk."

"Thank you," Erika whispered, struck to the core by his words.

They finished the rest of their loop around the plaza in silence before returning to her tent. Cara's snores still came from within and Erika hesitated to wake the Goddess. She feared going to the citadel alone—very little could stop Amina now that she was within the city. In fact, Cara might be the only one capable of going toe to toe with the queen. But the Goddess needed rest after their time on the road, after everything the two of them had been through, and Erika was about to turn away when a harsh cry came from within the tent.

Cara appeared a second later, still only half-dressed,

wings spread, amber eyes aglow with...something. The Goddess swung wildly from side to side, before finally seeming to notice Erika.

"*Erika!*" she gasped. "Something's happening, beyond the wall, with my people. They're *terrified!*" The words tumbled from her mouth faster than Erika could follow, then ceased abruptly. "Their voices..." Cara murmured, before her eyes widened. "*The fledgelings!*"

"Cara, what—" Erika tried to make sense of the Anahera, but Cara cut her off.

"*The fledgelings!*" she cried again. Abruptly, the Goddess hurled herself into the air, leaving Erika and the other Calafe staring dumbly after her.

Erika's heart pounded hard in her chest as she watched her friend spiral upwards, auburn wings flashing in the light of the rising sun. Panic spread through her soul as Cara disappeared beyond the rooftops, leaving her behind.

Whispers spread around Erika, growing quickly as the Calafe emerged from their tents in search of the source of the commotion, only to find their bedraggled queen standing in the middle of the street, eyes on the heavens. They followed her gaze, confusion in their eyes.

It was long seconds before the importance of Cara's words finally struck Erika. The fledgelings, the children of the Anahera...it couldn't be, could it?

Something swelled in her chest, a sudden hope, the glimmer of a possibility. Then she was spinning on Darien, drawing an aura of authority about herself, igniting the power of her gauntlet.

"Darien, gather as many of our warriors as you can, *now!*"

The one-armed warrior didn't hesitate to ask questions. In an instant he was turning from her, bellowing out orders. Despite the ramshackle camp and the ragged appearance of her people, they obeyed with the discipline of trained soldiers. Those still fit for battle cast aside loaves of bread and mugs of coffee in exchange for great-axes and broadswords. Within minutes, a force of a hundred men and women had gathered around Darien in answer to their queen's call.

Erika swallowed as their eyes fell upon her, taking in the glittering weapons and hard faces. Only once had she led soldiers into battle, when she'd forced Lukys and his Perfugian regiment to follow her south of the Illmoor River. It had ended...badly. But she could not hesitate now.

"Calafe, my friend needs our aid," she said shortly. There was no time for long speeches. "Follow me!"

At that she spun on her heel and raced from the plaza, praying that her new authority and Darien's respect amongst their people would be enough to convince these warriors to follow. It might have been her imagination, but there seemed to be a pause, before the pounding of boots finally chased after her. Her eyes on the sky, Erika exhaled in relief, but she couldn't count her blessings yet.

Above, she glimpsed Cara as the Goddess soared back over the city. Spying Erika below, she gestured violently in the direction of the gates. Then she was gone again.

Baring her teeth, Erika charged through the city after her friend. The Calafe ran with her, Darien drawing along-side her, others moving ahead. With the early hour, the streets were mercifully quiet, and those already outside stepped quickly aside at the sight of the charging Calafe.

Then they were bursting into the courtyard before the city gates. The gates themselves stood barred to the enemy without, though in truth they would make little difference as the Tangata could scale the walls in seconds. The guards on watch snapped to alert at the sight of Erika and her Calafe.

She waved urgently to them as she raced across the courtyard, gesturing at the gates.

"Lift the bar!" she bellowed. "By order of the queen!"

Knowing she had no power over these men, Erika neglected to say *which* queen. Panic showed in the eyes of the Flumeeren men at the sight of a hundred grizzled Calafe charging towards them. Whatever objections to her command they might have had were forgotten as Erika and her followers reached the gate, and the guards belatedly leapt to obey her.

The doors swung open with a soft squeal of old hinges. Erika caught a glance from Darien, the flicker of doubt in his eyes, but there was no time for explanations now—even if she had fully understood what was happening. So instead, she darted through the opening, and summoned the power of her gauntlet.

To their credit, the Calafe followed Erika despite her apparent madness, though it was definitely not her imagination this time that several hesitated. She could hardly blame them. Whatever her claim to the throne and the magic she wielded, Erika was still an outsider, yet to fully earn their loyalty.

Open ground stretched beyond the gates. The land around the city had been cleared just days ago in preparation for the siege, to ensure there would be no shelter for the Tangata to come creeping upon the defenders. The sun was just beginning to peek above the distant mountains, its heat washing across the land, lighting up the long grass...

...and the distant ranks of the enemy.

Erika paused to catch her breath as she looked across the mile that separated the city from the Tangatan camp. And in that pause, she caught a distant rumbling, as of a thousand feet pounding the earth, of a hundred voices raised in anger.

Icy fear lodged in Erika's throat, and she struggled to inhale as she glimpsed the cloud of dust rising from the horizon. Her stomach tied itself in knots and she scanned the sky, seeking, searching…

"There!" Erika shouted, pointing.

Cara plummeted from the air a half mile out, swooping towards the ground, wings snapping wide to slow her moments before she alighted amongst the long grass. Fist aglow with power, Erika set off at a sprint, though her lungs were already burning from their headlong race through the city. As Darien and the other Calafe glimpsed Cara, they chased after her, impressing Erika with their bravery.

Blood pounded in Erika's ears as she ran and she scanned the long grass ahead, searching, praying, hoping. It grew higher as they drew farther from the capital, untamed but for the few lines that were Flumeer's roads. Surely they must be somewhere…

Erika's heart lurched as a figure burst from the grass ahead, brown eyes wide, face panicked as she glanced back, urging others behind her to hurry.

Maisie, the Gemaho spy.

Such was Erika's shock, she almost staggered to a stop right there. She thought Maisie was dead, fallen in the Mountains of the Gods. How many more of her former companions were destined to rise from the grave this week?

Shaking herself, she leapt forward. Maisie's eyes widened as she glanced towards the city and finally noticed Erika and her Calafe, shock showing in her face, though it turned quickly to relief.

"Erika!" her cry sounded above the distant pounding. Only…that pounding was no longer so distant. *"They're coming!"*

Erika hardly heard the spy's words, as suddenly more figures were bursting from the long grass in front of her.

Gasps came from around Erika, then the Calafe were stumbling over themselves to stop, staring open-mouthed as the tiny Anahera darted amongst them, adolescent wings flapping uselessly as they struggled to keep pace with the human they followed.

Several of the Calafe reached belatedly for their weapons—the Anahera had sided with the enemy, after all —but these were quickly lowered again when they saw the terror in the eyes of the youths.

Only then did Erika and her people return their attention to the distant rumbling, to the pounding on the air, the vibrations of a rage so terrible Erika swore she could sense what Cara had never quite been able to describe in words.

The Tangata were coming.

"Calafe, on me!" Erika screamed, lifting her fist to ignite the light of the gauntlet.

The sight of her magic steadied their line as Darien fell in at her side. Maisie had vanished after the fledgelings. She was no warrior, and would be needed to shepherd the young to safety. That left Erika and her Calafe to deal with the enemy.

One hundred Calafe warriors and their mad queen.

Against a Tangatan horde ten times their number.

"Form up around me, weapons to the fore!" Erika bellowed, doing her best impression of Romaine when she had seen him commanding the Perfugian recruits.

The last of the fledgelings passed between the Calafe ranks as her followers pressed together, and Erika risked a glance over her shoulder. The gates were barely in sight, half a mile off at least. She gritted her teeth.

"Controlled retreat, weapons to the enemy!" she called.

Darien nodded alongside her, and though the Calafe were not trained soldiers, they began to withdraw, eyes never leaving the direction of the enemy. It seemed to Erika that they held a collective breath, waiting for the first of the enemy to emerge from the grass, to leap upon their line.

A shadow on the horizon drew her eyes to the sky, and her heart twisted as she spied distant wings, too far and too many to be Cara. The Anahera. She and her people might hold a few Tangata, but her hundred would be decimated by even one of those creatures attacking from above.

Then with a roar, the Tangata were upon them. The first exploded from the long grass and leapt at Darien, but Erika reacted without thought, directing a burst of power at the creature. The shriek of her gauntlet struck, bringing the Tangata to its knees, where a swipe of Darien's sword took its head from its shoulders.

Others soon took its place.

Step by step, the Calafe continued their retreat, struggling as the dark creatures launched themselves from the grass, as the strength of the Tangata sought to break their lines, to recover the fledgelings their master had worked so hard to capture. There were only a few at first, the fastest of their kind. They attacked in madness, driven to such a frenzy that they barely seemed to notice the warriors that stood between them and their prey.

But even mad, the creatures were more than a match for a tiny band of Calafe. Erika did her best to use the gauntlet to slow them, allowing Darien and his fellow guards to strike the finishing blows, but she could only protect the centre of their formation. On either side, the line was quickly buckling beneath the Tangatan assault.

"Hold!" she cried as they stumbled back, but Erika's voice was drowned out by the screams of her followers, by the deaths of those who had trusted her to lead them.

Chaos engulfed the Calafe as the tide of Tangata swelled. There was no time to glance back, to check how far they were from the gates, from safety. No doubt the guards would have barred their entrance by now anyway. Erika could only pray Maisie had managed to lead her charges to safety, that their sacrifice would not be in vain.

A scream tore from Erika's throat as she unleashed another burst of power at a creature that evaded Darien's sword. It crumpled before her magic and she screamed again, frustration building within, that after everything she had been through, this was how it would end.

She might have fallen then, might have lain down and died, but instead Erika lifted her gauntlet and fought on. She could feel the strength draining from her with each flash of light, but she would not surrender now. She would go to the void screaming, before she failed her people again.

Darkness fell across the battlefield as another Tangata came at Erika and she flinched back, raising her gauntlet to strike it down. Light flashed from her fist, but already more of the creatures were stepping up to take its place, snarls upon their faces.

She staggered back, sucking in a breath, struggling to stay upright, to gather energy for her next attack.

Before her strength returned, a sharp *crack* came from overhead, then a shadowy figured plunged from the sky. Another followed, then another, until dark wings all but blocked out the sky. Despair swallowed Erika as she looked upon their doom.

The Anahera had come.

❦ 28 ❦

THE SOVEREIGN

S tanding in the great throne room of Mildeth, Lukys
looked around at the gathered rulers and couldn't help
but feel himself an imposter. It was a familiar sensation by
now, but one made all the worse by the presence of Amina.
The woman stood pointedly opposite her throne, and even
now he could sense her eyes on him, could feel her disdain.
That emerald gaze seemed to pierce him to the core, to
know the doubt in his soul, regardless of the outward illusion he presented to the world.

It is not an illusion, Lukys, Sophia whispered. *You and I, we
deserve to stand here. It is only your own doubt that does not allow you
to see it.*

He offered her a smile at that, though they did not say
more. They knew now what Amina was, the danger she
presented to them. She might have been unfamiliar with the
mental powers of the Anahera and Tangata, but that did
not mean she was ignorant to them.

I just pray we made the right choice, Sophia, he replied finally.

She pursed her lips, eyeing the Flumeeren queen. *She*

will never be a friend to my kind, Sophia said at last. *Her hatred is too great. But...we had little choice, given the circumstances.*

Lukys nodded, though he could feel the whispers of other minds within, the memories of Sovereigns that screamed to strike Amina down before she could betray them. But...he wasn't sure they could have harmed Amina anyway. She wore the gauntlet of the Gods—or rather, of humanity, as Erika had explained to them. And with the strength of the Anahera coursing in her veins...

...well, he would feel better when Erika and Cara arrived. The pair might hate him for the decision they had made, but they were likely the only ones capable of controlling Amina now that she was within the walls. They had spent the night in the Calafe camp, but with sunlight streaming through the broad windows above, the pair should have arrived by now. The hour of their meeting had long since passed, and he could sense the patience in the room growing thin.

Not that impatience was the greatest of their problems just now.

In his mind, Lukys could feel the distant pounding, the weight pressing upon his emotions. The influence of the Old One. He could hardly believe the strength of her Voice, to reach them even here. He had tried to counter her, to fortify the courage of his people as she toyed with their fears, but even with the strength of the Sovereign gift, he felt as a pebble before the endless currents of the mountain river. He knew too little about those minds within, feared losing himself in their terrible depths.

Even without her influence, Lukys hardly knew where to begin with this meeting of monarchs, how he could possibly unite the warring factions within the city—let alone set aside the personal grievances between those present. Amina had not even allowed Zayaan into the meeting, claiming she would not recognise the authority of traitors, though the old advisor had run the city in her absence. It was a miracle she'd consented to the presence of Erika and Cara. And now they were late…

Lukys sighed, sharing another glance with Sophia. How far he had come since his arrival so long ago in Fogmore, when he'd first faced the Tangata. Romaine had saved his life that day, a whirlwind of power that had shielded him from death. How he missed the man, his strength, his conviction that what he did was right. Even now, he wondered what the man would think, how he would judge Lukys's decision to parley with the Flumeeren queen, despite everything the woman had done, the atrocities she had committed.…

He would understand, Lukys, Sophia said, interrupting his thoughts.

Would he? Lukys murmured, staring at Amina now. *She betrayed his people, destroyed his nation. She was probably behind the death of his family. No, I think Romaine would have killed her the second she set foot in this city. Who is to say we're right, to keep others from their vengeance?*

It is as Nguyen warned us, she replied. *Rulers must set aside personal convictions, their own grievances, for the greater good of their people.*

The words whispered into Lukys's mind, granting him strength, quieting the voice deep down, and finally he nodded. *We will find a way to save your people, Sophia,* he replied, recalling their conversation in Perfugia. *I promise.*

I know, Lukys, Sophia said in response. *I believe in you, in us.*

"Well!" Amina's voice broke suddenly over their conversation. "Had I known this alliance would involve so much standing around, I might have chosen war after all, and spared myself the boredom."

Lukys ground his teeth. "We are waiting——"

"I'm done waiting," Amina snapped. She strode the length of the chamber, passing Nguyen and Lukys and Sophia, crossing directly to her throne. There she paused, glancing pointedly at the others, before lowering herself onto the velvet cushion. Crossing one leg over the other, she entwined her fingers and arced an eyebrow in Lukys's direction.

"It seems the good Archivist will not be joining us after all," she continued. Lukys narrowed his eyes, suddenly suspicious that the woman had done something to Erika, but she continued before he could question. "I suggest we begin, unless you'd prefer we wait until your Tangatan friends break down the gates." The queen looked pointedly at Sophia as she spoke, and they could both sense the emerald of her hatred.

A soft growl, barely audible, whispered from Sophia's throat, but to her credit, she did not rise to Amina's bait. Instead, she took a moment to gather herself, then nodded her consent.

"I agree," she said firmly, looking to Nguyen and Lukys. "We can apprise the Calafe queen later of what we discussed—for now, there are urgent matters that must be addressed, before *Maya* seeks a final confrontation."

After a moment's pause, Nguyen inclined his head in concession, though Lukys read his concern in the yellowish tinge of his aura. Letting out a breath, he clasped his hands behind his back and positioned himself in the centre of their circle, attempting to draw the attention away from Amina.

"Very well," Lukys said, his words echoing from the high ceiling.

Beyond the throne, a great map of the valley around Mildeth had been laid out by the citadel staff, complete with tiny statuettes representing the warring factions. He moved to the edge of the map. Nguyen and Sophia joined him, and with an accentuated sigh, Amina abandoned the throne to stand with them.

The map had been updated in the night to show Amina's troops in the citadel, along with the arrival of the Tangatan army. Maya's forces seemed small beside their own, representing numbers rather than raw strength, but with the strength of the Tangata on her side, numbers were deceiving. The Old One had already surrounded the city by land, ensuring there would be no escape into the foothills. Lukys might have thanked the gods she had no naval ability, but...

...the gods themselves, the Anahera, would harry any attempt to flee by sea. Such was the power of Cara's people, it wasn't beyond reason to believe a single Anahera might sink a dozen ships....

Lukys shook himself. It would not come to that. They would make their stand here.

"With your soldiers, Amina, we should have the numbers to hold the walls for a time," he said softly. "Only..." He trailed off, glancing at the queen.

"Holding our own is not enough with this creature," Amina finished for him.

She crossed her arms, tapping one finger against her elbow as she stared at the red figurine placed in the centre of the valley, where their scouts suggested the Old One had stationed herself. Lukys frowned at the queen's words, wondering what she knew.

"My mother...revealed certain truths to my father, before he put the demon down," Amina elaborated with a smile. Lukys's stomach twisted, and he decided he was pleased that Cara had not come. The "demon" Amina spoke of had been Cara's mother too. Amina's father was the reason she had never returned to her people, to her first daughter…

Gritting his teeth, Lukys did his best to ignore the comment and nodded. "We are aware," he said, still staring at the red statuette.

Surrounded by the dense ranks of Tangata, Maya's position was unassailable. But he still carried Isabella's words in his mind, that perhaps there was a way to manipulate the creature, to separate Maya from her followers—before the worst came to pass.

"According to Erika, the Old One may already have been with child a month ago, when she invaded the Anaheran city. The gestation of her kind was often as short as three months before the Fall."

Amina lifted an eyebrow at that. "That is more than my mother knew," she remarked. "My father made sure of it. How could you know such details, *Sovereigns?*"

Lukys pursed his lips at the scorn she placed in the word, but he ignored the taunt. "We have our methods. Needless to say, there is no time to waste if these reports are true."

"Indeed," the Flumeeren queen replied, looking from Lukys to Sophia. "Though…if you can uncover such secrets, perhaps you might also unlock the secrets of the ancients, how they first cursed these Old Ones, removed their ability to procreate."

Lukys bit his lip, sharing a glance with Sophia.

"That…" Sophia started, then sighed. "They destroyed the world," she continued. "It had…consequences. The males of Maya's race, our ancestors, were made sterile."

"Then how did *your* kind survive, my dear Sovereign?" Amina pressed.

You don't have to answer her, Lukys said silently to his partner, sensing her tension, but Sophia only shook her head.

"Our ancestors splintered," she replied after a pause, recounting what she and Lukys had witnessed in that ancient memory. "Some, like Maya, searched for a cure amongst the ruins of ancient humanity, from their magic. Others...they chose peace, unity. They went to the remnants of humanity that had survived the Fall. They bonded, created new lives for themselves, peace. Only..." She looked up, catching the queen's eyes, holding her gaze. "It was not to last. Divisions appeared, tensions rose, and eventually those with Tangatan blood were ostracised, pushed out for their differences."

"A tale as old as time, it seems," Nguyen commented. "Even in the texts my own Archivists recovered, they speak of such divisions within humanity from before the Fall. Hatred without reason."

"Or maybe there was every reason," Amina interrupted, her eyes still on Sophia. "Perhaps your people betrayed the peace."

"Maybe," Sophia murmured. "Or perhaps it was humanity. Such details are lost even to our memory."

Lukys shivered as an uncomfortable silence fell, watching the swirling colours of Amina's aura. It was strange, how openly they displayed despite her Anaheran ancestry, as though this were a part of her she had no control over. It revealed the truth of her mind to Lukys, the hatred that contaminated her, the distrust she held for Sophia, for even the Anahera.

"Gladly, we no longer possess the power to destroy worlds," Nguyen stepped in, playing the peacemaker despite his own grudge against the queen. "So we cannot repeat the errors of the past. But that still leaves us with the question: how do we defeat this Old One?"

Silence fell at Nguyen's words as they exchanged glances. Lukys looked at Sophia, then drew in a breath.

"We might have a way."

"Oh?" Amina asked, one eyebrow raised.

He nodded hesitantly. "There is…something she wants. Or rather, *someone*. Her former partner. He was with her at the end, with those who sought a cure."

"I thought she was the last."

"She might be," Nguyen interjected. Clasping his fingers behind his back, he nodded to Lukys. "By the false gods, I hope she is. But does *Maya* think that? If she has slept all this time, perhaps this partner of hers did as well."

"Okay," Amina replied, eyes narrowed. "How does any of this help us?"

Lukys smiled, glad to be a step ahead of Amina in this at least. He opened his mouth to say as much, but before he could speak, the doors to the chamber burst open with a bang. As one, the four of them swung towards them, hands raised, weapons at the ready.

But it was only Erika. She paused a moment in the doorway, shoulders heaving, face slick with sweat, as though she had run the entire way there. Lukys frowned, taking a step towards her, before he noticed the tears in her clothing, the blood…

"Erika?" he asked, his concern growing with each pulse of his heart. "What—"

"Your Majesties," Erika spoke over him, advancing into the chamber, before stepping to the side.

Behind her, a second figure loomed in the doorway. Wings spread wide, Lukys thought at first the figure was Cara, but a second followed behind it, then a third. Steel rattled behind him as Dale and the other guards raised spears towards the creatures, but Lukys could only stare as the Anahera crowded in the chamber.

"May I present to you, the Anahera," Erika continued as though this were an entirely expected event. "It seems they have decided to join us in the fight against Maya."

❧ 29 ❧

THE FALLEN

A donis no longer struggled as his captors dragged him through the Tangatan camp. His body was an aching mess and he lacked the strength to even stand now. And his mind…

…his mind was a shrieking torment, a vortex of self-hatred and regret and…ecstasy, joy that he had won, that in the end he had achieved the impossible, freed the Anaheran fledgelings, freed the Anahera themselves.

The Tangata had beaten him for that, had unleashed their pent-up fury against the traitor in their midst. But in the end, their blows could not harm him, could not change what he had done, could not bring back the escaped children.

It was only when the silence fell, when his assailants suddenly retreated from him, that the darkness had invaded Adonis's mind. He knew what it was, recognised her touch. He'd clung to the memory of his freedom, the light of what he had done, and yet…

Adonis could not stand against her.

Now with each step his captors carried him closer to her

presence, to the darkness that bombarded his mind, crashing against his consciousness. With each passing second, his hope shrivelled, the light of his defiance dwindling, the despair in his soul swelling.

Until finally he was thrown to the ground in the centre of the camp. The sun rose slowly into the distant hills, but where Adonis lay was shadow, the sky blotted out, darkened by the figure before him.

Adonis's mind withered as he looked into the eyes of Maya. Rage shone from her face, and the force of her hatred battered him, tearing and rending at his consciousness until he felt the very fabric of his being coming apart, the substance of his mind unravelling…

Abruptly her mind released him and Adonis gasped, sinking to the ground before her, sobbing, shuddering.

You should have stayed dead, Maya's voice whispered into his mind, dark, deadly. *You have no understanding of what you have done, the danger you have unleashed. The Anahera are no different from humanity. They would see us exterminated if they held that power in their hands. They have already tried once before.*

No! Adonis struggled against her power, against the weakness of his own body.

But as he tried to stand, two Tangata leapt forward, capturing his arms, forcing him back down, to bow before their Matriarch. Even so, Adonis would not allow himself to be silenced, not so long as he still possessed his sanity.

These Anahera are not the ones you fought in ages past, Maya. Nyriah, her people they want only—

He broke off as her anger slammed into him again, the strength of the Old One's rage silencing his own Voice. He gasped as images invaded his mind, of the Anahera swooping down, fighting, battling against Tangata…no, not his people—Old Ones. Maya's people, from a time unknown.

The Anahera will fall, she hissed. *They will feel my retribution for the crimes of their ancestors. That is my sole purpose, Adonis, to see my enemies extinguished, to see those who betrayed my people cursed to extinction.*

Adonis struggled against those words, against the depth of her hatred finally revealed. But however he resisted, still he felt his own emotions responding, his own hatred swelling in answer to her call.

You too shall pay for what you have done, Maya's voice hissed in his thoughts, sending tremors through his very being.

This time when Maya invaded his mind, it was not words or emotions she pressed on him, but a pure agony, as though she had poured molten iron over his skull, as though she were running ragged blades through his veins, crushing his chest upon an anvil, tearing each nail from each of his fingers, peeling the skin from his flesh…

A scream burst from Adonis, harsh and unending, tearing at his throat, and he began to thrash. His captors released him and he fell to the earth, digging burning fingers into soft dirt, as though its dampness might extinguish the flames within.

But there was no escape from Maya. Eyes locked open, Adonis looked into the depths of her grey gaze and saw no mercy there, not a hint of the love she had claimed for him. Nothing but hatred, the rage of centuries.

Adonis cried and begged, pleaded for his fellow Tangata to save him, to strike him down and end his suffering. But his brothers and sisters stood in silence now, watching without emotion the fall of one they had respected, had followed. There was no Nyriah to save him this time, no Maisie to drag him from the muddy ditch. Adonis was alone, abandoned, discarded by all he had trusted.

No, rose the thought through the pain, *not abandoned. I*

chose to be here, to stand against the darkness, to help my people. To put right my wrongs.

Abruptly the pain vanished.

For a moment, Adonis thought he had succumbed, that the agony had driven the spirit from his body, freeing him from the punishment of the real world. But then sensation returned, the touch of the earth beneath him, the reek of the camp, the whisper of Voices nearby. Slowly he gathered the will to sit, and discovered Maya still standing over him. He flinched away, but she knelt beside him and reached out to stroke his cheek.

I feel your defiance, my mate, she said softly, *the hope you cling to.* Adonis shuddered as laughter whispered into his mind. *Fool. You think you have saved the Anahera? Their freedom will be short-lived. The human city will fall, then nothing will be able to protect those fledgelings from my vengeance.*

She looked into the distance then, where the stark walls of the city shone with the morning sun. *No, my dear Adonis, your resistance will fail.*

Adonis's eyes widened at her words and he struggled to retreat from her, but instead he found himself fixed in place, body trembling, unwilling to obey his own will. A sob tore from him as he found his eyes locked with Maya's, and felt the doors of her trap swing shut.

Consider this your reward, she continued, a hand falling to her swollen stomach. *For the service you provided me.* She smiled, and taking Adonis's hand, she drew him to his feet. The darkness surged, robbing him of will. *You will be the executioner, will stand at my side as we slaughter the humans.* Laughter rasped in his mind. *And when we capture your precious fledgelings again, it will be your hand that snuffs the life from their pathetic bodies.*

No...

He tried to resist her, to fight back, but his mind rang

with the vibrations of her Voice, twisting his emotions, changing him, until…

…Adonis felt a terrible shame within, a swelling horror as he realised what he had done, the trick the human had played upon him. She had manipulated him, turned Adonis against his own people, caused him to commit the greatest treachery the Tangata had ever known.

A moan tore from his lips as he prostrated himself before Maya, before all those who stood in witness. Crying out, he begged for her retribution, for her to send him against the humans, so that he might die in honour, might escape the knowledge of the terrible thing he had done.

And Maya stood before him, before all of the Tangata, and smiled.

Now you see, children. Her Voice carried over the crowd, to the ears and minds of the multitude. *Now you see the power of the humans, their corruption. Not even the greatest of us could resist. Their whispers must be silenced, their power crushed, until every one of their kind has been erased from this world.*

An ache swelled in Adonis's heart, a pain that threatened to tear him in two. Such was his shame, he could not look upon the eyes of his people, could not face their condemnation for what he had done. He found himself sobbing, begging.

Please, my Matriarch, he whispered. *Please, kill me. I do not deserve to live, after what I have done.*

Maya smiled down at him, and there was something in her eyes, a mocking laughter that he should have sparked something in him, something other than the awful, terrible shame. Yet there was nothing else within him, only an emptiness, a void where the rest of his mind had once been…

He begs for death, children, but am I not a merciful Matriarch?

Maya spoke again. *No, sweet child, I will not give you death, but life! I will grant you—*

Maya...

The Old One broke off abruptly, her eyes swinging to the west, the colour draining from her face. For a second, Adonis felt a spark of something within, a flicker of life, of will...

Maya, where are you...please...so weak...

Raxion! Maya's voice boomed across the open field, echoing through the minds of all present, searching, seeking. *Where?*

Images flickered through Adonis's mind, of twisting corridors, of endless darkness, of waves crashing upon cliffs. He shuddered, seeking the source, the mind from which they had come, but the images were already fading, the presence withdrawing.

Please... a last whisper reached them. *Others...hunting me.*

Abruptly, the presence vanished, and Adonis's mind returned to the field outside the human city. He gasped, the flickers of life returning to him as Maya's distracted mind released him. She stood looking into the distance for a moment longer, eyes wide, as though contemplating what they had just heard.

Then she turned her gaze back to Adonis, and the vice closed around his mind once more.

Well, well, well, she said at last, her Voice thundering in his mind. *What have we here? Perhaps I will not need your mongrel offspring after all, Adonis.*

———

A MILE AWAY, STANDING ATOP THE WALLS OF MILDETH, Lukys and Sophia gasped as they came back to themselves, as they surfaced from the depths of the Sovereign gift.

Lukys shuddered as he shared a glance with his partner, unable to believe they'd managed it, that their mad idea might have worked.

That ancient presence within was so utterly foreign, so unlike their own minds, a part of him screamed to hurl it from him. That mind had been an Old One like Maya, a *Chead* as it thought itself, but unlike Maya, it had chosen humanity over hatred. They had hoped the power of its Voice might have been similar enough to Maya's mate, Raxion, that she would not recognise the difference, not if they limited their words.

It seemed their gamble had paid off.

The trap had been set.

Now all that remained was to spring it upon the Old One.

✺ 30 ✺

THE QUEEN

Erika watched as the cliffs rose from the crashing waves. They stretched high overhead, towering above the swirling ocean waters, making even the masts of the ship seem small by comparison. Ripples ran through the stone, lines of gradient colours that seemed more a reflection of the ocean below than true rock.

It seemed too strange to be natural, and yet...the truly unnatural feature of the cliffs lay not in the layers of stone, but at their base. There, the strata abruptly gave way to plain grey stone, untouched by the invisible forces of erosion. This was the stone that defied nature, refusing to bend before the will of Mother Earth.

The stone left here by her ancestors, waiting for its creator's return.

A rowboat carried their unlikely party ashore. Cara might have ferried them across one by one, but she needed to preserve her strength for what was to come. Even so, Erika would have rather been anywhere but a damp rowboat seated alongside the Flumeeren queen. For her part, Amina had said nothing on the voyage, even as she suffered the glares of Erika and her Calafe guard. One-handed or no, Darien looked ready to drive a blade through the queen's cold heart at a moment's command.

Seated across from them, Maisie was similarly quiet. The Gemaho spy had said little since her victorious return, and Erika wondered what the woman had been through during her weeks of captivity. She doubted the Old One would have treated her prisoners any better than Amina. And yet...Maisie's morose silence seemed to go deeper than that.

Perhaps it was the Anahera. Freeing the fledgelings had released the adults from their bonds with Maya. They would fight for the enemy no longer. But while the creatures had professed their gratitude at the release of their children, the truth was, most were not warriors. A few had elected to fight with humanity on the walls of Mildeth, but many others had been needed to ferry their fledgelings to safety. And on this journey...

...well, of all the Anahera, only Cara was willing to face the presence of the Old One again. Erika just prayed their collective strength would be enough.

Clenching her fists, Erika shivered as she watched the light play across the threads of her gauntlet, and wondered if she should have done more. Perhaps she could have taken one of the fledgelings herself, as the Old One had. The Anahera would have fought for them then...

...but no, that would only have created a lifelong enmity between their peoples. If humanity was to survive, it could not be through darkness. They needed to be better than their ancestors, to rise above their terrible past and forge a new future, one where all could prosper.

The rowboat thumped down on the crest of a wave, shaking Erika back to the present, reminding her there was a battle to be won before any could plan a future free of war.

The sailors deposited them on the shore not far from the unnatural streak of rock. The four of them moved quickly, scrambling from the rocking boat onto the exposed reef at the base of the cliffs. Maisie stepped onto the slippery surface with her usual confidence, while Amina still somehow managed to move with the air of a queen. For Erika's part, she tripped stepping from the vessel, and would have plunged headfirst into the icy waters had Darien not caught her.

When she finally gained a purchase on the damp rocks, Erika did her best to ignore the smug smile on Amina's face. The meaning of that look was clear—that *she* was the true queen, and Erika nothing more than an imposter, the lowborn offspring of a courtesan rather than the daughter of a king.

The whisper of feathers on air announced Cara's arrival. She landed between Erika and Darien, keeping a wary eye on Amina. The young Goddess's distrust for her half-sister was obvious, a sentiment Erika could well understand. And for her part, Amina made no secret of her hatred for the Tangata and Anahera both.

With them all gathered, Erika finally turned her attention to what had brought them to this place. This had been the first ancient site Erika had explored in her quest to uncover the secrets of their Gods. Little had she known then the truth that waited.

The shadow of a cave marred the strange rock. In her explorations, she had discovered this was not one of the original entrances to the site, but had been exposed when a section of rock had finally given in to the unending pounding of the ocean waves. The original entrance was somewhere above. That was the entrance the Sovereigns had shown Maya. Cara had already checked its iron casing —it remained barred to the world.

The Old One had yet to arrive.

Shivering, Erika glanced at her companions to see whether they were ready. Lukys, Sophia, and Nguyen had remained behind in Mildeth—someone had to oversee the defence of the city, and they weren't about to trust Amina with the task. Given that neither had Erika's magic or the strength of an Anahera, the three had seemed the natural choice.

Even so, Erika found herself questioning that decision. They might have been as new to their roles as Erika, but Lukys and Sophia carried an air about themselves, a quiet confidence that lent strength to those around them. How she wished for such an ability, to squash her inner doubts and stand as a natural leader, confident in her command.

But Lukys and his Tangatan partner were far from them now, and instead it fell on Erika to see the Old One defeated. So after a moment's hesitation, she led their group up the shore to the cave. Stepping into the darkness, Erika found herself recalling her first visit to this place, the excitement of entering its forbidden darkness, the secrets that might lie within. She had been disappointed that first time, though she had known so little then. Perhaps she had missed something…

Erika shook herself, forcing her thoughts back to her more pressing danger. This was no expedition into the secrets of the past, however she might wish it to be. Maya might not yet have arrived, but she would not be far behind them. They needed to be ready before then, to find a chamber to make their stand. Clenching her fist, she allowed the gauntlet to light the way.

Cold walls swallowed them up, beckoning them further into the darkness. Erika's chest constricted as they stumbled ever deeper, her nerves betraying her. She would have preferred to face the Old One in the open, where they could see the creature coming, but their lie had to be believable. And this was the closest ancient site to Mildeth.

Well, the only one that could be reached by sea at least. There was another, the site where she had discovered the gauntlet and the map that had revealed the locations of other such sites. A shudder ran down her spine as she recalled the tale Lukys had told her, of how Maya had come to rule the Tangata. They had taken that map from Lukys's mind. Just as it had led Erika to the city of the Anahera, the map had led them to where Maya had lain sleeping.

And so the world had changed forever.

How she wished now she'd destroyed it, burned it where it lay and left sleeping demons buried. But it was too late for that now.

"So what do we do once we're inside?" Maisie murmured as they crept deeper into the tunnels.

"We get ready for Maya's arrival," Erika replied. "I explored this place for weeks, the first time I visited. It's empty, but there are some areas that could make for good ambush sites."

Alongside her, Cara nodded. Erika could read the tension in the young Anahera's wings, the way her feathers stood on end. Her eyes kept flicking to Amina, and Erika prayed her friend's distraction would not cost them against the Old One.

"I'm not sure what good we mere mortals are going to be," Maisie offered, nodding to Darien.

The one-armed Calafe grunted and reached down to pat his sword hilt. "I'll fight," he replied shortly. "There's no other choice."

Cara's eyes flickered to the man, while Maise offered soft

laughter. "I suppose that's true." She drew her own blade, a short sword, and hefted it.

Erika nodded. "Maya may not come alone."

Word from the Sovereigns was that the Tangatan army had remained outside Mildeth and was even now preparing to attack, but some of the creatures might have joined Maya on her journey. Though the Old One would outpace the weaker of the Tangata, there were some that could match her speed, at least for a time.

"If she has company, we'll need you to keep her followers distracted while we fight her," Erika added after a pause.

Maisie grunted. "Definitely feeling some second thoughts about joining this quest. Who knew a city under siege by thousands of Tangata would prove the *safer* option."

"There'll be no chance to run this time, Gemaho," Darien said, his voice hard. Erika grated her teeth. Though the blame for the southern war now fell squarely on Amina's shoulders, the Calafe would not be quick to forget how Gemaho had abandoned them in their hour of need.

"Enough," was all she said, and was grateful when Darien obeyed.

They were in the true tunnels now, where multitudes of passages branched off from the main corridor. This would be a poor place for an ambush—the side chambers they passed were too small, and the narrow hallways would only aid the Old One, making it difficult for more than one of their party to attack at a time.

"So this is one of your precious ancient sites, Archivist," Amina said as they moved through the corridors. She paused, eyeing another chamber as they moved past it, then wrinkled her nose. "Delightful. Truly, if your interest in dust and dirt is exquisite."

"These were the places where our ancestors created

beings like the Tangata and the Anahera," she replied. "The things we could learn—"

"Yes, yes," Amina smirked, waving a dismissive hand. "I'm sure you could discover another trinket or two, given time. But there are more efficient ways of extracting secrets than digging in the dirt, my dear Archivist."

Erika ground her teeth, but forced herself to ignore the woman's gibes. "Come on," she said instead. "I wish I had my maps. I think there was a larger chamber this way—"

She broke off as her light caught on something in the tunnel ahead. Freezing in place, Erika squinted into the gloom, struggling to pierce the darkness at the end of the corridor. Surely it had only been her imagination, her mind playing tricks in this haunted place.

As the others drew to a stop behind her, Erika raised her fist, and ignited the full power of her gauntlet.

❧ 31 ❧

THE SOVEREIGN

Lukys stood with Sophia on the ramparts of the Mildeth and watched as the Tangata gathered in the distance. Their rage radiated across the open fields, their hatred pressing against his mind. Maya had vanished, but her dark presence remained on the battlefield, her influence still touching those below, driving them to a frenzy.

Against the raging emotion rising from the enemy, he leaned against Sophia, drawing on her strength, on her love to keep the darkness at bay. Yet amidst her own consciousness, he could feel her pain, the terror she felt for what was to come.

A shudder ran through Lukys and he drew her closer, though the blue-stained armour they both wore was cold beneath his hands. In that moment, Lukys wished they could be anywhere else, that they had gone with Cara and Erika to face the Old One. But…he knew his place was here. They both did. He had not yet given up hope for the Tangata. If anyone could reach them through the haze Maya had cast over their minds, it was them. The future would be decided not just in that dark place beneath the earth, but here on this battlefield.

And humanity needed to win both to survive.

A roar rolled across the battlefield as abruptly the Tangata surged forward, their powerful legs sending them bounding across the open ground. Lukys tensed as their cries crashed upon the battlements, and releasing Sophia, he took up his spear. Travis and Dale and their other guards shifted around them, determined to shield their Sovereigns from the worst of the assault.

All along the wall, calls went out from sergeants and regiment leaders as the human forces prepared to face the deadly Tangata. Nguyen had organised their defences, placing the three surviving kingdoms on separate sections of the wall, with the Calafe waiting in reserve as reinforcements. The proud Calafe had not been pleased by the assignment, but Nguyen had pointed out their numbers were too few to stand alone.

Lukys couldn't help but agree. In fact, if it had been up to him alone, he would have seen Romaine's people far from the battlefield. Enough Calafe blood had been spilt in the last ten years. It was time the other kingdoms stood against the darkness.

Watching the Tangata charge, Lukys felt the emptiness of his failure, the pain of knowing those who came against them did so not because they desired war, but because a dark creature had fed them lies. The Tangata attacked now because they feared there was no other choice, because they believed humanity would destroy them if they did not strike first.

Maybe they were right. Maybe one day those like Amina would come to rule all the kingdoms of humanity, would seek the extinction of the non-human species.

Perhaps the Tangata were right to fear humanity, to loath them and seek their destruction.

Yet recalling the days he had spent in New Nihelm, living side by side with the Tangata, Lukys knew things did not have to be this way. There had been peace between their peoples, if only for a brief time.

Maya had stolen that peace, but if it had existed once, they could have it again.

Are you ready? he whispered to his partner, eyes on the approaching hoard.

No, came her reply. Yet he saw her gathering herself. *But I will fight regardless.*

Lukys drew in a breath, then called out for the archers to nock arrows. A sharpness touched his mind at the order as Sophia tensed alongside him, and he shuddered at the weight of what he was about to do.

But there was no other choice.

"Fire!" he bellowed.

The sharp *twang* of bows followed as arrows rose high into the air, only for gravity to take hold, plunging them down into the ranks of the Tangata. The first screams rose as a new colour blossomed amongst the chaotic aura of the charging enemy—the grey of pain.

Lukys... Sophia's voice came to him.

He pulsed a wave of reassurance to her, though he knew worse was yet to come.

Below, the Tangata line barely faltered, as many dodged the flashing arrows or continued regardless of their injuries. They charged into the teeth of a second volley, Voices raised in defiance. As they drew nearer, Lukys saw that many carried pieces of rock the size of his fist. Understanding struck him a second before the first drew back their arms in preparation for their own attack.

"Down!" Lukys bellowed, adding his Voice to the command.

The Sovereigns and their guard dropped even as Lukys spoke, his mental warning reaching them heartbeats before his spoken words. A second later, rocks flashed overhead and the sharp *crack* of stones striking the crenelations sounded over the cries of the enemy.

Heart beating hard in his chest, Lukys clenched his spear tight and lifted his shield from where it rested. Sophia and her brethren did not carry any weapons, and he gestured for her to take shelter behind his shield. Keria, Isabella, and the other Tangata did the same with their human partners.

Only then did Lukys have the chance to assess the damage to the rest of their forces. Those soldiers nearest them had been able to heed his warning, but he saw many others slumped on the stone battlements, great dents in their steel armour revealing how they had fallen.

Fists clenched, Lukys stepped back to the edge of the ramparts, shield raised cautiously in preparation for another volley.

Instead, a flicker of movement was the only warning he had before a Tangata launched itself over the crenelations. It would have had him then, if not for Sophia. The creature seemed almost surprised as she leapt forward, moving with unnatural speed to place herself between them. Cast all in steel, it would not recognise her Tangatan eyes, and her appearance gave it pause.

But only for a moment, as with a snarl, it charged the Sovereign. Sophia met the Tangata with an iron fist that stopped the male with an audible *crunch*. Then it was tumbling backwards, disappearing through the gap between the crenelations.

And as it fell, Lukys sensed a scream, a shriek from his

mate's mind, even as a sharp sob rent the air. He stepped forward quickly as she stumbled, a groan rumbling from the depths of her soul.

Sophia! He forced the words into her mind, and within he found a terrible pain, a shock at what she had done. *Sophia, are you okay?*

I...I killed him, she gasped, and Lukys gritted his teeth.

You did what you had to, he replied, pushing her behind his shield and aiming his spear at the gap in the crenelations. He would not be taken unawares again, would not force Sophia to... *This is not you, not us,* he said to her, embracing her mind, shielding her from the horror. *We wanted only peace.*

But even as he spoke the words, he saw the aura rising from the tops of the ramparts, the emotions of his fellow humans. They matched the dark hues of the Tangata below, a roiling squall of anger and hatred.

Lukys recoiled from the sight, though he felt the same emotions within, the war between his desire to reconcile— and the part that had feared and loathed the Tangata for so long. He had almost forgotten those emotions these past weeks, but now they came rushing back. And with them came a terrible realisation.

There could never be peace between their peoples.

Humanity would never tolerate Sophia and her kind, would not break bread with the creatures that had haunted their nightmares for a generation. Even if they could end this battle, it would only postpone the inevitable, would only delay the darkness...

Lukys...something is happening.

He shivered as Sophia's warning whispered into his mind, struggling to free himself from the dark thoughts. They clung to him, seeking to draw him back into their depths, but he resisted, clinging to the light of Sophia's consciousness.

As he rose, withdrawing his senses from the greater battle, Lukys turned his consciousness to those nearest him, on Isabella and Travis and his friends. Their aura shone with red and yellow, with fear and anger, but there was no hatred amongst them, no darkness.

This was the hope he clung to, that if these men and women could surrender their hatred, so too could the rest of humanity. That was the truth, not the whispers of his despair...

...or perhaps it was not his despair at all.

Looking out across the walls of the city, Lukys finally saw the pattern to the auras, the swirling of darker forces, and knew they were not the only Melders influencing this battle.

Maya's mind was at work here.

Panic touched Lukys and he scanned the surging bodies below, seeking the Old One, fearful suddenly she had not taken their bait at all, that she had remained with the Tangatan army. Without their strongest warriors, they would be helpless if she came against them, unable to match her strength, her speed...

...but no, her touch was present on the battlefield, but it remained faint, where before it had been a radiant glow at the centre of the Tangata, corrupting all it touched.

Where then? he whispered.

Sophia stirred alongside him, and he sensed her joining in the search for the Old One. The creature had disappeared from their view the day before, after their message, but surely if she were working her influence here, they could find her.

Perhaps if they worked together...

Reaching for Sophia's aid, Lukys shivered as their consciousnesses overlapped, the lifetimes of knowledge they possessed uniting within their twin minds.

And looking to the sky, they saw finally the darkness of the Old One, the tendrils of aura criss-crossing the battlefield, feeding the base emotions of the warring men and women. They rose from the gathered ranks, trailing towards the distant horizon.

Their hearts beat quicker, and as one, the Sovereigns set out after those threads. They could see the truth now, that Maya was far from this place, still somehow able to influence the battle, but…that influence was waning. With their united power, they just might…

There!

The Sovereigns touched the Old One's consciousness, but recoiled from what they sensed there. Not anger or fear, not even desire. Within Maya's mind they found only darkness, only a hatred that consumed all it touched. This creature's sanity had fled long ago, leaving only the husk of a person, a remnant with but one goal, one desire.

To destroy.

What is this?

The Sovereigns shuddered as a Voice grated upon their consciousness. They drew back, seeking to escape, but it was already too late. The Old One had sensed their presence. Their hearts twisted as her attention fell upon them.

Is that a human I sense? There was curiosity in her voice, confusion too. *No…something else? Not one of the Tangata…nor even the Anahera…something…older?* There was a pause, as though the Old One were contemplating something. *What are you?*

The Sovereigns shuddered as the pressure upon their minds grew, the Old One seeking to pierce the veil of their thoughts, to infect their minds with her madness. But they were not what they had once been, not a naïve boy who dreamed of war, nor the innocent Tangata in search of love.

Those parts still existed, but they were something else now. Something *more*.

We are the Sovereigns of Perfugia, they replied in unison, hurling the words at the Old One. *And we stand united against you.*

The Sovereigns felt a moment of satisfaction as this time it was the Old One who recoiled, the barriers of her mind rising to guard against their power. For a fleeting moment, they glimpsed something more amidst the madness, a flicker of gold. Fear?

Sovereigns? No...no, that is a lie. You are something else, yes, but... She trailed off, then a brilliant light flared, and Lukys sensed shock from the ancient creature. *Yes...I sense you now, Tangata, Chiara. What magic did you discover, that you persevere still?*

Something responded within the Sovereigns at those names, a roiling deep within their souls, as consciousnesses long dormant struggled to wake. They were the names of those who had stood in the circle all those centuries ago and opposed Maya, the first to have passed their memories on to their descendants, to form the tradition of the Sovereigns.

Shivering, Lukys tore himself from those memories, from the drowning ocean. As he did so, he felt his consciousness separate from Sophia's, emerging from the depths of the Sovereigns. Suddenly alone, he found himself drifting before the Old One, before their enemy.

And for the first time, Lukys sensed the images flicking through their enemy's thoughts, of a cavern cast in darkness, of chambers deep beneath the earth.

To his horror, Lukys recognised that darkness.

She was already in the tunnels beneath the earth, the ancient site in which they sought to trap her.

But it was his friends who were walking into a trap.

Cara! he screamed desperately, reaching for the young Anahera. *Beware!*

❧ 32 ❧

THE QUEEN

E rika cried out as a face appeared in the darkness. A voice behind echoed her—then Cara was there, hurling her back, spreading her wings to fill the narrow corridor.

For just a moment, Erika longed to retreat, to turn and flee back the way they'd come, to escape the tunnels, the darkness, the *history* of this terrible place.

But then she saw Darien standing alongside her, face hard, eyes on the creature that lurked in the darkness. His blade was already in hand, ready to face the enemy, and Erika knew she could not flee. Her duty was here in this darkness, to her people, to humanity.

Drawing in a breath, Erika turned and stepped up alongside Cara. Movement came from their other side as Amina joined them, barely able to fit in the narrow space. Erika cursed inwardly. This was the last place they wanted to face a creature such as Maya.

Laughter whispered in the darkness, low and haunting, empty of mirth or joy or…anything. Hairs rose on the back of Erika's neck as she watched Maya emerge from the gloom. Her long hair hung around her shoulders, bleached of all colour in the light of the gauntlet, and her eyes…her eyes were like two empty voids, watching them from the face of the Old One.

"Magic wielder," the creature whispered, and the darkness fixed on Erika. "I know you, do I not?" She nodded, taking a step closer. "Yes, the human who escaped with the young Anahera, the same one I see here, I suppose."

A growl came from Cara and Erika quickly grasped her friend's arm, steadying her. This creature was far more deadly than those Cara had once fought, the pair she had defeated alone. Those had been weakened by their long sleep, while Maya…Maya had been awake for months now.

No, if they were to attack, it must be together.

Though…Erika's stomach twisted in horror as her suspicions were confirmed. The Old One was with child. And while only a month had passed since the City of the Gods, Maya looked to be ready to give birth any day now.

"It was a clever ruse," the Old One continued, leaning her head to the side. "Luring me away from my followers, bringing me here." She cackled suddenly, advancing a step. "Or was it I who lured you here? My greatest enemies all gathered in one place, ripe for the slaughter?"

A chill spread through Erika at the creature's words. That couldn't be true, could it?

The laughter continued. "Your scheming matters not, human. The Tangata are mine now. They will destroy your precious city, whether I am with them or not." Her voice hardened and she took another step. "As for you…well, I will ensure your deaths are long, for taunting me so with the promise of my mate."

Erika shuddered as she felt something dark touch her mind. Her fear responded to that touch, swelling to terror. Even as she recognised the touch of the Old One, had known to expect it from Lukys and Cara's warnings, still she found herself trembling, her knees shaking, the strength fleeing her limbs…

… abruptly, the sensation lessened, dwindling, as though someone or something had turned off the tap of her terror.

The Old One didn't seem to notice, though, as turning to the walls of the tunnel, she ran her hand across the stone.

"What memories these places hold," she said softly. "You have no idea the atrocities humanity committed here, the ghastly experiments they committed against our kind, against *her* kind." She paused, leaning her head to the side.

Cara screamed. Erika spun to the Goddess, expecting an attack, some surprise assault from the darkness. Instead, she found Cara staggering backwards, wings thrashing, fingers clawing at her face, mouth stretched wide as her amber eyes lit the darkness. A moan rattled from the back of her throat, building into another scream.

The Old One was doing something to the Anahera, showing her something. Before Erika could react though, Cara's screams died away, leaving only the echoes calling back to them through the endless tunnels. The Goddess stilled, her wings still stretched wide, poised as though about to flee. The rasping of her desperate breaths filled the silence.

"Cara." Erika took a step towards her friend, hand outstretched.

A shriek came from the Anahera as she leapt back, eyes wild, their colour swirling from yellow to grey. Erika froze, as behind her, the Old One's voice whispered in the darkness.

"Now she knows," Maya murmured. "Now your pet has seen the truth, human. Do you think she will forgive the terrors your kind committed upon her ancestors, the torture and abuse and death?" She turned her attention to Cara. "Her people tormented ours by the thousands, child, tore us limb from limb and put us back together, again and again, all for the pursuit of greater power. Will you serve her still, even knowing their crimes? Or will you finally throw off your chains?"

A tremor shook Cara as some of the light returned to her eyes, the yellow glow, though as she looked at Erika, a new emotion appeared in her friend's eyes.

Fear.

"Cara," Erika said urgently, seeking to drown out the Old One, though the creature might even now be whispering into the Goddess's mind. "Cara, it's me. You know me. I am not my ancestors. I will not allow my people to repeat the mistakes of our forefathers."

"Won't you?" Cara whispered, the words seemingly torn from the depths of her throat. Her eyes fell to the gauntlet on Cara's hand. "Truly? You wield their magic, have dug into their hidden places, sought their secrets."

"Yes, child, see the truth," Maya's voice came again. "See them for what they are—wild, reckless. This creature would do anything for the power of her forefathers, would commit any crime for their secrets."

Erika opened her mouth to deny the charge, but found the words would not come. She swallowed, wondering... how much truth there was in Maya's claim. She looked again to Cara, knowing a part of her could not deny the Old One's words, only...

...that was the old Erika, was it not? The Archivist who had dug so recklessly into the past, who would have done anything to fill the void left by her father's death, by her exile.

Erika was no longer that woman, but she had responsibilities of her own now, to her kingdom, to her people. If the powers of the ancients could save them...

"I..." Erika trailed off, struggling to find the words. "I...

we are not them, Cara," she said finally, the words lame, even to her.

"Aren't you?" her friend replied, and Erika saw her eyes flicker, shifting to where Amina stood nearby. The Flumeeren queen stared back, face betraying none of the emotion hidden within. "Aren't you *exactly* like them? Didn't your people torture my mother, twist her, break her, *murder her*? And all for what? For her knowledge, for the secrets she possessed."

Erika let her hand fall to her side. Cara stood staring at her with those soft yellow eyes, and she could see the pain there, the hurt the Goddess had carried since the day they'd realised the truth, had discovered the fate of her missing mother.

"You're right," Erika said at last. Her eyes caught the queen's, and she saw the slightest of smirks there, the satisfaction. This woman held no regret for Cara's pain. "Some of us are terrible," Erika continued in a whisper. "All of us have that capacity, whether we be human, Tangata, or Anahera. But I swear to you, Cara, there are others amongst us who want to do better, who would create a world for all of us." She drew in a breath. "But I can't do it without you, Cara, without your light to guide the way. Please, I need your help."

She trailed off, watching the silent Goddess, staring into those golden eyes. Hesitantly, Erika offered her hand again. The moment stretched out, a silence hanging in the air as the others watched on, waiting.

Until finally, Cara reached out and clasped her hand around Erika's.

"Okay," she whispered.

Laughter answered the pronouncement. "So disappointing," Maya rumbled. "I thought for sure the child would throw off your shackles, human." She grimaced. "Alas, it was not to be so. Her kind were always weak, their will easily corrupted." She paused, then turned, the dark pits of her eyes fixing on another. "And what of you, half-blood queen? Are you ready to embrace your true power?"

Footsteps sounded in the gloom as Amina advanced into the light of Erika's gauntlet. Her smile did not falter as she looked from Erika and Cara to the Old One. She shook her head as she appraised the creature.

"All my life," she snarled, "I have been waiting for your arrival, *Chead*. You think I would join you now?"

33

THE FALLEN

Hidden in the darkness, Adonis listened to the thrum of Maya's Voice. She had brought him with her, her repentant servant, the only one she had trusted to bring to this place. Watching from the shadows, he listened to her converse with the humans and wished she would unleash him, set him upon the vile creatures. He could feel her strength within him, the swirling of her hatred…

…then abruptly, he felt it weaken.

An inner gasp escaped Adonis as he emerged from the pain, from the crushing agony of his own regret, as Maya's influence over his mind retreated.

A shudder shook him as he returned to himself, looking across the tunnel to where the humans stood. What did the creatures think they were doing, coming here, thinking they could face the Old One alone? The Anahera might fight for a while, resisting the power of Maya's Voice, but even he could sense the divisions amongst the others. The Old One would turn them against one another before any managed to strike a blow.

She played the calm Matriarch now, but when they had arrived in this place earlier, her rage had been terrible to behold. To discover her mate's absence, that the humans had tricked her, manipulated her...

...no, none would leave this place alive. Maya could have crushed them already, could have broken their minds as she had his. Why she had not already, Adonis could not comprehend. Neither could he understand why her influence on him had lessoned. Her Voice still touched him, fixing him in place where he stood hidden in the shadows. But the unrelenting agony she had used to torture him had at least vanished.

He was not surprised to see the human and young Anahera from the mountains, the ones that had escaped. Even less so the half-blood queen. After witnessing her fight on the river, Adonis had known she would come.

But why had Maisie followed them here?

Beyond the three with power, she stood with another human, armed only with a simple blade. No magic or strength to protect her, just a regular sword, barely enough to fend off a feeble human, let alone the strength of the Old One.

When he'd first seen her, he'd wanted to scream for her to run, to flee. But even with his mind restored, his Voice remained mute, unable to reach out in warning to the Anahera, let alone the Voiceless Maisie. He couldn't save her this time. He couldn't even save himself.

Instead Adonis remained hidden, locked in his master's mental grip, waiting for what was to come, to witness the doom of humanity and his own kind both.

"Give up, Maya." To his surprise, it was Maisie who finally spoke. "You're all alone, outnumbered. Your time has come."

Laughter answered the human's words. Adonis might have laughed with the Old One. Little did the poor human know the darkness she faced.

"Human, it seems I underestimated you. I should have realised one of your kind, even injured and alone, would find a way to survive. Had I known Adonis could be so easily influenced by your words, I would have killed you both that day." Maya's words turned to a cackle. "But you are wrong, my dear child. I am not alone."

At her words, Adonis felt a compulsion, the pressure returning to his mind as the Old One refocused her attention on him. Though her Voice was weaker than it had been earlier, it was still enough to propel him forward. Head lowered, Adonis stepped into the light of the human's magic. A hiss of inhaled breath followed his appearance.

"*Adonis.*"

Despite Maya's compulsion, Adonis's head jerked up at that, surprised at the emotion in Maisie's voice. But his ears did not deceive him, as looking upon the swirls of her aura, he read the impossible rainbow of the human's soul.

He wanted to speak to her, to ask what had become of the Anaheran children—but instead the full force of Maya's Voice returned, crashing upon him like a landslide. And instead of reaching out with his Voice, a soft rumble came from his throat and he drew back his lips, the hatred in his heart responding to Maya's own. In that moment, Adonis saw again the truth, that this human was the creature who had tricked him, that had caused him to betray his own people.

Fists clenched, teeth bared, he took a step towards the human.

"Adonis," the human gasped, retreating from him. "No…"

Anger raged within Adonis, at his naivety, his foolishness, that he had allowed this pathetic creature to manipulate him, to trick him. He wanted to reach out and tear her apart, to finally earn redemption.

Only Maya's Voice held him back.

"I suppose it was for the best," the Old One mused, her words mocking as she addressed the human. "Tell me, how are your new allies, the Anahera? I do not see them here, apart from their rebellious daughter." Her smile grew as the humans said nothing. "Oh my poor dears, did they abandon you?" Laughter echoed through the tunnel. "It is good to know they shall never change. The Tangata might be weak and foolish, but at least they are not craven."

Her words pierced the fog of Adonis's thoughts, and for a moment he was as a man drowning, struggling to keep his consciousness above the miasma of Maya's power. He clenched his fists, yearning to turn and strike at his captor, but...

...instead all he managed was a growl. Maya laughed again, though this time it seemed her mirth was directed at him.

"For what it's worth, human, know that the Anahera will not escape me," Maya whispered. "When your civilisation burns and the world belongs to me, I will have my servants hunt them down, bring them my retribution. Just as extinction beckons for humanity, so it will come for them."

A growl answered Maya's words as the winged one straightened, eyes flashing in the darkness. "The only extinction that beckons is yours, Maya."

Silence fell as the Old One regarded her foes, a smile touching her lips. "An unusual alliance," she mused. "I have read your hearts, know your minds. If this is the best your kind can send against me, I am not impressed. Three women, rejected, spurned by their own blood, by their people. How far the world has fallen." She spread her hands and grinned. "But very well, children. Come to me, and I will gladly grant the death you seek."

Snarling, Amina leapt at the creature, Erika and Cara just a step behind.

❊ 34 ❊

THE SOVEREIGN

A snarl tore from Lukys's lips as a Tangata leapt at him, evading his guards and reaching for his throat. Reacting faster than he'd thought himself capable, Lukys spun his spear and drove the point up through the creature's heart, sending it screaming into the void. But he barely heard the creature's Voice as it cried out—his attention was only half on the events in Mildeth, the assault upon the walls.

The other half was far away, tangled in the minds of his friends, supporting them as they fought in the darkness. The queen had led the charge against the inhuman Old One, Erika and Cara joining in the battle while Maisie and the Calafe Darien held back. Yet with Maya's Voice filling the underground tunnels, they would have been incapable of throwing a single punch without his own Voice to reinforce them.

Yet despite his efforts, they were losing.

He could sense their furious battle, the exchange of blows and screams. But even as those in the caverns struggled, Maya worked her mind upon them, peeling at the layers of their consciousness, feeding on their base emotions, seeking to turn them against one another.

Only Lukys's desperate efforts kept her from succeeding, as he used all the strength of his Voice to bolster his friends' courage, to keep the Old One from their minds.

His efforts were slowly failing, as Maya crept through the gaps in his defences, or tore them apart when a distraction on the walls drew his mind back to Mildeth. Her raw power, her mastery, was far beyond Lukys's amateur efforts, even with the memories of the Sovereigns crowding him. This was a fight he was destined to lose, and yet he struggled on, did his best to keep his friends safe, if only for a moment more.

Alongside him, Sophia struggled as well. On the battlefield of Mildeth, she fought for the hearts and minds of the human defenders, of her people. But despite the distance, despite her own innate knowledge as a Tangata, she too was losing. The passion of battle was too great, the fear and rage and hatred too deep between their peoples. Maya had only to nudge the minds of the warring factions to drive each to ever greater madness.

But like Lukys, Sophia would not give up, would not surrender so long as hope remained. If only they'd had time to practice this ability, or had greater allies to support them. The Anahera who had remained in the city had raw ability, but the creatures were unpractised, easily distracted by the chaos around them. Perhaps together—

Lukys gasped as the overwhelming strength of Maya pressed against him again, her hatred washing through him, and for a moment he felt as though he stood alone, that he would be consumed...

...screaming, he tore himself from the battle in the caverns, surfacing for a moment on the walls of Mildeth. His vision flickered, clearing in time to see a Tangata leap over the crenelations. Quickly Lukys moved to shield Sophia from the bloodshed. He felt her pain with each death, but he could at least spare her the agony of fighting her own brethren. For now, at least.

But despite the memories crammed into his skull, Lukys was still human, and his strength was waning. Their guard were struggling too. He saw Travis fighting desperately at Isabella's side, glimpsed Dale down on one knee as Keria stood protectively over him with another of the Perfugian guard, fighting off a maddened Tangata.

Slamming the butt of his spear into the face of another Tangata, Lukys reversed the weapon and drove the razor tip through its throat. It fell back, crumpling to the ground, and he forced his will back to the cavern, even as he felt his friends wilting.

His protection was failing. Eroded by distance, he could not match Maya's strength, not for long. Sooner or later, she would find her way into the hearts of one of the allies. When that happened, their fate would rest on the strength of that soul, on what lay in their heart, whether they had the will to resist...

Thinking of the mistrust held between the three women, Lukys shuddered. He gathered himself for one last effort, then hurled himself at the darkness surrounding his friends. He would not surrender, would not abandon them to the Voice of the Old One. He held the knowledge of generations in his mind, the will of all the Sovereigns who had come before him. It would be enough.

It had to be.

Withdrawing from the battle atop the wall, Lukys found himself back-to-back with Sophia, with his love. Without seeing her face, he could sense the tears in her eyes, her pain as she tried again and again to find the love in her people's hearts, to remind them of the peace of New Nihelm.

They're dying, Lukys, her voice came to him.

He scrunched his eyes closed, turning to hold her tight, even as chaos reigned around them. They fought and fought and would keep on fighting, but he no longer knew why. They were losing, crumbling. Maya could not be defeated, would destroy them all. It was inevitable.

Why suffer, why continue?

Why not finally give up, and have peace?

"I can't lose you," Sophia whispered to him, lips warm on his cheek as they held one another.

Lukys tightened his grip on her and said nothing. What more was there to say?

You do not have to perish with the rest.

A shudder slid down Lukys's spine as the Voice of the Old One spoke into his mind. He tried to force it away, to close himself to her, but there was an exhaustion upon him now, a weariness he could not simply shrug off. It left cracks in his consciousness, gaps through which the Old One continued to whisper.

I sense my brethren, the true strength of the Chead, entwined in your souls. Surrender to it, give yourself to the power. Return to me, brother, sister, and we will rule this world as we were always destined.

Lukys's skin crawled as she spoke, and something within him stirred in response to her command. Opening his eyes, he found Sophia staring back at him, saw the terror upon her and knew she felt that same stirring, like a giant that had long lain dormant, now waking...

An icy cold seeped through Lukys as he found himself frozen, his body torn between the memory of a creature long dead, and his own self. Looking around, he saw the bloodshed upon the battlefield and felt that creature grow stronger, sensed it gathering, its anger, its rage...

No!

With an effort of will, Lukys fought back, clinging to

Sophia, sensing her own battle, her own fear. Instinctively, he reached out for her, their minds mingling, uniting in their battle against those other consciousnesses, filling them with strength…

…and with relief, they sensed those other minds subsiding, returning to the depths, to dreams of a world long since passed.

Letting out a long breath, the Sovereigns found themselves standing once more atop the walls of Mildeth, arms clasped around one another. They shivered, thankful for their sanity, and wondered…they were a hundred miles from the battle beneath the earth. Why then had Maya turned her attention towards them, tried to bring them to her side? Their minds raced, their thoughts as one as they came to a singular conclusion.

She fears us.

It was a spark of hope in the darkness of night. Together, the Sovereigns realised they no longer felt the oppressive weight of Maya's Voice, the darkness that had weighed on their thoughts these past days. Something had changed, a discovery of fresh power, of strength that kept the Old One's influence at bay.

We work as one.

Realisation struck, the truth that had been staring them in the face, ignored, avoided for fear of what it might mean. Separated, they could not stand against the Old One. What they had been doing, dividing their attention between their friends and the battle for Mildeth, it was not enough. Maya's mind was greater than either of them alone.

They needed to act as one. And yet…

We must decide, the Sovereigns thought together. *We must choose.*

The thought struck fear into their souls, and for a moment Lukys found himself separated from Sophia, though her emotions still roiled alongside his own, raw, exposed. He felt her pain, her fear, but beneath that, a steely resolution.

We cannot abandon our friends, she whispered, and Lukys saw her attention was not on their battlefield now, but had turned to that dark place, where Erika and Cara and the others were now fighting for their lives.

For a moment, Lukys watched the three fighting, their magic and power flashing in the darkness.

Then his mind returned to look out over Mildeth, at the thousands of lives joined in battle, at the terrible hatred shared by Tangata and mankind alike. Hatred that had been born from the mouths of men, crafted by callous rulers to bring war from peace. Maya was only the latest of those to exploit these peoples, to use them for their own purposes.

But what if that hatred could be healed, if the minds of humanity and Tangata alike could be opened, so that they saw one another not as the monsters of childhood tales, but the men and women they truly were?

What if they could bring peace from war?

If the Sovereigns could heal the wounds of centuries, not all the power of the Old One could tear them asunder again. Humanity, the Tangata, they would live on, would survive and prosper in a new world.

In that moment, Lukys realised it was not the battle beneath the earth that their fates rested upon, but the one before him. Turning to Sophia, he reached out to embrace her.

No, he whispered, and felt her frown, her confusion. *No, it is our people*, all *of our people, that we cannot abandon.*

What about our friends? she whispered back, though he sensed the swelling of her hope.

He kissed her then, and as he did so allowed their minds

to unite, to become the Sovereigns, to feel that joyous sense of Oneness.

We must trust them to do their part, the Sovereigns said, even as they released their protection from the caverns, turning their attention instead to the battlefield. *Our attention is needed here.*

And together, the Sovereigns reached out to undo the destruction wrought by Maya, by Amina, by kings and queens and Sovereigns past, by all those dark rulers that had come before them.

❦ 35 ❦

THE QUEEN

Light burned in the darkness as Erika and Amina ignited their gauntlets. The brilliance of their power reflected off those unnaturally smooth walls, catching on Cara's scarlet feathers. Erika's heart raced as her strength rushed into the strange links of the gauntlet, its power gathering, preparing to strike. In the City of the Gods, she had seen Maya resist its magic—but back then Erika had been weak, exhausted. Let the Old One stand against her true strength.

She exchanged a glance with Amina, who nodded. There was no love lost between them still, but the queens would stand together, at least against this enemy. As one, they raised their magic, preparing themselves.

"Ahhh!" A cry of joy, of victory, burst through the chamber as Maya suddenly straightened...

...and Erika staggered, a weight suddenly falling upon her, a crushing darkness, terror and despair that burnt away all hope, all thoughts of resistance. Tears welled in her eyes and she watched as the power bled from her fist, slipping away until the light all but died. Only the softest glow remained, casting their world in shadow.

A whimper slipped from Erika's lips as she sank to her knees. Sobs came from nearby and she saw that Cara had already crumpled, arms wrapped about herself, wings spreading to hide her face. The sight sent terror rushing through Erika, and she felt desperation, a need to act, to protect the young Anahera she had come to see...come to see as...

"And so we come to the end."

Maya's voice sounded in the darkness, banishing everything else from Erika's mind, leaving only the despair. On her knees, she looked up as footsteps approached, as the terrible eyes of the Old One fell upon her.

"I admit, your Sovereigns resisted far longer than I thought possible." She smiled as she stood over them. "But I knew their true nature would reveal itself eventually, that they would choose themselves over their friends."

A cry tore from Erika as she felt the world shrinking about her, as childhood terrors rose to drown her, as she came to realise her every hope, every dream had been a lie, the foolish whims of a child. She had never been a queen, did not deserve the love of her people. She was no one, a pretender, a fool for denying the majesty of this creature before her.

"Still," Maya mused. "I will have to deal with them eventually. Who knew my old rivals would be so cunning, as to find a way to thwart me even now, long after they were gone? I will have to prise that secret from their hosts before I rip them apart."

The Old One leaned her head to the side as a whimper came from nearby, and the dark eyes fell on Cara. "So considerate of you to lure yourselves out here, so far from your friends and followers."

Erika shuddered, shrinking farther and farther towards the floor. Her entire being unravelled as she relived her every mistake, her every terrible decision, the lives she had cost, the evils she had committed. Again and again she had led those who'd trusted her to their deaths, and now...now she had done it again, had brought Darien and Maisie and Cara to this place, had failed them, failed herself, failed her people.

The Old One stepped past her, advancing on Cara. The Anahera was sobbing, trying to crawl away, but Maya caught her by the wing and dragged her back, laughing, cackling as she threw the girl down in front of Erika.

Pain burst within Erika's heart, threatening to tear her apart. Desperately she sought something, anything to sustain her, some spark amidst the suffocating despair. But she couldn't breathe, couldn't think, couldn't see anything beyond the darkness, the doom. Not a hint of love or hope or joy. It was all gone, washed away, sponged from her soul.

She watched as Cara sobbed on the floor, unable to summon the will to defend herself, and knew that her friend would die, that here, now, Erika had truly failed her.

No...

Somewhere in the depths of her soul, a piece of Erika fought against that thought, resisted. She had made a promise, had sworn...sworn to protect her friend, to do better, to *be* better. Somehow, her hands found the cold stone beneath her and she froze, no longer sinking, no longer slumped in defeat. Teeth clenched, she struggled, fought to push herself back, to rise again.

The weight upon her redoubled, the despair swelling within, trying to crush that spark, to drown her. Erika clung to its light, to its determination, even as she felt it slipping from her, knew that no matter her strength, this was an enemy she could not fight, not alone...

…but she was not alone. Her eyes found Cara, lying on the ground beside her, saw the Old one pinning her wing beneath a boot, saw the death shining in the creature's eyes.

Desperately, Erika sent up a plea to the sky, to the Gods she knew did not exist, had never existed…and yet still she begged, pleaded…

Please, give me the strength to help her.

But of course there was no answer

Erika cried out as the Old One slammed her boot into Cara's chest, punctuated by the sharp *crack* of breaking bones. The Anahera doubled up from the blow, gasping, sobbing her pain, but still she did not fight back, could not. Another blow landed, then another, the harsh *thud* of each impact whispering through the tunnels, until Erika was forced to squeeze her eyes closed, unable to watch, to witness…

Very well, human, a voice—no, voices—whispered into Erika's mind. *You have…proven your word once. Perhaps you are proof that humanity truly can change.*

And suddenly, the spark to which Erika clung exploded, sweeping outwards, washing back the darkness. Where before there had been despair, Erika found an unlikely hope, an unyielding joy for the voices in her mind, the possibility of a future. The weight of responsibility no longer felt so heavy, the doom she had foreseen not so inevitable.

And she found herself rising.

We will not see another world Fall, the voices of the Anahera whispered to her. *This Old One, she is too strong, too powerful. We cannot risk leaving the fledgelings, not again, but this, at least, we can do. Stop her, Erika of the Calafe.*

"Impossible," Maya whispered as she swung to see Erika on her feet.

Erika reacted without thought. Light burst from her gauntlet and she threw out her hand. Screaming, Maya staggered back, retreating from the power. Erika had not gathered enough to strike the creature down, but the attack still served as Erika wished, driving the Old One away from her friend. Quickly she advanced, placing herself between Cara and the Old One.

A groan came from Cara as, trembling, the Goddess rose. She clutched at her chest and one wing hung limp and broken, but despite her obvious pain, the Anahera stood, teeth bared at the creature who opposed them.

We will watch over you and Cara, came the voices again, followed by a pause. *The other...she clings to the darkness. She will not let us in.*

"So the Anahera have found their courage after all," Maya murmured as she straightened. "No matter. Their Voices will not be enough to save you, human."

Erika had a moment to process those words before a figure joined Maya in the darkness. A dark smile crossed Amina's lips as she looked at them. Erika sensed the vibrations in her mind, could almost read the words of Maya as she gestured to the queen.

"Kill them."

And smiling, Amina advanced.

———

HATRED BLEW THROUGH ADONIS LIKE A STORM UNLEASHED, tearing every other emotion from his soul. Setting his sights on Maisie, he advanced with a snarl, hands outstretched. He made no move to rush—the human could not escape him, could not fight him. Trapped by the Voice of the Old One, she could only stand there and die, just as her friends were dying even now.

Indeed, she watched his advance, eyes wide with fear. Then abruptly she spun—and vanished.

Adonis staggered to a stop, confusion penetrating the haze of his mind, struggling to comprehend what had happened. The human had no power—how could she have resisted Maya's Voice, let alone disappeared into thin air?

Movement came from nearby, and he spun as a one armed man charged him. Adonis's eyes widened at the creature's nerve, but it stood no chance against his power, and brushing aside a blow from the man's broadsword, he struck the human's chest.

The man crumpled, collapsing to the floor with hardly a sound, and Adonis turned back to the darkness.

Back to the hunt.

His ears caught the soft thump of retreating footsteps and he grinned, striding up the tunnel after his quarry. The human might resist Maya's mental powers, might have been capable of vanishing from sight, but she could not hide from his other senses. He trailed after the whisper of her soft movements, after the sharp scent of her humanity. No, she would not escape.

The chase carried him away from where Maya and her new servant battled against the Anahera and the human. Adonis's master did not need him to defeat two such as them, though as the distance to Maya grew, her presence upon his mind lessened again, retreating as it had before, until only her Command remained, the order to hunt, to kill. A growl rumbled from Adonis's throat as he stalked the tunnels, seeking his prey, desperate to finally watch her feeble life fading into the dark. She would pay for corrupting him, for luring him from the path of his Matriarch.

"You're a fool, Adonis." The human's voice chased him through the shadows, taunting him, ever just out of reach.

He growled, bounding forward, before he realised her scent no longer hung in the air of the tunnel. Retreating, he found the side passage down which she had fled, and continued after her.

"A lovestruck idiot, lost, alone, *weak*," Maisie mocked. "Better you had died than this."

They continued the chase, Adonis ever just behind, though he sensed at times the shift of movements, the human's presence. She had no stamina, this creature, especially not with the aftereffects of her injury. This could not last—eventually she would fall, would stumble or trip, and reveal her position. Laughter rasped from his throat as he imagined his fingers closing upon her soft flesh, her screams as he wrought his revenge.

"Nyriah, she would weep to see she died for nothing." Her voice came again, and this time the words struck Adonis like a hammer, bringing him to a halt. "You are a stain upon her memory."

A tremor wracked Adonis and he swung this way and that, his snarls echoing in the narrow corridor. Where was she? How he longed to destroy her, to cease her tormenting—

There!

He leapt, bounding forward at a flicker of movement. The human had cried out, but there was no escaping Adonis now, as his fist met with flesh. He heard a soft *crunch* as of breaking bone, followed by a *crash* as glass struck stone. Abruptly, whatever magic had protected Maisie vanished and she appeared before him, broken wrist clutched in one hand, eyes wide.

She retreated from him, cursing beneath her breath, but the rock was damp beneath her feet and she slipped, collapsing to the stone. Adonis loomed above her, breath hissing in and out as he drank in her fear, her terror. The time had finally come, his vengeance, his redemption.

"They're alive," she said suddenly, eyes wide as they met

his glare. "The fledgelings, they're safe. She'll never find them. Thanks to you."

Adonis stumbled to a stop. Her words pierced the darkness upon his soul, the fog of his mind. Those words, they should have enraged him, driven him to a fury, for they proved the magnitude of his treachery.

Instead, he felt a thrill, a sharp joy that swelled within, growing, swirling as it burned up his hatred, his anger. A gasp tore from his throat and he staggered back from her, shuddering, struggling.

"I know you're in there, Adonis," Maisie's words chased him.

Placing her good hand on the stone, she pushed herself up, her legs struggling to support her. One was slightly crooked, its bones healed poorly. She was so weak, he should never have let her live. And yet...

"I know you can hear me," she spoke again, taking a step towards him, reaching out a hand. "I know you don't want to do this."

Another shudder shook Adonis and he twisted away from her, then back. A moan built in his throat, a pressure, a battle within that threatened to tear him apart. The pain in his soul grew to a crescendo as the twin forces of Maya's Voice and his own did battle.

I...can't... he whispered to himself.

And still the eyes of the human watched him.

❧ 36 ❧

THE SOVEREIGNS

The Sovereigns shuddered as they looked across the battlefield, taking in the chaos of war. Fear and rage and hatred swirled, mixing and swelling as human and Tangata clashed, the screams of the dying and the victors rising until it seemed they were one and the same. Watching the flicker of their auras, they couldn't help but think it was true, that a part of both of their souls was lost with the death they dealt.

The darkness of Maya, and those who had come before, had consumed these pour souls. Even now as the Sovereigns worked to sever the Old One's influence, the darkness fed upon itself, upon the battle, upon the pain and loss and death. These men and women, they no longer wished to see the light, to believe in a better world.

A piece of the Sovereigns broke with each death, with the loss of every brother, every sister. In their minds' eye, the terrible waste of war was laid bare, revealed for the tragedy it was, brothers and sisters murdering one another. Looking upon that horror, they knew they had made the right decision.

And together, they reached out to grasp the scarlet threads of rage, the emerald lines of hatred. Speaking as one, they sought to crush those dark emotions, to press them back, to contain them in the bounds of compassion and empathy that had once held them in check. Across the battlefield their Voice rang out, muting those terrible passions, trying to heal the wounds their foe had dealt.

Only as they came to an end and looked back did the Sovereigns realise the futility of their actions. As they moved from one part of the battle to another, the fighting paused, but only momentarily. For as the people looked and saw the dead and dying around them, their hatred crept back, and the battle was re-joined.

No, they thought to themselves, watching the chaos resume, the darkness sweeping through the ranks of human and Tangata alike, all across the walls, except...

...except where they themselves stood, surrounded by the glow of their guard. Of all the souls on the battlefield, the Perfugian recruits and their Tangatan partners alone stood untouched by the darkness. Instead, they shone with the rosy hue of hope, of joy and love. And looking upon their friends, the Sovereigns realised their mistake.

We cannot hold back the darkness, but we can spread the light.

Gathering their power, they swept back into the chaos, immersing themselves in the surging emotions, feeling the hatred that had torn them asunder, that had led humanity to first attack the Tangata, that had unleashed the Tangatan rage upon humanity. But it was not those emotions, those memories, they sought this time. They were entrenched, experiences that could not be ignored, would never be forgotten.

Yet there were other emotions amongst them, buried deep by Maya, smothered by her hatred. Buried, but not destroyed. One by one, the Sovereigns dragged them from the depths. Images flickered through their minds as they passed above the battlefield: a Tangatan man and human woman in one another's arms; a human spear raised above a helpless Tangatan child, withdrawn; even images of themselves as they walked the streets of Mildeth and Ashura. Memories still fresh, suppressed but not forgotten. Now they returned at the bidding of the Sovereigns, to remind the people of what *could* be.

More and more, the images of hope rose from the past, of families left behind, of children and loved ones waiting, praying for their return, of joys forgotten in the depths of their darkness. The reasons they had first taken steps down this path, but which had been forgotten in the pursuit of Maya's conquest.

Amidst it all, the Sovereigns felt their own joy swelling, their memories sweeping outwards to join with the others: the warmth as Lukys danced with Sophia in the courtyard of New Nihelm, the joy of the children in the streets, the hope they'd felt, watching their peoples protect one another, and a future they had once envisioned.

Of peace between their kinds.

Atop the walls of Mildeth, Lukys opened his eyes, sensing a change had come over the battle. Beside him, Sophia stirred too. Blinking, he struggled to adjust to his return, to separate the links of his mind from his union with Sophia. Relief touched him as he found Dale back on his feet, Keria at his side. And Travis too, standing nearby, an enormous smile on his face.

Lukys frowned at the sight, and straightening, he stepped cautiously to the edge of the wall. And only as he stood there, looking out across the battlefield, did he realise the change that had drawn them back, the impossibility that had come to pass on the walls of Mildeth.

Silence.

———

Erika screamed as the energy gathered in her fist, burning, boiling, blinding. With another cry, she threw out her arm, directing it at the blur in the dark that was the Old One. The figure staggered, but the Old One's momentum still carried her clear of Erika's magic.

Laughter whispered from the shadows as the figure straightened and Erika panted, struggling to gather her strength. The harsh *thunk* of blows on flesh carried from elsewhere in the dark, as Cara and her half-sister did battle.

She caught a glint and rustle of feathers as the two darted past. In the narrow corridors, Cara's wings were only a hinderance against the maddened Amina. Light flashed as the queen snarled and unleashed a burst of her own magic. Twisting, Cara somehow managed to avoid the debilitating effects of the gauntlet, her smaller size and agility aiding her against the larger woman.

A *crack* followed as Amina's fist collided with the Anahera's cheek, sending her crashing back. Erika winced and in her mind the voices that aided her rose to a cacophony, the Anahera's terror swelling.

Clenching her teeth, Erika forced herself to ignore them, to turn her back on Cara's plight. She had to believe in her friend, trust she would survive, would distract Amina long enough for Erika to do what needed to be done. There was only one way to win this fight—by killing the Old One.

With Darien down and Maisie vanished, somehow, impossibly, that task had fallen on Erika's shoulders.

She balled her gauntleted hand into a fist, allowing the power to grow, to light the dark. Its brilliance revealed Maya standing a few feet away, smile still stretched across her lips, eyes glimmering in her magic's glow.

"You know you cannot win, human," she rasped, "and

yet you fight on." She shook her head. "Such is the arrogance of humanity."

Abruptly she darted forward. Erika screamed, hurling herself to the side and bringing up her fist, unleashing the power. Light flashed from her, silhouetting the Old One, tearing a scream from Maya.

Then Erika collided with the wall of the tunnel and tears of pain sprung to her eyes. Stumbling, she struggled to see, to spot the Old One before she attacked again. Laughter sounded in the narrow confines, but Erika's magic must have had some effect, for the Old One retreated again, merging with the dark. Words echoed through the tunnel and Erika swung this way and that, chasing shadows.

Nearby, Cara screamed and hurled herself at Amina, catching the queen about the waist. Amina stumbled but did not fall. Instead, she bared her teeth and clenched her fists together, then brought them down on Cara's back, driving the Anahera to her knees.

A snarl tore from Cara as she released the queen and tried to leap away, but the half-blood was faster still, catching one of the Goddess's wings as they fluttered outwards. Cara screamed as the queen dragged her back, before several feather tore loose, freeing her.

She staggered away from the queen, spinning, eyes wild as blood dripped from the ends of one wing. Glimpsing the beginnings of madness in her friend's eyes, Erika cursed, but there was nothing she could do for Cara, nothing she could say to draw the Goddess back from the edge.

Instead she turned and sought the Old One.

"It is not arrogance that makes us fight," she whispered, more to herself than in answer to Maya's whispers. "It's hope." She swung her gauntlet in an arc, seeking out her foe. "Maybe I cannot win. Maybe you'll kill me. But it won't end here, Maya. Even in death, my people will remember my sacrifice. They will fight on against you. Maybe one of them will have the strength to defeat you."

Laughter answered her words and Erika suddenly felt foolish, sensed the ridicule of her enemy. Even with the support of the Anahera, she sensed her doom. She could not win this battle, would find only death down here in this darkness. The Calafe would forget her brief reign—if they survived to remember anything at all.

And Maya would persist, would give birth to more of her terrible kind, nearly as strong as herself. Then it would only be a matter of time before they took the world.

A scream built in Erika's throat as she foresaw that dark future. Another flicker of movement came from a nearby corner and she threw out her hand, unleashing the gathering power. Light burst from the gauntlet, catching Maya midstride.

The Old One staggered as the power struck, bending her in two, freezing her to the spot. Shocked, Erika kept on, pouring her energy into the gauntlet, feeding the magic. Gripping her wrist with the other hand to steady herself, she staggered forward, knowing this was her chance. A dark sound whispered from the Old One as her frame bowed, as her body shook, trembled...

... then straightened.

Erika stumbled to a stop as the Old One's laughter echoed around her. Abruptly the creature darted forward, catching Erika by the wrist and yanking her hands towards the ceiling, directing the gauntlet's power away from her.

"Ahhh, but I had forgotten that sting," the Old One hissed, leaning in close so that they were face to face.

Erika flinched away from that face. Her power had not been without effect. Scarlet tears ran from Maya's grey eyes and her cheek twitched with the aftereffects of the pain. Yet she still stood, teeth bared, that terrible insanity watching Erika from the grey depths.

A scream came from nearby, and Erika's heart twisted as she saw Cara go down. Before she could recover, Amina leapt forward and landed upon the Anahera's back. Grasping the youth by the hair, she drove her face into the stone floor. Screaming, Erika struggled to free herself from Maya's grip, but the Old One only smiled, amusement playing across her lips as she too watched the end of the battle between sisters.

Snarling, Amina drew Cara's bloodied face back, then slammed her into the stones again. And again and again, until finally the Anahera lay limp beneath her.

Only then did the Flumeeren queen rise. Magic lit her fist as she gathered power there, readying herself to finish the Anahera.

"*No!*" Erika screamed, fighting hopelessly against the Old One's sheer strength. "Amina, don't you see? She has made you the very thing your father raised you to stop!"

To her surprise, Amina glanced up at that. A frown played across the queen's face, but her hesitation only lasted a moment. Her eyes met Maya's, and something seemed to pass between the pair, before Amina turned back to Cara and raised her fist once more.

"Witness, my dear human, what becomes of those who stand against me," Maya whispered.

"No."

Erika jerked as a voice spoke from behind them...

...then a blur charged from the darkness, and slammed into the Old One.

THE TANGATA

The breath burst from Adonis's lungs as he collided with the Old One, hurling her back, freeing the human from her grasp. He attacked again, driving a fist into his master's face, straining to do the impossible, to stand against Maya's Voice, against her power. Yet even as he struggled, Adonis felt her mind turning towards him, felt the full force of her consciousness as it focused on him...

Movement came from the floor as Maisie helped the other human to her feet, yet Adonis could not stop to consider them. He launched himself at Maya again, snarling, screaming, determined to stop her, to prevent her from leading his people to disaster—

Light exploded across his vision as the Old One finally recovered, her shock turning to rage. She moved faster than thought, faster even than his Tangatan senses could follow, and abruptly Adonis found himself on the cold stone, the metallic taste of blood filling his mouth.

"Adonis!" Maisie screamed.

His heart lurched at the thought of Maya turning her gaze upon the human, and snarling, Adonis pushed himself back to his feet, placing himself before his foe. Maya's eyes widened, as though unable to believe his defiance. Even Adonis struggled to comprehend it, the animalistic desperation that fuelled him. The buzzing of her Voice increased in pitch, scratching at the layers of his mind, but fists clenched he fought back, clinging to his freedom like a drowning man to a log.

Gathering himself, Adonis charged again, determined to stop her. But this time the Old One was ready. She caught his fist in one hand, a look of disgust on her lips, as though she considered it beneath her to spar with one so low as him. Her fist came up, and not all Adonis's speed or skill was enough to avoid the blow. It collided with the side of his head, sending him careening into the wall. Red flashed across his sight, and this time when his vision cleared, Adonis found he no longer had the strength to stand.

A scream pierced his sluggish mind, and teeth clenched, he raised his head, struggling to remain conscious. Light burst from the fist of Maisie's friend as she unleashed the power of her ancestors, though this time she used it not against Maya, but the other, the half-blood that had fallen to the Old One's power. The queen's face contorted as the magic caught her, and she staggered, clutching her ears, crumpling to the ground.

The light faded as quickly as it had been unleashed as the human lowered her arm. Adonis frowned, his addled brain confused, struggling to track the players in the room. Nearby, Maya appeared equally as surprised, but the human ignored her, focusing on the fallen half-blood.

"Amina, get up!" Her voice echoed loudly in the narrow space. "We need you!

On the ground, the half-blood queen stirred, and Adonis realised that her eyes had cleared, that the human's attack had disrupted Maya's hold on the woman. The Old

One realised it at the same moment, unleashing a scream, she leapt towards them.

Recovering with the speed of the Anahera, the half-blood surged to her feet to meet the Old One, turning aside a blow meant for the human. Maya stumbled, and light lit the darkness as the human raised her gauntlet. This time there was no mistaking her target, and Maya snarled as the power of the ancient humans struck.

Adonis had already seen Maya resist that terrible power, but roaring, the half-blood ignited her own weapon, the matching gauntlet she wore. Too late, the Old One realised her peril, as the half-blood queen unleashed the magic of the second gauntlet.

A terrible scream shook the tunnels beneath the earth as Maya fell to her knees, hands clasped to her ears before the assault of the twin magics. A snarl hissed from her lips, and even as blood spilt from her eyes, she tried to rise, to leap at one of the two, to bring them down.

But even the strength of the Old Ones had its limits, and Maya reached hers now, her feet slipping on the smooth ground, sending her crashing back to the cold stone.

Only then did she turn, her bloodied face twisting, her desperate eyes searching the dark, finding Adonis. They shone as their gaze met, as she looked upon his fallen figure. Even through layers of his mind, the defences Adonis had raised against her, he heard Maya's call as she placed a hand to the mound of her stomach.

Adonis, please! she begged. *Please, save me! Save our children!*

His heart wrenched at the words, and despite everything she had done to him, to his people, Adonis almost went to her, almost stood and struck down the human and her awful magic.

But he resisted. He knew it could not be, that the Old One's words were but ash upon the wind, her lies greater than any humanity had ever told. She would see him dead, would murder his people, slaughter thousands to feed her hatred. Even the children she carried would be consumed by her cause, discarded in her pursuit of her revenge.

No, Maya could not be allowed live, or she would doom them all.

And so, though a part of him was breaking, Adonis bowed his head and sat back. Closing his eyes, he waited for the end.

Until finally, the vibrations of the Old One ceased, and silence fell over the ancient tunnels. Her presence, her touch, vanished from his mind.

It was done.

The threat to his people, his world, was dead.

And all it had cost was his own future.

Voices whispered in the darkness as the humans conversed. He wondered if they would kill him, but finally they seemed to decide to leave him, that they would return to the surface. Still he did not move, barely breathed as their footsteps retreated, finally disappearing into a distance too great for even his enhanced senses.

Only then did Adonis finally lift his head and look upon the creature he had loved, that had lifted the hopes of his people to the heavens, that would have born his children. Sobbing, he dragged himself across the floor to where Maya lay and cradled her body against him, held her tight.

And wept for the future that might have been.

EPILOGUE
TWO WEEKS LATER

S tanding on the shores of the Illmoor, Erika looked to the north, where a fleet of ships was slowly disappearing into the morning fog. Raising a hand, she bid farewell to Nguyen and the Gemaho as they returned to their lands. What they would find there, no one could say— Amina had disappeared after the fall of the Old One, fleeing into the tunnels. She must have learnt something of her own mental powers during that desperate battle, for not even the Sovereigns had been able to locate her since.

Erika could only shake her head at the thought. Perhaps it was better that the woman had vanished. Though she longed to bring Amina to justice, there were still many in Flumeer who supported her. Had the queen chosen to resist, she could have started a civil war amongst the Flumeeren people.

As it was, a fragile peace had finally come to the four kingdoms, to human, Tangata and Anahera alike. Erika couldn't help but wonder whether it would last, if the darkness that had so stained their history would rise its ugly head once more, but for now, she was willing to give it a chance.

And so she led her people south, back to the vast forests and wilderness of Calafe. Despite their fears of what they would find there, her people had followed, had placed their faith in their young queen and set out on a journey to reclaim their homeland.

Though perhaps *reclaim* was too strong a word.

For nearby, journeying separately, yet never far from the Calafe column, came the Tangata. Their numbers were greatly reduced from the host that had marched north to assault the Flumeeren capital, numbering similar now to the Calafe. Despite the efforts of the Sovereigns, distrust still lingered between the two groups, remnants of a hatred fostered over a decade of war, and yet…

…here and there, Erika saw where the groups had combined, where children of each race played as one, drawn to one another by a shared curiosity, by a desire to discover, to explore the unknown. And where the children went, the parents soon followed, nodding greetings to their former enemy.

Watching such scenes, Erika felt hope for what they would discover once they reached New Nihelm. With both groups decimated by the Old One's campaign, there would be no shortage of housing, and Erika's heart quickened at the thought of seeing her childhood home again, the future she might discover there.

A shame Maisie and Cara had decided not to join her. Cara had set off in search of her people, promising she would come find Erika in New Nihelm. Erika worried for the young Anahera, but she had faith the Goddess would return.

As for Maisie…she too had not been seen since the death of the Old One. She had ventured alone back into the tunnels, to seek out the Tangata that had saved them, but…the pair had never re-emerged. By the time the party had gone looking for them, both had vanished—along with the body of the Old One.

Erika feared for her friend, but Maisie had trusted the Tangata…had perhaps felt more than that. Erika could only hope Maisie had discovered a safe place, had found joy in the peace of the wilderness, in companionship with Adonis.

As for herself…Erika shivered, looking out across the broad expanse of the Illmoor, at the swirling mists. To the north, she had built a life for herself, had had status and authority as the queen's Archivist. But she was no longer that woman consumed with advancement, obsessed with power. Erika might still wear the gauntlet of her ancestors, but in the darkness beneath the earth, faced with the madness of the Old One, she had finally set aside the follies of her past, and become a queen in truth.

So looking out across the Illmoor, Erika smiled, bidding one last farewell to the woman she had been, to the queen's Archivist…

…and turned to lead her people forward into the wilds of Calafe.

———

ADONIS MOVED CAREFULLY THROUGH THE TREES, TREADING softly, creeping closer as the deer lowered its head to tear a clump of clover from the ground. Its head came back up as it chewed and he froze in place, watching, waiting. He was almost close enough now, just one more second…

…the deer lowered its head again, and silently Adonis darted forward, crossing the dozen yards in a heartbeat. Leaping forward, he slammed into the creature's back with all the power of the Tangata, and felt a satisfying *crack* as the beast's spine snapped at the impact.

The deer struck the ground with a *thump* as Adonis stood

over it, panting softly, his breath fogging in the dawn air. After a moment, he looked around, checking for wolves or other predators that might be interested in his meal, before returning his attention to the fawn. Slinging the dead beast over his shoulder as though it weighed no more than a sack of feathers, he set off through the forest.

Maisie had a fire burning in the cave when he returned, and a smile touched her face at the sight of him. Rising, she crossed the stone floor and greeted him with a kiss, before wrinkling her nose and gesturing to the carcass he carried.

"Did you have to kill Bambi?"

Adonis creased his brow to show his confusion, and Maisie laughed, gesturing with a hand to the depths of the cave, where they were preparing a larder for the winter.

"Don't worry," she explained as he wandered back to lay out the carcass for butchering. "It's just a story from our children's tales. I'm glad we won't be running out of meat when the snows arrive."

Grunting his agreement, Adonis returned to the fire and embraced the woman. She drew him into her arms in response, her brown eyes lifting to meet his, lips parting to draw him in. They kissed, and he felt the rush of blood pounding in his ears, the burning in his veins…

"Waaaah!"

Flinching, the pair broke apart as a shrill cry echoed from the stone walls. It wasn't long before a second voice joined the chorus of screams, followed by a third. Cursing, they crossed to where they'd stacked a pile of furs high near the fire. Leaning down, Maisie lifted a baby in each hand, while Adonis took the third. They stood together like that for a while, rocking the children gently in their arms.

"You know, Adonis," Maisie said as the cries of the children slowly faded. A smile touched her lips as she looked up from her burden. "They have your eyes."

———

Lukys strode along the docks of Mildeth, Sophia at his side, the last of the Perfugian forces marching around them. Two weeks had passed since the end of the war and all of his people were excited to return home, to see again the family and friends they had left behind, to enjoy the peace they had won.

They would have left sooner, but these few regiments had remained in Mildeth with their Sovereigns, aiding the city with its injured, helping bring food to the displaced, and ensuring Zayaan and the other nobles would cope with managing the kingdom once they left.

Though in truth, Zayaan probably had more experience in that regard than either of the Sovereigns. Their presence had mostly been to guarantee the stability of the city. From now on, Flumeer would be ruled by a council selected by the people, though the first elections would not be for another year, once the damages from the war had been repaired. Until then, Zayaan and the others who had led the city through the invasion would continue.

But from today, that would no longer be Lukys or Sophia's problem. Today they would finally return to Perfugia to lead their own people. Despite all they had done, the thought still stirred doubts in the backs of their mind, but they would not shirk their duties. Already they had lingered here too long.

Ahead, Dale and the rest of the Sovereign guard led the way up the gangplank to their ship, while on the docks, Lukys and Sophia turned to bid their goodbyes to Zayaan. The man had insisted on an honour guard to see them off, after all they had done for the kingdom. They lined the docks around them, some hundred knights garbed all in golden armour.

A smile touched Lukys's lips as he met the eyes of the old man. Despite their rough start, the man had proven surprisingly flexible in his worldview, and had adapted quickly to the presence of the Tangata in his city.

"Thank you, Zayaan, for everything you have done," he said softly. "We could not have won without your aid."

It was true. For the lives they had saved avoiding a battle for the city, they owed this man a debt.

For his part, Zayaan only inclined his head. "I only did my duty, Sovereign," he said softly. "I am glad if it contributed in some part towards our victory."

"You did more than that, Zayaan," Sophia murmured. "If ever you have need of Perfugia, you have only to call for us."

"Of course, Sovereign," he replied, dipping into a short bow before straightening. "I bid you good fortune on your journey."

Lukys chuckled. "I should hope so, since it's only a day's voyage, but thank you all the same." Turning to Sophia, he offered his arm. "Shall we, My Lady?"

A smile lit up his partner's face as she accepted his arm, and together they turned towards the gangplank. Before they could start towards it, however, Zayaan's voice called them back.

"Sovereigns?" he said. "Perhaps there is *one* thing you might do for me?"

"Oh?" Lukys asked, frowning as he turned back to the elder man.

"Yes," the man replied, a smirk crossing his face. "One last favour…"

Lukys's frown deepened, but before he could respond, sudden movement came from around them as the Flumeeren knights drew their weapons. Lukys and Sophia leapt back from them, but as they turned towards their ship, they found more of the steel-garbed men barring their path. Heart racing, Lukys swung on Zayaan, teeth bared. Already he was reaching for Sophia, seeking to join their thoughts, for the unity of the Sovereigns.

"What is this?" the Sovereigns snarled, hands coming up in preparation for a fight. Neither had thought to carry a weapon, but they were not without defence.

"My duty," Zayaan replied, his voice suddenly hard, his words harsh. "To humankind."

"Don't do this," they warned. *"You must know we will stop you. Your people will not lay hand on us."*

"No," Zayaan snarled, but still he did not retreat.

Fear struck the Sovereigns then, that there was more to this trap, and desperately they thrust out with the power of their minds, seeking to turn the hatred of those around them aside, to still—

Lukys screamed as a terrible pain exploded through his chest, stumbling, staggering on the wooden dock. Suddenly his strength was gone, the unity shattered, and in its place...agony. Sobbing, choking, he sank to his knees, gasping, hands clutching at his chest, seeking the wound...

...but finding himself whole.

"Did you think I had forgotten you, Tangata?" a cold voice spoke from behind him.

Desperately, his mind an agony of broken glass, Lukys twisted, seeking out the voice, and found Amina standing behind him, the visor of her gold-embossed armour raised, spear in hand...

...the other end of which was piercing Sophia's chest.

A gasp slipped from Lukys as the agony within redoubled, and he reached out a hand, desperate to reach his partner, to save her. But with an awful twist of her blade, Amina tore the spear loose, splattering Sophia's blood across the docks. For but a moment, she swayed on her feet, stumbling, turning, her grey eyes meeting his.

Lukys... For the briefest of moments, he felt her mind again, sensed her fear.

Then she was falling, tumbling down, striking the wooden boards with a terrible, awful *thump.*

"*No!*"

Lukys screamed as he sensed her presence vanish, her touch upon his mind dissipate to nothing. He made to stand, to hurl himself at the queen, but the agony of their separation struck him afresh, robbing him of strength, of will, and instead he crumpled alongside his partner, sobbing, pleading, gasping.

The thud of footsteps approached as he lay there, but still Lukys did not look up, could not tear his gaze from the empty eyes that stared at him from the face of his beloved.

"Kill me," he whispered, vision blurring, the void within tearing him apart.

"Oh no, my dear Sovereign," came Amina's whisper. "The monster had to perish, but *you*, you are far too valuable. The knowledge, the lost secrets you hold in that head of yours, they will change everything. With your help, Flumeer will finally take its place as the rulers of this world —and myself as its rightful queen."

Even through his pain, Lukys felt his panic rising, his terror for what this woman might be capable of with the Sovereign gift. But even as he tried to lift himself from the void, the pain redoubled, tearing him apart again, and he slumped back down.

Only then did another Voice reach him, a distant cry of desperation.

Lukys! It was a moment before he recognised Isabella. Distantly, he sensed her panic, her fear. *What is happening?*

A moan escaped Lukys and he scrunched his eyes

closed, wishing he could block out the world, the agony, the loss. But there was no escaping this horror, at least...not for him.

The Flumeerens have betrayed us! he screamed into the void, uncaring of who heard his words. *Flee, warn the world, Amina has returned!*

Then something hard and unyielding struck Lukys's skull, and the world turned to darkness.

———

WELL THAT'S THE END (FOR NOW!) BUT TO FIND OUT HOW the Tangata were born and this world ended, check out the prequel with Reborn.

NOTE FROM THE AUTHOR

Ooof. That hurt to write. Goddamn bad guys, they never give up do they? But there was no way the scheming Amina was going down without taking **someone** with her, and given how much she hated the Tangata…
…well, you saw how things went down.
Obviously I'm not quite done with this world yet. In fact I'm hoping to begin work very soon on my next series in this world. There'll be a time skip again, although no where near as long as with the secret sequel (***The Evolution Gene***). So you'll get to see your favorite characters again soon.
Well, most of them...
In the meantime, if you'd like to discuss my dastardly plot twists with other readers, be sure to join me on Facebook or my newsletter…

FOLLOW AARON HODGES
Join Aaron Hodges on his newsletter to r**eceive TWO FREE novels and a short story!**
https://aaronhodgesauthor.com/newsletter

Reborn

AARON HODGES

REBORN

BOOK ONE

THE EVOLUTION GENE

ALSO BY AARON HODGES

The Sword of Light

Book 1: Stormwielder

Book 2: Firestorm

Book 3: Soul Blade

The Legend of the Gods

Book 1: Oathbreaker

Book 2: Shield of Winter

Book 3: Dawn of War

The Knights of Alana

Book 1: Daughter of Fate

Book 2: Queen of Vengeance

Book 3: Crown of Chaos

The Evolution Gene

Book 1: Reborn

Book 2: Havoc

Book 3: Carnage

Descendants of the Fall

Book 1: Warbringer

Book 2: Wrath of the Forgotten

Book 3: Age of Gods

Book 4: Dreams of Fury

The Alfurian Chronicles

Book 1: Defiant

Book 2: Guardian

Book 3: Conquest

The Swords of Heaven and Hell

Book 1: Darkstrider

The Four Circles

Book 1: Help! My Wizard Mentor Had A Heart Attack And Now
I'm Being Chased By A Horde Of Giant Spiders!

The Untamed Isles

The Path Awakens

www.ingramcontent.com/pod-product-compliance
Lightning Source LLC
Chambersburg PA
CBHW072205130726
47910CB00011B/1962